Freckled Venom

Copperhead

Book 1

Freckled Venom Series

JULIETTE DOUGLAS

Dedication

To Rodney Bleidt and J. Jordan Phelps
Without you, this book would still be in the computer gathering
dust bunnies. Many thanks, hombres.

Prologue

THE BIG GREY'S RIDER slid the horse to a stop in front of Vern Edward's office. The town was quiet in the darkness with only a few coal oil lamps flickering outside of businesses, reflecting their weak light across the walkway into the street.

The rider's boots quickly landed in the dirt. A young girl darted for the stairs leading to the marshal's office. With her legs wobbling she tripped on the steps, landing on her knees as a loud sob escaped her throat. Pushing herself up, she stumbled towards the marshal's office door. A blood-crusted hand began pounding on the wood as a strangled voice desperately whispered, "Vern? Vern...open up..."

Chapter One

SHOD HOOVES ECHOED dully on the wooden expanse of bridge hovering over the White River. The dry road muffled four hooves as they hit the dirt, creating tiny billows of dust. Noting the change in tempo, hands gently tugged on the reins bringing the big grey to a standstill. The horse shook its head in protest making the leather creak as the grey shuffled impatiently; the bit in its mouth jangling like keys on a metal ring.

Crows cawed in the treetops at the disturbance. The warm sight, smells and sounds of a dry Indian summer surrounded the pair - pungent aromas of sun-warmed grasses and dried leaves rattled against each other in the slight breezes. A rich earthy smell of one season coming to a close and another one blossoming filled the air, mingling with the soft burble of water flowing around and under the bridge.

As the boy struggled to push himself off the grey's neck, he gazed through bleary eyes towards the main street of the town. He tapped worn boot heels to the grey's ribs, urging her forward.

Memories rose through his tired brain of how he had turned to a life of flushing fugitives out of the brush. He remembered reading a newspaper tacked to a board outside the newspaper office in that same town. His eyes drifted toward the wanted posters that had been attached there. A hand reached up, ripping them from the nail. With that action, a bounty hunter had been born. *That had been nine years ago,* the boy thought as he continued riding through his old hometown.

He noticed the clapboard buildings had weathered over the

years, the whitewash fading into the grain of the wood. Items were stacked outside as they always had been at Ezra's General Store, even after all this time. Rolls of wire, kegs of nails, a barrel of brooms, shovels and rakes littered the front porch. Metal and wooden buckets sat outside the double doors as did stacks of grain-filled burlap sacks. Bow saws hung on the exterior walls. A bench to sit on and chat was situated under one of the big plate glass windows showing displays of items within the store's interior.

The store still sat across the street from the log building housing the town marshal's office. *Vern's office,* the lad recalled sadly. His eyes rested on a huge brass plate suspended between two poles next to the hitching rail in front of the marshal's office. The boy wondered where that had come from.

Looking further down the street, the lad noted that the oak sapling at the corner of the town's red brick bank had now grown into a huge tree. The smattering of once small trees surrounding the livery stable had grown, too, lending colorful shade to the building that also penned the livery's stock.

About a week and a half ago, he had let his guard down for just a split second after capturing his bounty. The prisoner had surprised him, firing the pistol that he had managed to grapple away from the kid. The bullet had ripped a deep gash into the boy's arm. That prisoner had died at the quick reflexes of the boy that day. Since then, exhaustion more than the pain from the wound had been taking its toll. Dropping his chin to his chest, the lad knew he needed to rest and find someone totake care of his arm, but not now, not when he was so close to finally capturing his next bounty.

Gathering strength from somewhere deep inside his small body, the boy nudged the grey into a walk. Riding past the general store, his eyes focused on the water trough that was leaking, saturating the parched ground around it.

Fever and exhaustion fogging his senses, he didn't notice the

3

wagon being driven hell-bent for leather from the alley behind Ezra's store that was coming straight at him. He quickly jerked hard on the big grey's reins. Unaccustomed to the rough treatment, the horse snorted and half reared in protest. Harness and bits jingled like sleigh bells on the two mules pulling the wagon, who were startled by the grey's sudden actions. Leather on the mules strained against their sudden twisting movement. The front axle of the wagon groaned in protest as the mules backed up, their hooves churning dirt, creating a brownish-yellow haze in the air that settled over their backs like fine flour. The mules continued their backing up, turning the front wheels sideways. The left metal wheel rim squealed as it rubbed against the buckboard's wooden side, almost jackknifing the cargo.

The driver yelled at the boy, 'Watch what yure doing! Ya numbskull!" Slapping his mules' rumps hard with the reins and making them jump, he shouted at the team, "Here now...you jackasses!" The harsh sound of his voice made eight hooves dig hard into the dirt. The wooden framework of the buckboard groaned as the mules struggled within their harnesses to pull the heavily laden wagon back into line. The driver gave the boy another hard stare as he drove the team past the lad.

The boy noted the quiet stares from half a dozen folks watching him dodge the loaded wagon but paid them no attention. After a few moments they went on about their business. With pain and fever dulling his otherwise sharp senses, he barely noticed the doors opening and closing, voices chattering and the laughter that flowed around him. The grey moved obediently further along the street with a slight tap to her ribs, then slowed at the gentle pull on the reins. Looking up at the large painted wooden sign, the boy noticed splintered bullet holes scattered within the faded red and gold lettering. *Stewart's Saloon,* the sign read. He didn't recollect the name from his past. His eyes tracked down, spotting two small signs beside the batwing doors of the establishment. A picture of an overflowing beer mug was painted on a slab of weathered wood; the yellow paint was chipped and flaking off. *On Draught*, the faded words read below the mug.

Slowly guiding the grey to the hitch rail, the boy slid painfully off the saddle, staggering, trying to keep from falling. He momentarily rested his fevered forehead on the cool leather of the stirrup fender. The lad heard footsteps hesitate behind him on the wooden walk, then hurry on. Hoping to gain strength the youngster breathed in deeply, then straightened, tossing the reins over the rail.

Stepping up on the scarred boardwalk, he weakly grabbed the porch post, steadying himself as he threw a look over his shoulder to view the town's landscape. Turning and leaning against the post for support, he faced the street. From this vantage point, his gaze roamed and bounced across the still familiar scene he remembered from long ago. *Not much has changed in nine years,* the lad thought with a heavy sigh. Sighting someone watching him from in front of the town marshal's office, he exchanged curious stares with the stranger. The youngster blinked then squinted, focusing tired eyes on the male figure down and across the way. The man leaned comfortably against the porch post with his arms folded across his chest. The lad noticed he carried his large frame well, with wide shoulders that tapered down into a narrow waist. He was wearing a light-colored shirt displaying a badge that flickered briefly when the sun hit it. Long legs were encased in dark pants. The hat resting on his dark hair did not hide the expression of open curiosity blazing from unusual eyes. Even from that distance, the lad could see the penetrating blue gaze that had zeroed in on him.

Dropping his own gaze from the close scrutiny coming from the man across the street, the boy turned and took a few steps towards the bat-wing doors. Hands gripping the edge, he stood on his tiptoes peering over the top, inspecting each man in the place with his tired, unfriendly, burnt coffee eyes. Patrons were scattered amongst the ten or so wooden tables. His eyes drifted slow-

5

ly around the room noticing the smoke that hung halfway to the rafters with thicker pockets hovering over some of the tables. He heard the quick sound of a deck being shuffled, cards slapping the table and the clink of glass upon glass with the soft murmur of conversation and laughter that drifted through the patrons. All this mingled with the scents of old sweat, stale smoke and whiskey.

Canvassing the interior some more, the lad found what he gathered might be the exit doors leading off the main floor of the saloon. One door was to the boy's left behind the big pot-bellied stove. *Probably the alley,* he surmised. The other exit was six feet or so located the right side of the bar. *Store room,* echoed his mind. The bar was L-shaped with the corner of the L next to the stairs heading up to a second floor. A short balcony ended halfway above the bar area. The bar sported a deep rich dark look, though it was heavily scarred and shiny from numerous wipe-downs, sweat and spilled liquor.

Throwing a glance at the gaudy framed nude woman portrait gracing the wall behind the bar, one red-gold eyebrow inched upward in the boy's otherwise flat expression. Pushing through the bat-winged doors, he took a few steps further into the room, stopping as the chatter slowly died. The boy directed a hard look toward the patrons, who had turned in their chairs to stare at him. After a few moments the light cadence of his boots resumed as he walked over to the far edge of the bar where he could keep the three exit doors in his view. With his back against the wall, a hand dug five cents from his pocket and threw the change on the counter. The coins skittered with a dull metallic rattle against the wood before landing flat on the surface.

"Water," the boy stated in a soft husky tone, while his eyes continued to scope out the patrons.

Mike the burly barkeep, used stubby fingers to gather the coins, creating a scraping noise against the bar as he pushed them back toward the youngster.

"We don't serve kids in here," he said, pointing to the sign

6

that hung over the bar. His square open face then refocused on the lad.

The boy glanced up at the sign, then his threatening dark eyes zeroed in on the barkeep. "All I want is water, then I'll be on my way," the lad answered in a voice edged with hardness beyond his years. He pushed the money back toward the barkeep.

Mike sighed as he reached under the counter. His thick palm wrapped itself around the handle of an earthenware pitcher. A glass tapped the bar as the sound of water filled the tumbler. Mike pushed it toward the kid and watched as he drained the glass in one long gulp. The boy gestured for a refill; Mike complied. Once again, the youngster emptied the glass and gestured for yet another refill. Mike filled it up again. This time the kid just held the glass with his eyes closed, opening them and taking a few more sips before closing them again. Throwing another curious look at the boy, Mike then turned, pulling the towel off his shoulder and wiping the top as he moved down the length of his bar.

The town marshal for White River, Rawley Lovett, stepped off the walk heading for Stewart's. His boots raised puffs of yellow-brown haze with each step he took. On the way, he waved acknowledging Joe Jenkins, a local homesteader, as Joe rode by. The lawman's ears picked out the draft horse's plodding gait amidst the town's early afternoon bustle.

Reaching the latest four-legged newcomer to his town, Rawley rubbed the horse's jaw, his eyes taking in the sleek lines of her build. With a wide forehead, refined nose and eyes of dark colored heartwood, her barrel chest, long body and legs added to her beauty. *No cow-horse, this one,* Rawley thought. His hand lingered on the jaw of the big grey as he turned and gazed at the door of the saloon. Giving her one last pat, he dropped his hand as one boot then the other climbed the steps heading towards the bat-wing doors.

Pushing his way through them, his glance caught the other patrons watching him; he nodded slightly at their questioning

7

gazes. His languid gait kept him moving toward the bar and towards Mike. He noticed kid plastered to the wall at the end of the bar; he seemed to be counting on the wall to hold him up. One hand was wrapped limply around a half-empty glass of water.

Out of habit, a thumb tucked itself into a back pocket as Rawley rested an elbow on the bar. He nodded a greeting to the barkeep. Half turning, the marshal's warm blue eyes continued to scope out the lad. Rawley's brow creased noting the dusty wide brimmed hat pulled low, concealing part of the boy's face. *Been ridin' for a while,* Rawley thought as he took in the boy's dirty coat.

Something told the youngster to look up and when he did his eyes locked on to the man who had watched him from across the street. Briefly his eyes darted to the badge on the marshal's shirt, then fluttered closed again as he dropped his head.

In that split second, Rawley saw dark eyes that were way too cold and hard for a kid that couldn't be no more than fourteen or fifteen years old. *That's not good,* Rawley thought, wondering at his tough visage.

Mike came over and leaned into the marshal, saying, "I told him, Rawley. Said just wanted water, be on his way."

Rawley nodded, still watching the drooping shoulders and head of the boy. "Thanks, Mike. I'll take it from here," he said.

Continuing that slow unhurried gait, Rawley stopped to stand alongside the lad.

Feeling a presence, the boy's eyes opened and he looked up. His eyes continued to rise until they found a rugged, handsome face staring intently at him.

Rawley grinned. He knew he was tall, but to a half-growed kid, he probably looked like a giant.

"Long trip, son?" He asked the boy softly, noting a face smothered in freckles and peach fuzz. *Must be a redhead and not even shaving yet,* Rawley surmised, continuing to watch the youngster.

8

The kid looked down at his glass as fingers wiped some moisture off the sides. He shrugged one of his shoulders encased in the oversized dusty brown coat.

"Well finish that water and head on out of here. This is not a place for young boys," Rawley said.

"I'll leave when I'm good and ready, mister," a husky voice replied.

The marshal glanced down, spotting the partially hidden rig by the overgrown coat. A black brow quirked up as he noted the well-worn leather and shiny grip buckled around the boy's waist for a cross-draw. *This kid won't see age twenty if he's a hired gun or whatever else he's been doing. Where do kids get these crazy ideas?* Rawley asked himself.

"We have rules in this town. I'm here to enforce those rules. Finish up," he warned the boy sharply.

Turning and then narrowing his eyes, the lad made a defiant stand, seeming to dare the marshal to throw him out of the saloon.

As the boy turned, Rawley made a split-second decision, suddenly reaching for the lad's pistol.

Sensing the marshal's motives despite his debilitating fever, the adrenaline kicked in. The boy quickly threw the water into the marshal's face giving him the few seconds he needed. Rushing the man, surprising him, two palms hit the marshal in the chest catching him further off guard. Falling backwards Rawley took the brunt of the fall, landing on the scarred planks with a thud and an explosion of air out of his lungs.

Expecting gunfire, chairs scraped and boots scuffled as Mike's patrons hurried out of the way. They watched as the boy's momentum neatly carried him through a somersault over the marshal's head and shoulders. Mouths dropped open and eyes followed the boy who landed on his feet, running. Bat-wing doors protested the use of force from the lad as they banged against the outside wall causing the big front window to rattle, then bounced back swinging and squeaking.

9

Jumping over the steps, his boots landed with a dull thud in the dirt. One hand pulled the reins from the rail and grabbed a fist full of mane. The mare turned instinctively, the boy hopping on one leg with her movement, trying to land his foot in the stirrup and lock the other hand onto the saddle horn. Finding both, he vaulted easily into the saddle, dust flying from the overgrown coat. Worn heels jabbed into the horse's ribs, making her grunt as she quickly escalated into a hard run. A rapid drum roll seemed to echo against the buildings with the sound of the fast paced horse. Shoes of the grey glinted through billowing yellow-brown dust leaving a trail of haze following the pair.

Rawley scrambled up just in time to see the boy do the quick mount and head northwest through town.

Mike came to stand next to the marshal as his eyes, too, followed the boy. "Don't see many men get the best of you, Rawley, but that boy sure escaped, easily," he finished up.

Flashing a determined smile at Mike's remark, Rawley said, "Yep. Gonna find out what this is all about. See ya later, Mike."

Chapter Two

IT DIDN'T TAKE Rawley Lovett long to find the boy who had stopped at the riverbank. That grey mare stood out like a sore thumb against the fall foliage. Sitting in the saddle, the marshal continued to scope out the kid from his viewpoint. His eyes squinted, watching the lad grimace every time he applied a wet bandana to an apparent wound; Rawley wouldn't know for sure until he got a closer look. Heels tapped the bay's ribs lightly moving him alongside the mare.

Quietly dismounting and throwing the reins around some river brush, Rawley moved to the edge of the short bank, his boots dislodging dirt and loose shale. He walked toward the youngster. A slight breeze gently lifted the dried leaves left on some trees, rattling them. The wind ruffled his dark hair that hung over his shirt collar. Water burbled on its way downstream, blending with the warmer than usual Indian summer temperatures. Rawley heard a trout slap the water upstream. He stopped about ten feet away from the boy, a little to the side so the kid would see him.

Hearing gravel and sand crunch beneath heavy boots, the boy swiveled his head. The man he'd landed on his backside in the saloon stood not ten feet away. In one fluid motion, the kid stood, drew his weapon and began retreating.

Rawley didn't want to hurt the boy, just curious, was more like it. But if he was wounded, the kid might need help. He threw his hands in the air, displaying a non-threatening pose, saying as he did so, "Now son, looks to me like you took a bullet, maybe I can help," Rawley offered, continuing to slowly take steps toward the boy.

Backing up, replacing the distance between himself and the

marshal, his gun aimed squarely at the man's broad chest. A husky voice ordered, "Back off, mister! I don't cotton to shootin' lawmen, but will if I have to. Now you jus' back off," he threatened.

Rawley continued to push the boy toward a piece of driftwood on the bank behind him, large enough to trip the kid and allow the marshal to get the jump on him. "Now son, I don't want to hurt you. Just take a look at your arm. That's all," he said once again, forcing the kid closer to the driftwood.

"Mister, I'm warning you," he gritted. The heel of his left hand settled on the hammer, pushing it down. The cylinder rolled with a soft metallic click, the round stopping under the nipple emphasizing his words.

Rawley's steps hesitated, then resumed, pushing the boy back.

"I don't care to go to the rock pile for shootin' a marshal, but when I let fly with this shooter, I don't miss. Back off!"

"Now, son..." Rawley began.

"I'll tell you one last ti..." the threat ended in mid-sentence as the boy's heel caught on the driftwood, tripping him. Sand and gravel crunched as the kid landed hard, air escaping from his lungs with the impact. His finger compulsively pulled the trigger as the gun danced out of his grip and skittered across the rock-sand surface. The boy's hat flew off to reveal long, copper colored tresses.

Intent on quickly retrieving the weapon before the kid could, Rawley jumped the driftwood. Picking up the pistol and tucking it into his waistband, he turned to say something to the lad. He stopped suddenly, stunned by what he saw lying on the ground.

"Well now, lookie here! Not a boy a-tall, but a freckled face girl!" He exclaimed softly.

Strolling over, he pushed his hat back on his head as he stood gazing at the girl lying there with her eyes squeezed shut in pain. The marshal squatted next to her, "You gonna let me take a look at that arm now?"

Eyes the color of burnt coffee flew open at the soft baritone of his voice, then gazed at him with pure hatred. Rawley blinked at the venom he saw oozing out of those hostile dark depths. "Well what's it gonna be?" he asked offering a hand.

The girl gave him a *Go-soak-your-head* look.

Exhaling at the girl's resistance for help, Rawley stood and prompted with his fingers as he said, "Well?"

The redhead took in a ragged breath of air, expelling it slowly as she grabbed his hand. As she stumbled rising, he caught her and led the girl back, easing her down on the piece of driftwood. Kneeling beside her, Rawley pushed the sleeve higher to examine her wound; a bullet had left a wide crease in her upper arm.

Rawley glanced quickly at the girl's face. Her eyes were squinted shut with her mouth drawn creating a pinched look. He touched her cheek with his hand; she jumped.

A balled fist caught him right below his ear. Surprised at her quick reflexes, Rawley landed on an elbow grinding into the sand. She whisked her weapon from his waistband and headed toward her horse.

The marshal struggled against the sand and the surprise of being clobbered by a girl. He finally just stuck his long leg out, tripping her. She stumbled, sprawling into the sandy loam.

He scrambled toward the girl, hand reaching to grab one booted ankle while the other gripped her arm, flipping the girl on her back. Sand flew sprinkling the two of them like rain. Rawley's weight landed on her thighs, pinning her. He jerked her freckled fists above her head pushing them into the sand and held them there and yelled making the girl blink. "Will you just cut it out! I'm trying to help you! Now just knock it off!"

Venom flashed from dark eyes as she struggled against the marshal. It was no use; he had her pinned good. Expelling the breath she had been holding, she snarled, "Get off me, ya big galoot. You're heavy."

13

Surprised at her comment, Rawley mulled that one over for a few seconds. Most women would say, *'You're hurting me.'*

The marshal shook his head. "No. Not till you let me help you," he said watching as her eyes closed again. He felt her try to struggle some more, then relax. The girl was going down fighting, he had to give her that much. *She's gotta be feeling awful.*

"You gonna fight me anymore?"

Shaking her head, the girl's husky voice whispered, "No."

"Good. I need to get you back to town to see Doc," he said. Standing, gazing warily at the girl waiting for her to spring up and run, he was surprised when she didn't, remaining still with her eyes closed. Rawley retrieved her belongings, walked back and knelt beside her, pulling the girl into a limp sitting position against him. She felt hot, like she had a fever.

Gathering the redhead into his arms, Rawley walked back over to his bay and the grey mare. Placing her on his saddle, the girl slumped forward across the neck of the horse. While holding onto her, Rawley reached for the reins of both horses. After mounting behind the girl and pulling her back to rest against his chest, he began to move out.

The girl whispered something.

Tilting his head, Rawley leaned in asking, "What?"

Licking dry lips, she swallowed. "Fancy will follow. Wrap reins...horn...," her words trailed off as her head flopped back against his shoulder.

A brow quirked up when he heard her words. He knew some horses could be trained to follow like a dog. Rawley looked at the grey, "Well now. So your name's Fancy, huh? You gonna follow me, if I do as your rider told me?"

The mare rolled her lips back, slurping as if she had been given a piece of peppermint candy, then shook her head, blowing.

Rawley knew the animal couldn't understand a word he said, but the horse's response made him smile.

14

Wrapping the reins around the horn, he said, "All right then, let's go."

A few moments later the marshal hitched around in his saddle and sure enough that mare was following behind him. He grinned.

Chapter Three

REINING UP IN front of Lydia's Millinery and Ladies Apparel Shoppe, Rawley swung off his bay. Doc's office was located above Lydia's store. Pulling the girl off the saddle, he carried her in his arms to the stairs.

Watching the marshal ride in with someone in his saddle, Billy ran over to him asking, "Hey Mister Rawley, what 'cha got there?"

Everyone considered Billy Adkins the town street urchin. Very seldom did he attend school, always working odd jobs since his father couldn't stay away from the bottle long enough to find steady work. Somehow Billy felt responsible for his father, which weighed heavily on his shoulders, causing them to slump. He looked and acted older than his age. His rangy build also helped to hide his fourteen years. Long stringy brown hair hung over his shirt collar, framing a thin, angular but pleasant face. His brown eyes peeped from underneath bangs that constantly fell into them. Dirt-crusted fingers were always pushing his hair away like a re-peated tic. If he saw bath water twice a year, it was a miracle.

Billy asked again, "Where'd that girl come from?"

Stopping and turning toward Billy, Rawley answered, "Kid from the saloon." His gazed shifted to the folks stopping to stare at him carrying the redheaded girl.

Brown eyes popped. "But I thought that wuz a boy..." Billy pointed at the girl in Rawley's arms. "Ya mean her wuz a he? Er, I mean, he is a her?"

Giving Billy a withering glance at his confusion, Rawley re-plied, "Yeah..."

"But that kid set you on yure backside..."

Rawley exhaled noisily, "Billy...jus' you never mind...Go put them horses up for me, will you?"

"Sorry, Mister Rawley," Billy said, gathering the reins of the bay and grey.

Shifting the girl once more in his arms as he climbed the stairs to Doc's office he thought, *Damn, what else is gonna go wrong today? A kid slamming my back against the floor in Mike's place, ready to shoot me on the riverbank, then turning out to be a girl and it ain't even noon yet!* He sighed inwardly.

Stopping in front of the door, he kicked it and then rapped several times in rapid succession with the toe of his boot as he yelled for Doc to open the door.

The door flung open. "What in tarnation ya hollering for?" Doc groused, then stopped, seeing the girl in Rawley's arms. "Well don't just stand there, bring her in! Put her on the table."

Quickly stepping through the door, Rawley made a beeline toward the leather-bound exam table, gently lying the girl down. He straightened up and scanned the now familiar office, orderly but dis-orderly chaos evident. Doc's roll-top desk was cluttered with files and opened medical journals. The bookcase was filled to overflowing, papers spilling over the edges of the shelves. He could smell the fresh brewed coffee in the pot on top of a small pot-bellied stove. The only place not cluttered was the medicine chest and bureau where Doc kept his supplies.

Rawley's eyes swung toward Doc. "Took a bullet. Seems to me she's running a fever from it."

Doc pulled on his ear as he watched Rawley remove his hat and swipe his sleeve across his brow. Doc asked dryly, "When did you get your medical degree, Rawley?"

"Huh?"

"Well, you seem to have already diagnosed the patient. Why bring her here?" Doc teased in his crusty way.

Eyes tapered as Rawley gave the prickly bachelor a dirty look. "Because you have the know how to treat this, ya ole

17

crank," he answered.

Doc chuckled. "Uh-huh..." Pulling his specs out of their protective case, he hooked them over his ears for a better look at the girl's wound.

Rawley grinned. Doc had become a good friend, a cranky, crusty friend, but a good one. The older gentleman always seemed to wear a frumpish and harried look about him; grey hairs sticking every which way from running his hands through it once too often. Stubble surrounded an untrimmed salt and pepper mustache, creating a bushy overhang for his top lip. Sharp, intelligent hazel eyes and a gruff demeanor belied a soft heart.

Dabbing and flushing the wound with some carbolic acid, Doc poured more onto gauze, then wrapped the wound with it, ripping and tying two ends together, holding it in place. Rawley waited patiently.

Looking up, Doc addressed the tall man in his office. "Do you know when this happened?"

Rawley shook his head. "Nope...first time I ever laid eyes on the girl was today in Mike's place," he replied.

"This the boy in the saloon that sent you backassered?"

"Shad-up, Doc."

Giving a low chuckle, Doc's palm rested lightly on the girl's forehead and neck. "Got a mess of freckles don't she," he began, then added. "Running a fever. Pick her up for me and let's put her in here," he said, leading the way into a room for his patients. Scratching his stubble watching Rawley place the girl on the bed, he told him, "Need you to run over to Mike's place and fetch me some ice."

"Ice? What for?"

"Need to bring the fever down," Doc said, tugging on his ear as he grinned at Rawley.

"Oh."

"Well, I hain't got all day, boy! Get a move on!" Doc groused.

Doing as he was told, Rawley quickly left Doc's office, picking his hat up from the exam table and resetting it on his head. Reaching for the crystal and brass door knob, he let himself out. Wood steps drummed out a rhythmic cadence as he descended to street level.

Mike's saloon sat catty-corner to the bank; Rawley headed off in that direction.

***

BIG PALMS RESTED on top of the swinging doors as Rawley peered into the hazy dark recesses of the saloon, looking for Mike. When the barkeep came out of his storeroom toting a large crate, Rawley hurried over to him. "You got any chipped ice in that block house of yours, Mike?" He asked.

"Ice? What for?"

"You sure are nosy...ya know that, Mike?"

The barkeep gave a toothy grin.

Rawley scowled at Mike. "Doc needs it for the girl. Uh...I mean the boy to bring his fever down." *The less folks know I was tackled by a girl, the better,* he thought.

Mike gave him a confused look. "Boy?"

"Yeah. You know...the one that was in here earlier today."

"Oooh," Mike gave the marshal a smug look, "That boy."

"Shut-up, Mike. You got that ice or not?" Rawley asked impatiently.

"Hey...Rawley!" A voice called out from across the room. "That boy sure set ya right smart on yure backside, didn't he?" Subdued laughter filtered throughout the room.

Turning at the voice, Rawley picked out Joe Jenkins as the one who had spoken. Ignoring the man, the marshal re-faced the bar, placing both palms on top and muttered, "Damn girl! Already causing me trouble and I don't even know her name yet."

Mike sidled in next to Rawley, "Wait a minute, did I hear you say girl?"

19

Rawley gave the barkeep a dark look. "Shut-up, Mike," he hissed out of the corner of his mouth.

Eyes grew round in a square face. "You mean that boy was really a girl? A girl set ya on yure arse?"

The marshal shot Mike a, *You're dead, if you say one more word,* look.

Ignoring the nonverbal threat, laughter rumbled up from within a deep chest, "Hey...boys..." Mike began.

Grabbing the barkeep's thick arm and dragging him toward the storeroom, Rawley growled, "Shut-up, Mike! You want to make me the laughing stock of this whole town? Now, get me that ice. Doc is waiting on it," he finished, shoving Mike through the door. "Alright, alright, ya don't haft ta be so testy about it," Mike said. A thick click sounded as he lifted the heavy metal handle of the ice house door built inside his storeroom. Picking up a wooden bucket, he disappeared into the cool recesses of the room. Moments later he returned and handed the full bucket to Rawley.

Words were thrown over his shoulder as Rawley hurried out the saloon's doors, "Thanks, Mike!"

Mike shook his head and smiled. Wiping his hands on his apron, he walked over to Jenkin's table. Laughter roared as the barkeep told his tale.

***

DOC HAD ALREADY laid towels on the exam table in anticipation of Rawley's return with the ice. When the marshal burst through the door, Doc motioned silently to fill the towels with the ice. Few words passed between them until Doc handed Rawley the first rolled and ice filled cloth. "Put this one under her neck and across her shoulders," he instructed.

Lifting the girl's head, Rawley got his first really good look at her.

She's a pretty girl, he thought. *Cute, really. Cute as a speck-*

led pup with all those freckles. Her long and dark lashes feathered out to a red-gold color. Her auburn hair that had also turned coppery with the sun framed her petite face.

Standing back, thumbs automatically tucked themselves into his back britches' pockets, Rawley continued to observe the unconscious girl. He figured her height at about fifteen and a half hands high, maybe a hundred and fifteen pounds. Not much to go on; all he knew was that she was quicker than lightening and knew how to handle a gun, a horse and herself.

"Rawley, we ain't got time ta be gawking."

"I ain't gawking, I was thinking, ya old coot," the marshal fired back.

Doc hid his grin as he handed over more ice filled compresses, then whirled suddenly, retreating into the main office. Doc returned shortly with a bowl filled with the rest of the ice and a little water. Motioning toward the girl's rig, he said, "Take off that gun belt. Don't think she'll be needing that here."

Rawley did as instructed thinking all the while how he always felt naked without the weight of his sidearm tied to his leg. As he pulled the belt from beneath her, he noticed her hip bones pressing against her britches', surmising the girl had been traveling a lot and not eating much. Walking a few paces and placing the belt on the back of a chair, Rawley turned and continued to rack his brain for possible reasons why a girl of fourteen or fifteen would be traveling alone and showing up here in White River. There were none.

Dipping the cloth into the icy water and wringing it out, Doc continued to wipe her forehead and neck. He repeated the process, then laid the cold cloth across her forehead. Doc stood, pulling on his ear and chewing on the ends of his mustache, gazing at the girl and thinking.

Interrupting the older man's thoughts, Rawley asked, "Well…now what?"

Glancing quickly over at the tall man, Doc answered, "Now,

21

we wait," as he proceeded to walk to his desk and sit. The chair squeaked as he swiveled around to face his cluttered desktop.

"I'm gonna go get her things and check on her horse."

Giving a dismissive wave of his hand, the old coot said, "Fine...fine."

Chapter Four

EVENING SEEMED TO have descended upon his town, Rawley noticed as he hit the street angling down toward the livery. His eyes were scanning the slowing bustle of businesses closing up for the day. Tomorrow would be Saturday. Folks would be coming into town from the outlying areas to pick up supplies for the next week's projects. Walking past Mike's place, the marshal noted the silence. *The quiet before the storm,* he thought, continuing on toward the stable across from his office.

Strolling through the barn's sliding door, Rawley stepped into semi-darkness with the approaching night. The air was warmer inside than out and brought pungent aromas drifting across his nose. Fresh and old manure, the sweet smell of hay and dried oats and newly oiled leather. He could hear mice scurrying, his footfalls disturbing them.

Stopping by the head of his bay, Rawley rubbed his neck. The other boarders looked at the human with mild interest. The grey mare turned her head, hearing footsteps cushioned by strewn hay; she eyed him as he came toward her. As he gently touched her jaw, he spoke softly, "You're one nice piece of horseflesh. You know that?" Watching the grey munch feed, he added, "Wish you could talk and tell me your rider's name." His hand rubbed gently between her ears.

Rawley continued, "A little rest and some food and your owner will be good as new. Maybe then I can get some answers out of her. You just rest and take it easy. You'll be here a few days yet." The horse nuzzled and butted Rawley's chest, making him smile.

He turned to the girl's saddle hanging on the stall partition. It was an old saddle, the seat and fenders worn and shiny from long hours of riding. Rawley pulled the rifle out of its boot, giving a low whistle as he did so. A Sharp's carbine, no less. Damn thing could knock the strips off of a skunk at five hundred yards; almost too much fire power for a young girl to be toting around.

The marshal had a lot of questions that weren't being answered. *Well, let's see what she has in her saddlebags,* his mind asked. He opened one side and found nothing there that might tell him something, anything. Same went for the other side, except for a couple of boxes of linen encased cartridges for the rifle, percussion caps, powder and shot for her pistol.

In the gear bag, there was just the normal trail stuff anyone traveling would carry. Soot blackened coffee post, plate, fork, tin cup, store bought ground coffee, little bags of salt and pepper, dried jerky and a small bag of beans. He untied the bedroll, found her rain gear and shook it out. Nothing there either. *The girl's a mystery, that's for sure.*

Turning back toward the mare as he began re-rolling the bedroll, he commented, "Sure wish you could talk. I need some answers. Like why is a girl, fourteen or fifteen wandering the country all by herself? And why does she carry such a high-powered rifle?" He cocked a brow at the mare, "Bet you know...but ain't talking." Rawley grinned at his one-sided conversation.

Tying the blanket back behind the cantle, Rawley's hand caressed the worn saddle.

A thought suddenly occurred to him. Sometimes folks hid stuff in the leather or padding of a saddle. Rawley pulled it off the partition and began examining the worn leather. No hidden compartments and no slits, the stitching was still intact with no indication of being altered. He sighed inwardly, replacing the saddle on the wall. Turning, he faced the mare again, leaning his body against the saddle and folding his arms across his chest. "Well, Fancy since you can't answer my questions, guess I'll just have to wait until your rider wakes up," he said. "I get the sneakin' suspicion your owner doesn't want anyone to know who she is," Rawley declared. He threw the girl's saddle bags over one shoulder and then picked up the Sharps and headed back toward Doc's.

***

STEPPING INSIDE DOC'S office he noticed the room was empty. His footsteps led him into the girl's room where Rawley saw Doc bending over her. He continued toward a chair, depositing the bags on the seat and leaned the carbine against the wall. Rawley then walked over to Doc. "Well?" He asked as he removed his hat and began twirling it around on his fingers.

Glancing at the marshal, Doc straightened, squinting bleary eyes at him replying, "The ice seems to be working. She doesn't feel as hot as she did when you first brought her in." Nodding at the gear on the chair, he asked, "Find anything?"

Rawley shook his head. "Nah...I get the feeling the girl doesn't want anyone to know who she is. I even checked the saddle for hidden compartments; nothing," he replied scratching his head. "The girl's a mystery. Comes into town looking like a boy, slugs me in the chest, runs, threatens to shoot me where I find her, hits me again out there. I don't know..." His head gestured toward the rifle, "Carries a Sharps carbine. An awful lot of firepower for a young girl. Rode in on one mighty fine piece of horseflesh. That mare can't be stolen, she's devoted to the girl. Looks like they've been together for a while." Rawley sighed, "Ain't getting any answers real fast."

"Humph," Doc intoned. He remained deadpan as he offered up, "Ya always was a sucker for a pretty girl, but ya like them frilly ones. Hain't never seen you with one loaded with freckles and a side-arm though..."

Rawley shot Doc a dirty look, "That's 'cause we ain't got no freckled redheads in town 'cept her, ya old crank!" Then he added quietly, "I'm just curious, is all."

Hazel eyes holding a glint of humor, Doc moved back to his

25

desk in the other room.

Rawley followed, "I'm gettin' some supper, you want I should bring you something from Maddie's?"

Doc shook his head no.

"Alright, see ya later, ya old coot," Rawley said fondly.

Doc just smiled.

Chapter Five

RAWLEY LOVETT HAD been the town marshal in White River, Wyoming for two years now. The previous marshal, Vern Edwards, had passed away during the time he'd been deputy for Sam Luebker up Montana way. Sam had received word from the folks here in White River on Vern's death since Sam was the closest to a relative Vern had. Good friends were hard to come by and harder to keep out here. The rest became history and Rawley Lovett became town marshal of the little hamlet.

Finding a home in the community had felt good to him. But now he had a mystery girl on his hands, and that was bugging the stew out of him.

Entering his office, Rawley stared at the tall wooden drawer cabinets that held all kinds of information. Vern Edwards had been a stickler for organized files. He figured that out when he'd first taken over the vacant position and Rawley was grateful for that. Vern even set up a missing persons file. Lot of folks disappeared out here, whether on purpose, by foul play, or by not being prepared for these hard winters.

The drawer groaned in protest at being pulled open. His fingers deftly separated the folders until he found the section he wanted. Pulling A through G, he laid them on his desk. Pouring himself a cup of coffee, Rawley settled into his chair as it squeaked with his weight. He began sifting through the papers.

Most had physical descriptions, some having artist-drawn pictures or reproductions of tin-types. Flipping quickly through the pages, he set aside the ones he needed to take a closer look at. Absentmindedly he licked his thumb again, resuming his search. When he reached the C's he ran across one that piqued his interest. Rawley's hands became quiet as he read the notice. His eyes widened as he read.

MISSING
Lacy Carrigan, granddaughter
Anyone having information on whereabouts
Contact Justin Carrigan at Carrigan Ranch
White River, Wyoming
Reward Offered

Rawley settled back in the chair. It squeaked in response, disrupting the silence along with the rhythmic sound of a clock ticking away the seconds. Lacing his hands behind his head, he began to think. *That notice was dated nine years ago,* he pondered. No one mentioned Justin Carrigan having a granddaughter; *out of sight, out of mind.* He knew Justin's son Adam was a drunk, having to lock him up every now and again for him to sober up enough to be able to ride back to the ranch. But Rawley didn't even know Adam had been married or that he had a daughter. More questions than answers began filtering through his brain.

Rising abruptly making the chair pop, Rawley grabbed his hat and the notice and hurried out the door back to Doc's. The doctor had been here for fifteen years, he might be able to fill Rawley in.

He took the steps two at a time, his boots marking a hurried cadence against the wood as they climbed. When Rawley opened the door, he spied Doc: chair tilted back, feet on his desk, sound asleep. Coming from Doc's open mouth were little snorting noises. Rawley grinned thinking. *Wide enough to catch flies.*

Moving toward the girl's room, he peeked in on her. Continuing to her bedside, Rawley bent down and gently touched her forehead, it was much cooler. Doc still had the ice around her. His fingers moved to the towels - touching them, they were wet but still cold.

Leaving the room, Rawley walked over to the edge of Doc's desk. Grinning mischievously, he swept the old crank's feet off the top. The chair protested squeaking loudly as feet clunked to the floor, waking Doc up.

"Confound it! You young whippersnapper!" Doc growled. "Can't an ole' body get a little sleep?" He sputtered.

Rawley made a shushing noise, finger held to his lips. "You'll wake the girl, Doc," he whispered loudly, his eyes teasing.

Rubbing his scruffy chin and cheek, Doc replied, "Humph, she's not gonna wake for a awhile yet, anyhow." His hand waved toward the coffeepot. "Since you so rudely woke me, you can just pour me a cup of coffee," Doc gruffly stated.

The marshal complied, handing the cup to Doc. He poured one for himself and then proceeded to sit on the edge of the desk. He took a sip, then offered up, "The girl's cooled off nicely. I'll have to remember that ice trick of yours," he said dryly, watching Doc over the rim of his cup.

Doc harrumphed, blew his coffee, then took a sip. He squinted up at the marshal. "You said she'd cooled off some?"

Rawley nodded, sipping.

"You sneak in here just to gawk at a pretty girl while she was unconscious?"

"No, grumpy," Rawley said smiling at Doc's response. "I came to ask you some questions." Taking the paper out of his shirt pocket, he handed it over for Doc to read. "Know anything about this?"

Taking the folded paper, Doc opened it. He reached for his specs and hooked them over his ears and scanned the writing.

"Remember anything?"

Eyes peeked over the rim of his specs at the lawman. "Just that she was fourteen when she disappeared," Doc answered. "Carrigan was pretty upset."

"Who? Adam?"

"No...Justin, the grandfather," Doc said.

"Not her father? What about the girl's mother?" Rawley inquired.

"When Marie took her own life, Lacy disappeared. That's when Adam began drinking real heavy. It's a wonder he's still alive," he finished.

"What caused the mother to take her own life?" The marshal prodded.

"Don't know," Doc replied. "The Carrigans' kinda kept to themselves. Vern didn't leave a file on it?"

"Didn't check yet. Found this going through his missing person files. Decided to see what you remembered."

Setting down his coffee, Rawley shifted on the desk. Folding his arms, he gazed at the ceiling then asked, "Any foul play suspected? Kidnapping? Ransom asked for? Family or ranch hands suspected?" His steady blue eyes refocused on Doc.

"Thunder, boy! You're firing questions faster than I can answer!" Pulling on his ear, Doc thought for a moment, "Vern didn't talk about it much. Kept whatever he found out close to his chest." Doc glanced up, his eyes becoming shrewd, "Now that he's gone, you can't pick his brain, huh? Like you're doing to me? You young whippersnapper!"

Flashing that quick smile of his, Rawley answered, "I know, that's why I'm here."

"You think the girl might be Lacy Carrigan?"

A shoulder rose nonchalantly, "Maybe...maybe not."

They both turned as the sound of footsteps clumped up the stairs. The door opened and Billy burst through. The town urchin bent over with his hands on his knees trying to get his wind back. Looking up, the boy panted, "Doc! Mr. Bramlett..." Billy hauled in more air straightening, "...Said come quick, the babies are coming!"

Keeping his seat watching Doc gathering his things, Rawley asked, "Aren't they a bit early?"

Ignoring the marshal, Doc directed his words toward Billy, "Son, go hitch up my buggy."

"Yes sir...Doc!" Billy answered as he turned on his heels and went clumping back down the stairs the way he had come.

"Good kid, that Billy. Too bad we can't do something to straighten out his Dad," Doc said.

"Yeah, I know. I pay him to do odd jobs for me. Feed him once in a while. Hopefully, he'll see there are other things to life than living in a bottle," Rawley said.

"Humph!" Doc retorted, stuffing instruments into his bag. He turned toward Rawley and quipped, "Think you can keep from staring my patient to death until I get back?"

Warm blue eyes smiled, "Who me?" Rawley teased.

"Thunder, boy! Yes you!" Doc groused giving the marshal a dirty look, "And take those wet towels offen her. But iffen she wakes up...don't scare her haft ta death either!" He warned.

Rawley grinned at the old grouch.

Doc pointed to a shelf, "Medicine and fresh bandages on that shelf. Make sure you change it once a day."

"I'll do my best, Doc. How long will you be gone?"

"You see that you do! Don't know. Only the second time we's had twins in White River. Babies is funny sometimes. Never know what they'll do. You know where I'm at if you need me," Doc said. Nodding toward the door of the girl's room, he added. "Times like this, wish there was two of me," he sighed. Shrugging into his coat and grabbing his hat, he rushed out the door and down the steps.

Rawley stood on the stoop watching as Doc climbed into his buggy and drove off toward the Bramlett's homestead. Then he turned and went back into the office and the girl's room, proceeding to remove the wet towels. Stepping back, thumbs hooked into his back pockets while he gazed at the unconscious girl he asked softly, "Who are you? Where did you come from?"

His gaze drifted along the length of the girl noticing her

31

boots. He took them off, and covered her with the quilt; that's when he noticed how small her feet were. Rawley chided himself, why did this girl pique his interest so hard, he couldn't figure. The girl remained a mystery to him and he wouldn't be satisfied until he finally had some answers.

Chapter Six

A MOAN AND rustling brought the marshal out of a light sleep. Stretching the kinks out of his back and neck, he rose from the chair in the girl's room and moved quiet as a cat toward the bed. He watched as her eyes opened and blinked. Stepping closer, Rawley spoke softly, "Well...now...welcome back."

She nearly jumped out of her skin at the sound of his voice. Turning her head she noticed it was the same man she'd fought on the riverbank and slammed his back to the floor in the saloon. She stifled a groan, closing her eyes again. "Where am I?" She asked, her already husky voice deeper with hoarseness.

"Doc's office," came the simple reply.

Her tongue eased out licking dry lips. "How...how long have I been here?" Her mouth felt as if she'd been sucking on cotton for a month.

"Two nights and three days."

"Oh...I've got to leave," she said, struggling to sit up and throw the tangle of covers off her legs.

Placing a big palm on her shoulder and gently pushing her back into the pillows, Rawley said, "You're not going anywhere."

"Don't touch me, mister!" she croaked, angrily swatting at his wrist. Dark intense eyes continued to glare at the marshal. A few moments later her gaze dropped from his hard scrutiny of her. Closing her eyes, she whispered, "Water. I want some water."

"Alright, but you stay in bed, you hear?" Rawley ordered.

Hearing footsteps move and fade, the girl struggled up into a sitting position. With her head spinning wildly from the slight movement of just sitting upright, she tried to stand but couldn't.

She slid to the floor and crawled on her knees. She just made it to the wall and her gear, resisting the urge to pass out. Eyes clamped shut to still the spinning in her head, she rested against the wall, one corner of the window sill digging into her shoulder. After taking a few deep breaths, she grabbed one boot pulling it halfway on. Stopping, she muttered, "This is gonna be harder than I thought."

A pitcher and glass held in big hands came through the door followed by the marshal's body. Glancing at the now empty bed, his gaze swiveled to find the patient sitting against the wall by the window. He caught eyes going round when she spotted him.

Damn, he's a big one! She thought. But she'd tangled with big men before, surprise and smarts had gotten her out of those situations in the past. *It'll work again, but not now.* She sighed inwardly, looking at the boot halfway on her foot. She didn't think she could make it to the stable, wherever that was, much less saddle her horse. *But I have to try.* Looking up again, his eyes caught her attention. *As beautiful as a blue Wyoming summer sky,* the girl thought.

Rawley paced towards her, those eyes blazing hard at her sitting with her back against the wall. "Thought I told you to stay in bed?"

Brown pools tapered into venomous slits. "You don't tell me what to do, mister!" Her voice rasped out.

Rawley squatted his long frame next to her, pouring water into a glass, then offered it to her saying, "Uh-huh...being as sick as you were and now weak as a newborn kitten, you can't even get your boots on."

Downing that glass during his little speech, she handed it back to him for a refill as she wiped the dribbles off her chin. With one hand, she struggled to pull the boot on retorting, "Like I said, mister...you don't tell me what to do!" Sitting back to rest, she took the second filled glass from his hand and gulped that one down, too.

Watching her, Rawley threw his two bits worth in, "Sure..." he said, dragging the word out. "But you don't leave here 'till Doc gives the okay."

Freckles drew closer framing those dark eyes. "Like hell!" she snapped. Grabbing the other boot, she struggled to get that one on, making her short of breath. *I am weak,* she thought. *But I'll never let him know that.* Chasing outlaws, she learned a long time ago, you never let them see your weaknesses. All of your senses had to be on constant high alert to survive. She felt the marshal watching her, not saying a word, just watching. That made the hairs rise on the back of her neck, sending shivers down her backbone.

Observing her struggle with the second boot, Rawley decided to let her fall flat on her face, figuring that wouldn't take too long. He stood and ambled back into the main office, spinning Doc's chair around, he sat and leaned back. Lacing his fingers behind his head, Rawley waited.

The girl swallowed and exhaled softly, watching the marshal exit with his smooth lazy gait. *I'm leaving, I don't care what he or anyone else says.* Rolling to her knees, she used the side of the chair to pull herself up, tottering as she came to her full height of five feet, two inches. Slinging the saddle bags and gun belt over one shoulder, she swayed, quickly grabbing the back of the chair with her hand to steady herself. She closed her eyes for a moment to quell the spinning in her head. Opening her eyes, they flitted to the bed she wanted to crawl back into, but wouldn't. She'd tracked the Dillard brothers back to her hometown and right this very moment they could be on another killing spree. She couldn't let that happen if she could help it. Gritting her teeth, she picked up the carbine with her sore arm and taking a deep breath, squared her shoulders and headed for the door.

Suddenly, a fit of dizziness had her crumpling to the floor, rifle clattering out of her hand, bags and gun belt thudded to the wood as she moaned.

35

When she fell against his knees, Rawley sat up, but it took all he had not to reach out and stop her fall. *She wants to be a tough one...I'll just let her be one,* he thought.

After a few moments of the redhead not moving, he reached out and pulled her into a sitting position against his knees. She swatted weakly at his hand.

"Alright, girl, that's enough," he stated in his soft baritone, then added as he stood and swung her into his arms, "You're through showing how tough you can be for today."

His words made her mouth drop open.

Standing alongside her bed, the marshal's eyes took on a teasing quality as he unceremoniously dropped her on the bed. The redhead came up swinging. Rawley caught both fists and pushed her back against the covers. "I said enough. You hear me? Enough!"

"You dropped me, you bastard!" she fired back.

The air peppered with tension seemed to hang between the copperhead and the tall lawman, one full of defiance against any authority, the other wondering what the hell this kid was all about.

Finally, the girl tried to jerk her fists from the marshal's big paws and he let her go.

Rawley picked up one ankle to remove her boot. The other aimed a solid kick, connecting with his wrist. Dropping the ankle, he exclaimed, "Oww!" Backing off, shaking his hand, he stared at it, then at her. His eyes turned to frost as his face hardened "You damn little spitfire! That hurt!"

Giving the marshal one of her famous blistering looks, she silently tugged off her boots, tossing them across the room where they landed with a clunk under the window. Lying back down, she rolled, over, presenting her back to him.

A deep frown creased Rawley's face, *Damn, she has a temper! And it don't take much to set it off, either,* he thought. One hand continued to rub his wrist where the heel of her boot hit. His voice said something different from what his mind was really thinking, like turning her over his knee and warming her backside good. "You rest some now. I'm sure your little escapade wore you out."

The girl jumped when a warm palm rested lightly on her shoulder. She moved away from his hand, hanging to the far edge of the narrow bed.

He shook his head at her stubbornness, then said, "I'll bring you some supper later." He moved toward the door, glancing back at the thin frame of the girl hugging the edge of the bed. He'd met some hard women in his time, but this one might just take the cake.

Chapter Seven

WHEN THE GIRL awoke again, she surveyed the semi-dark room. A coal oil lamp was lit with a low flame keeping most of the room in shadows. Glancing around some more, she noticed that her gear had been placed back on the chair. Looking nearby, she spotted the tray of food on the bedside table. The girl slowly sat up, then threw off the covers. This time the dizziness wasn't as bad.

Lifting a checkered napkin off the plate, she saw biscuits and a couple of pieces of chicken along with a glass of milk. Reaching for a chicken leg, she took a bite, the flavor tickling her taste buds. Her stomach growled, making her reach for a biscuit. She picked up the glass of milk and drank some washing the food down with it. She couldn't remember the last time she had milk.

Feeling the room beginning to crowd her, she stood slowly to her full five-foot two inch frame. The dizziness she had felt earlier seemed to have disappeared. Taking the half-eaten biscuit, milk and another piece of meat, she opened the bedroom door. Seeing no one in the office, she made her way to the front door, then her hand quietly turned the knob and pulled. Standing to the side, she peeked around the jamb. The town seemed quiet as she stepped outside and softly pulled the door closed. She took a few steps and sank to the stoop. Leaning her head against the stair railing post and closing her eyes, she listened to the sounds of the night.

Every once in a while, she would hear the clip-clop of shod hooves, horses nickering softly in the stillness, a dog barking, voices drifting through the air. A soft breeze lifted copper tendrils and brushed them across her cheek. Scents wafted across her nose; wrinkling it, she tried to distinguish the smells. With her eyes still tightly shut, the girl began to play the game she had taught herself long ago to sharpen her senses. Sitting straighter, she lifted her face to the breeze as she began to think. *Wood smoke, I smell...food?* But she wasn't able to discern what might be cooking on those stoves. A freckled nose sniffed the air for other scents picking out barn smells. *The sweet smell of dried hay and oats, fresh and old manure and the warm horsey scent that came from her big friends.* She used to love spending time in the barn when she was little. She slumped tiredly back against the stair post. *Memories, don't even go there,* she scolded herself.

Giving another tired sigh, she thought of the time lost in tracking the Dillard brothers. Exhaustion combined with being clipped in the arm by a bullet had landed her in the doctor's office. *The trail will be really cold by now,* she thought, fuming.

Making one of his sweeps through the dark town, the marshal continued his languid gate towards Doc's office. The town was putting itself to bed; even Mike's place didn't have the normal roar that accompanied the saloon.

Approaching Doc's stairs to his office, Rawley glanced at the window and saw the soft light continuing to filter through the curtains. As he neared the steps, something else caught his eye. He did a double take, noticing a figure sitting on the stoop. Slowly he climbed the stairs, stopping two down from the girl. The marshal eyed her with curiosity.

Feeling the vibrations of footsteps on the stairs, she opened her eyes and sat straighter, watching his approach. Her eyes tapered. She really hadn't paid attention to his appearance before, but now...*Damn, he's handsome,* she thought, *even in the dark.* In the night, it seemed even darker hair curled over his shirt collar and below that collar, broad shoulders tapered into long legs. Her eyes noted the pistol positioned low for his long arms, the holster tied to a muscular thigh. One big palm rested on the curved grip, the other lightly on the railing. His hat shadowed the upper half of his face; she didn't like the fact that she couldn't read his eyes. *The eyes are the window to one's soul,* her mind said. Eyes drifted to the half-smile playing along his lips, she snarled, "What are you laughing at, you big galoot?"

Hooded and hollow, thought Rawley of the dark eyes surrounded by a million freckles. Those eyes were also expressionless, void of all emotion except when she became angry, and that piqued his curiosity even more. Rawley's grin grew wider at her snippy comment as he moved to sit next to her. Seeing the glass of milk, small chicken bone lying beside it and a half-eaten biscuit in her hand, he said, "I see you ate some meat, too."

The girl nodded.

"Good. That'll help get your strength back up," he said. "You were one sick pup," he added, hoping that would bring out a response. Silence greeted his ears, so he offered up, "My name's Rawley Lovett, town marshal."

Jumping when the man said his name, she gave him a short side-ways look, then returned her eyes to the street, taking a nibble of biscuit in the process.

His voice, deep and velvety soft in the quiet night, continued, "Turn around is fair play. I told you who I am, now it's your turn," he said.

That deep baritone sent shivers down her backbone. *Smooth as warm caramel,* the girl thought.

She shook her head, "No. The less you know about me mister, the better off you'll be," she replied in that husky voice of hers.

Pushing his hat to settle on the back of his head, he focused steady eyes on her, observing. *Trying to prove she's tough as nails.* Changing tactics, he asked, "How'd you get that bullet wound? You running from someone?"

Scoffing, she replied, "Pffftt...hardly."

"Well, I'd like to know who I'm speaking to..." he said, pressing further.

"Like I said, mister, the less you know, the better off you'll be," she answered.

"Well, need to call you something 'sides *Freckle Face*." The comment met his ears with silence. His brow quirked up when he saw her eyes narrow in the filtered darkness. He thought he'd get a rise out of her with his words; it didn't work. "Reckon I'll just call you Sunshine, since you seem to be so sour all the time," Rawley said.

Again, the girl remained quiet.

Reaching out to help her stand, Rawley said, "Okay, Sunshine it is. Need to get you back to bed."

Stopping his hand, the redhead spoke softly, "No...I want to sit here for a while." Cutting a quick side glance at the man next to her, "The room was closing in on me."

Giving a low chuckle, Rawley agreed with her, "I know how you feel. I used to sleep under the stars more often than not. But now I kinda like having a roof and four walls. 'Specially when it's colder than a witch's..." he stopped and quickly rephrased, "Uh, colder than blue blazes out," he finished. *Well that didn't even get a response.*

Standing, the marshal offered, "I'll check on you when I finish my rounds." He turned and headed back down the steps. Halfway down Rawley stopped and turned, looking back at the girl. In return, she gazed hard at him. A black brow cocked, then he resumed his descent.

As Rawley sauntered back across the street thinking about the girl outside Doc's office, his thoughts kept returning to her dark eyes that revealed nothing. Creating an illusion of cold deadness, empty of all feeling, masking the emotions from within. *What in her past had made the girl go dead inside? More questions and no answers once again,* Rawley sighed inwardly.

She relaxed some watching the marshal head off across the street. Sam Luebker had mentioned Lovett before when she had worked for Sam. Lovett was a half-breed, with a Cheyenne mother and a white trapper father. 'Good man,' Sam had said. Smart, honest, good at tracking and detecting, liked solving the puzzle of a crime.

The girl fondly remembered the man she'd worked for, recalling how she had met the sheriff in Montana Territory when she brought some fugitives in for the bounty. He'd hired her to be his deputy. *Go figure.* Sam had taught her how to detect, solve murders and track criminals. 'Learn to think like 'em,' he said. Following his advice, she became even better at what she did.

When she was little, Vern Edwards was her friend and the town marshal in White River. She knew Vern had passed away a few years ago. The town apparently hired this Rawley Lovett to take his place, probably through Sam. Even though the distances were great and handshakes were far and few between, friendships remained.

Rawley Lovett could never find out she was really Lacy Carrigan and granddaughter to the biggest bastard around, Justin Carrigan. That's why she had to leave White River as soon as she could, before her grandfather found out she had returned, even if it was for just a short while.

Lacy sighed. Thinking of her grandfather had opened old wounds and then constantly being on guard with the marshal seemed to tax her even more. She laid back on the stoop, her arm across her eyes. Lacy pushed the thoughts of her grandfather back into the darkest recesses of her mind where they had resided for nine years. Rolling on her side and making a pillow out of her arm, she drifted off, exhaustion claiming her mind and body.

Late hours were gracing the clock's face as Rawley checked Mike's saloon one last time. Turning, he thumped down the steps on his way back to Doc's to see how the girl was making out.

Quietly Rawley took the steps two at a time, stopping just below the stoop. *Sound asleep,* he thought. Noticing that this time she had come out in her stocking feet. *No boots, wasn't gonna run just yet*, his mind mused. Stepping lightly, he knelt beside her

42

as long fingers lightly brushed the hair off her face. He smiled and then handsome features drew into a frown. This redhead was really beginning to bug the stew out of him. He wasn't getting any straight answers from her. The words she had thrown back at him made him even more determined to find out who she was.

Gently picking her up and heading inside, Rawley placed her on the bed. Covering her, he straightened and continued to study her. His mind flitted back to the piece of paper he'd shown Doc. There wasn't any description on that old notice he had found in the files back in the office. Nine years is a long time and a person can change a lot in those years. *If someone wanted to hide, it's not hard out here,* he thought. Something happened out at Carrigan Ranch to make Lacy run away. He wondered if this girl just might turn out to be this missing Lacy Carrigan.

Closing the door, Rawley hung his hat on the rack and made a beeline for the bunk in Doc's office. As his hands laced behind his head, Rawley reminded himself to go through Vern's files on this case. Giving a long yawn, he mumbled, "That's for tomorrow," and closed his eyes.

Chapter Eight

AWAKENING WITH A start, Lacy's hand fumbled beneath the covers searching for her pistol. She then realized where she was, sleeping in a real bed for once. Lacy relaxed and took note of her surroundings before rising. Dust particles danced in the filtered sunlight streaming through the eyelet material framing the window. Sunny speckles covered her gear still on the chair. The last thing she remembered was falling asleep on the stoop. *The marshal must've brought me in last night,* she concluded. Her mind changed gears thinking, *Coffee, I need some coffee.*

Sitting up, Lacy flex her injured arm, noticing that it was on the mend. She placed her stocking feet on the floor and stood without swaying. *That's good.* She hadn't felt good since that yahoo grabbed her rifle and fired, the bullet leaving a deep crease in her arm. Lacy had returned fire, killing him. *Enough memories, all they do is hold you back,* repeating her mantra to herself as she moved toward the closed door. Peeking her head around the doorjamb the office looked empty, not noticing the marshal sound asleep on the bunk behind the exam table.

Stocking feet padded toward the little pot-bellied stove. Opening the stove's door Lacy stirred the coal with a poker she found in a bucket with kindling. Adding the kindling she continued to stir until the flames began licking at the dry wood. Pouring fresh water into the coffee pot, she rummaged around for some ground coffee. Her hand clicked earthenware and tin cups together looking for that elusive bag of coffee. Finding it, Lacy unwrapped the string that kept the cloth bag closed. Her fingers peeled aside the cloth, allowing the rich odor to float up. Sticking her nose closer, she inhaled the wonderful aroma. Fingers found a small scoop within the bag; filling it, she poured it into the pot. Flipping the lid back down with a slight click, she returned the pot to the stovetop.

Lacy ran her fingers through the tangled mass of copper hair as she walked back into her room. After digging her comb out of her saddle bag, she worked the snarls out and braided the strands into a thick rope. Catching a whiff of herself she thought, *Scheesh, I need a bath. I stink.*

Returning to the stove and selecting a tin cup from the shelf, Lacy poured the first cup of coffee she'd had in over a week. Inhaling the aroma, she walked over to the window, peering out as she sipped the brew. Pulling the curtain aside on the closed window, Lacy gazed out on her hometown below. She observed the silent bustle of the street. She noticed two women standing on the walk across the way, hug each other, then began talking and waving their arms as if in a silent mime show. A buckboard drove by, leaving a dusty trail in its path. Another woman joined the first two, creating a trio of silent mime actors. As the three moved off down the street. Lacy turned at the window, her eyes following them until they disappeared. She sighed wistfully.

Rawley had sat up, but remained on the bunk watching the copper-headed girl's movements for some time. Gauging by the patched elbows and frayed sleeves of the black and checkered flannel shirt, he figured she had been traveling long and hard. A patch of winter wool peeked from the V just below her neck. The wool once red had faded to a dusky pink. Well-worn corded britches finished the girl's ensemble. "Well, Sunshine, you must be feeling better this morning."

That deep, soft baritone from across the room startled her making the cup fly out of her hands. Her feet did a quick dance, hopping away from the hot liquid. Her eyes watched the tin cup hit the floor, bouncing with a *ping-ping,* rattling as it settled down. She spun. Pin-pricks of sparks seemed to dance in dark eyes alluding to her quick temper as they focused on him. Grab-

45

bing a towel from the wash basin, she mopped up the spilled coffee. Picking up the cup, she stared at it, then at several others on the shelf. Glancing over her shoulder at the marshal, her eyes narrowed. *Maybe if I give him this cup, he'll catch the plague or something, since it landed on the floor. There ought to be enough germs floating around here,* Lacy thought. And that's exactly what she did. Refilling the cup, she ambled over to the marshal and presented it to him.

A lopsided grin reached to crinkle crow's feet etched deeply next to black framed eyes. "Why…much obliged, Sunshine."

Giving him a contemptuous look, Lacy padded back to the shelf where she retrieved another cup and filled it. Strolling back toward the marshal, she leaned against the exam table, crossing one stocking foot over the other. She threw one of her best blistering looks at the half-breed over the brim of her cup. Sam had said she could throw the nastiest looks he'd ever seen. *Could make a skunk roll over and play dead.* At least that's what he'd told her.

Hiding his smile, Rawley sipped his coffee. The girl just stood there, shooting mean looks at him, not saying a word.

Lacy continued her close scrutiny of the big moose. Dark hair tousled, stubble gracing his rugged face, shirt pulled halfway out of his britches from tossing around trying to sleep on the hard bunk. *He's handsome in the dark, but in the daylight…*she cut the thoughts off, no way would she allow herself to continue thinking them.

Giving herself a mental shake, Lacy cleared her throat. "I need a bath, I'm getting kinda rank. Know where I can get one?"

The soft husky voice pulled Rawley out of his own thoughts of her glaring at him. "The hotel." he said.

"How much?" She asked.

"Four bits."

The girl winced.

"You don't have any money, do you?"

Looking down into her cup, the redhead shook her head, "No. I'll just go down to the river and get washed up, then be on my way." Spinning on her stocking toes, she went back for a refill, bringing the pot and refilling the marshal's cup too.

Cocking a brow, Rawley announced, "It's getting a little cold to go swimming, don't cha think?"

She shrugged, "That's all that's available to me, so...I guess I'll go there."

The marshal stood, making the girl look up, way up. "Tell ya what, I'll fix you a bath in my quarters," he offered.

Eyes gazed at him warily as she asked, "Why?"

"You said you wanted a bath. Apparently you have no money, seems to me the most logical answer."

"You're being nice?"

"Why not?" he returned.

Eyes tapering once again, Lacy just knew he had to have an ulterior motive. But, oh how she wanted a bath in hot water, not some cold stream. Mulling it over for a few moments longer, she finally agreed, "Alright." She threw another scathing look in his direction as she went to gather her things.

Spying that last expression, Rawley thought, *Girl still wants to fight, trying to intimidate me with all those crazy looks she's been throwing.* Doc had told him he had the patience of a saint. This one might push his buttons but so far, she hadn't hit the right ones...*yet.*

Chapter Nine

ENTERING HIS OFFICE with the girl on his heels, Rawley continued toward his quarters throwing her gear on his bed.

Lacy stopped short gazing around the long ago familiar surroundings. When she was little, she used to visit Vern every chance she had. The interior was much as she remembered. Pot-bellied stove by the front window, always a perking pot of coffee sitting on the top. A small table stood against the wall with a shelf above for cups, coffee grinder and a bag of beans. The big desk still resided where it had always been, in front of the door to Vern's quarters, where the marshal now stood, arms folded, leaning against the jamb watching her. Lacy's eyes flitted to the wooden file cabinets where haphazardly stacked papers lay. She glanced down the short hall, door at the end and one to the right. Snowshoes and fishing poles hung on the opposite wall. Focusing back on the main room, she saw a shut door that closed off the cell block. The rack of rifles on the wall next to the cell block was secured by a chain and lock. Keys to the cells rested on a peg underneath the gun rack. Lacy sighed inwardly; she had been gone a long time and this marshal had kept everything as she remembered from her childhood. *Memories,* Lacy thought, *Don't go there.*

Continuing to study the girl, Rawley knew from her expression that she was familiar with this office or dozens like it, making his curiosity about her nudge him a little harder.

Feeling Lovett staring a hole into her head, Lacy pulled herself out of the memories by taking in air for her starved lungs. Flicking him a glance, she walked over toward the stove and opening the door, laid more kindling inside, then stood there watching the flames begin to grow.

48

Bending and picking up the two metal buckets for heating water, Rawley headed out to the pump in the back, leaving the girl to snoop if she wanted to.

***

HANDING THE GIRL a bar of soap and a towel, Rawley gestured at the tub. "All yours," he said, closing the door quietly. A hand absentmindedly scratched the stubble on his face as he headed toward Ezra's store to pick up fresh clothes for the redhead.

Sinking into the water, Lacy sighed in pleasure. It had been a while since she had been able to take a real bath and she was going to savor the moment. She had just finished rinsing her hair when a knock sounded at the door. Before she could reply, it opened and the marshal's head peeked in. Surprised, Lacy drew in a big breath and ducked under the water. Stepping further into the room, Rawley waited for her to resurface, she didn't. Walking over, he grabbed a handful of hair, pulling up a sputtering suds-filled face. She came up floundering like a fish on dry land, hands gripping the edge of the tub, splashing water over the sides leaving puddles on the floor.

"Just wanted you to know I have fresh clothes for you," he said, tossing the package on the bed.

Lacy blinked, then slid back down in the tub until the water met her chin. A hand rose through the suds and swiped the soap from her face.

"I'll be back with some breakfast soon," Rawley added, closing the door once again.

Swallowing, Lacy glanced at the package on the bed then back at the closed door. Air escaped loudly from her lungs.

Feeling almost normal again from the bath and new clothes Lacy stepped into the office. Satisfied that the marshal remained gone picking up their breakfast, she let her eyes roam across the familiar room again as she placed her bags and gun belt on a chair next to the desk. She rested the rifle across the top edge.

Flicking a glance toward the haphazard stack of papers and files on the wooden cabinet, Lacy refocused on the piles littering the marshal's desk instead. She rolled her eyes to the beamed ceiling above saying softly, "Sam, he sure ain't as neat as you and Vern were, is he? Nope." Lacy answered herself as fingers began rifling through the papers, looking for what she didn't know, but would when she found it.

The sound of a door opening made her whirl, one arm reached for her pistol hitting the coal oil lamp sending it crashing to the floor. The smell of coal oil filled the air. Lacy stared at the shattered lamp, watching the coal oil spread and soak into the planked flooring. She glanced over at the marshal, her eyes turning cold at what he had made her do.

Sitting the basket down on the table, Rawley turned, pushing his hat back on his head and stared annoyingly at the girl. "That's twice today. A little skittish aren't you?"

A rosy hue began climbing through a million freckles while dark eyes flashed her quick temper. "Don't you know better than to sneak up on people, you big ox," she retorted, bending down to pick up the broken glass.

Sighing, Rawley walked over. He bent his large frame down to help, but did not see the girl rising. The back of her head hit him square on his chin making his teeth clack, sending him reeling backwards a few steps.

"Ow! You stupid idiot. What do you think you're doing! You jackass," Lacy railed at him, rubbing the back of her head.

"I could say the same for you Sunshine," the marshal returned, rubbing his jaw and moving it around to see if it was broken. "Got an awfully hard head, don't cha?"

Spinning with the broom in her hand Lacy threatened him, "I ought to rearrange your smug face for that!" shooting Rawley another black look before sweeping the glass into a pile.

"You sure are a prickly one, and so early in the morning, too.

Must've been sucking on lemons during your sleep last night. Got up even more sour this morning, huh?" Rawley razzed the girl.

Ignoring the man's barbs, Lacy looked around for something to sweep the glass into.

Rawley picked up an old circular, knelt and curved it into a scoop. Lacy swept the glass into it, then stepped back so they wouldn't bump into each other again.

Dumping the remains into a trash bucket, Rawley walked back to the girl and removed the broom from her hands. He led her by the arm to his chair and not very nicely, shoved her down. The chair squeaked with the sudden impact.

Lacy half came off the seat, ready to lay into the marshal. Catching the quick movement, Rawley pointed and ordered, "Sit."

Dark eyes danced like fire. "You don't talk to me like I'm some damn dog, you bastard," she hissed, settling back into the chair.

His head spun and eyes narrowed when her heard her words. Rawley bit back a sharp retort, deciding it was best to ignore the spitfire's comments. Retrieving the medicine and bandages he'd brought from Doc's office, Rawley squatted his long frame next to the girl.

Her eyes still festering with anger, Lacy clamped her teeth together tight. His touch stirred emotions in her, feelings she had not allowed herself to have in a long time. She had shut down her insides after what her grandfather did to her. It was safer that way, but this...this half-breed was making her feel again. Lacy did not want to feel. If she felt, then the awful memories came back. *Memories will slowly kill you,* she reminded herself.

Lacy kept her bad arm relaxed as Rawley re-bandaged it. The other, her right hand, remained clenched and hidden behind her. Lacy tried to control her fear with being touched by a man, but the harder she tried, the faster her heart banged and ricocheted off her ribs. She focused her eyes on the ceiling, hoping that the mar-

51

shal couldn't hear that heart drumming away on her insides.

Rawley felt the tension in the girl; it seemed to permeate the air around her. He picked up on the fact she did not like him being so close. Whatever had happened to her in the past had something to do with men, he figured. She was a prickly little cuss and that remained a fact; at least with him she was.

He finished tying off the fresh bandage and then patted her hand saying, "There you go Sunshine, ready to tackle the world." Rawley gave her a quick smile as he pulled his long frame upright.

Lacy frowned, "You always so happy?"

Turning at her question, Rawley grinned answering, "Never helps to carry resentments and grudges, makes you sour."

Bouncing out of the chair, "I'm not sour, I just...just have a lot on my mind," Lacy lied, rolling her sleeve down and buttoning the cuff.

"Uh-huh," he answered, not believing a word the girl said. "Breakfast is getting cold." Seating themselves at the table centered between the cellblock and the front door, Rawley enjoyed watching the girl tuck into her food. Grinning at his plate, he decided to see if he could get a rise out of her, she just might slip up and give him some information. Stabbing at his eggs, Rawley casually ventured a statement, "You know, that chip on your shoulder has turned into quite a boulder," cutting her a look across the table. "Must be heavy carrying that around all the time."

Lacy's fork stilled in midair. "I don't have a chip and if I did, it's none of your business," she responded tartly.

"You made it my business," he began, wagging the fork in her direction. "Slugging me in the saloon and, I might add, several times since then." Eying her, the marshal continued to press, "I could have jailed you for ten days, counting all the times you slugged me."

"What?" Lacy cried. "You could not."

"Assaulting an officer of the law? You bet I could, Sunshine," he returned sternly.

Eyes hardened at his ridiculous name for her. Lacy launched herself upward, sending her chair crashing backwards. Slamming both palms on the table, she leaned toward the lawman.

Ah...ha, thought Rawley, *got her.*

"My name is not Sunshine, it's Lacy, you big moose," she shouted. Then realizing she had just given him a clue to her true identity, she quickly straightened up.

Tilting his chair back on two legs, he folded his arms across an expanse of chest and gave her a lopsided grin. Rawley said, "Well...well, I finally got a straight answer out of you."

Color blazed across a million freckles as Lacy's hands edged under the top. Giving a heave, she upended the table, sending food, dishes and coffee all over the marshal as he too, toppled backwards in his chair.

Quickly comprehending the trouble she had just put herself in with the marshal, Lacy whirled, hastily grabbing her gear and flew towards the door.

Shoving the table off his legs, Rawley scrambled, boots skidding as he tried to gain a foothold on the slippery floor. His strides instantly closed the gap as he swiftly reached out with one long arm, fingers stretched and closed around the collar of Lacy's shirt, yanking her off her feet. Saddlebags, gun belt and rifle thudded and clattered to the floor. Spinning her around, he shook her vigorously. Lacy's head bounced back and forth like a rag doll. "You snarlin', spittin', damn little wildcat!"

Blinking and trying to refocus her eyes, Lacy's anger rose. As she flicked a glance at the egg and coffee dripping from his chin, then rose to take in angry eyes that had turned to ice, as frozen as a mountain stream in winter.

Feeling the quick shift in the girl's weight, Rawley turned in the nick of time, taking a knee meant for his crotch on his thigh.

The marshal had anticipated her move. *Damn,* Lacy's mind

went blank, *Now what?* She brought a worn heel down hard on his instep. Rawley winced, but still stood his ground. *Damn, double, damn.* She racked her brain for more of what Sam had taught her. She'd never had to go to plan 'C' before; the first one usually brought 'em down like a sack of rocks.

"You want to fight like a wildcat?" A voice low and deep with anger answered his own question, "Well...I'll just cage you like one."

Rawley's hand grabbed the cell keys off the peg while he kept a tight grip on Lacy's arm dragging her toward a cell. Throwing all one hundred and fifteen pounds into reverse, Lacy locked her knees to resist his strength. Her fingers dug into the door's framework like a hay hook. It didn't work. Her boots still slid and scraped along the wood floor.

Flinging open the metal door, Rawley shoved the copperhead in, making her tumble to the floor. Lacy bounced up, but not quick enough; the door slammed into her face with a heavy clank. Thrusting the key in the lock Rawley turned it, tumblers clinked into place, sliding the bolt home. Cold, hard, blue steel zeroed in on the spitfire standing behind the bars giving him her own wicked look.

Hands balled into fists, nails digging into her palms, Lacy didn't back down from his stare. Instead, she moved forward and spit.

As he wiped the spittle off his face, Rawley's tone dropped even deeper and softer in his anger. "Sunshine, you've got one hell of a bad temper. You'll stay in there till you simmer down or hell freezes over."

The office door banged open and Rooster slid through, crowing, "Marshal?" Rooster had become the town's gadfly. A thin, wiry fella, with a shock of stiff, sooty, grey hair crowning his head; the reason someone back down the line had begun calling him Rooster.

Turning, both Lacy and Rawley stared at the man whose eyes

54

were large 'O's with his mouth hanging open as Rooster surveyed the tossed chairs, upended table, food and broken dishes all over the floor. His befuddled look settled on the marshal with egg and coffee splattered on him with a girl in the cell. Rooster scratched his head. "What the hell happened here?" breaking the tense silence that filled the office.

"Had a difference of opinion with a wildcat," Rawley replied, nodding over his shoulder at the girl as he hung up the keys. Standing in front of Rooster, Rawley scraped a glob of hardening egg off his cheek, staring at it while he asked, "What 'cha need, Rooster?"

"Rawley, I stopped by the Clancy's place for a visit...they've all been murdered," Rooster said in a rush.

"What?"

"Someone came in and well...they's all dead! Ever last single one of 'em."

Lacy moved closer to the bars, gripping them tightly, eavesdropping.

"Give me a chance to get cleaned up, then I'll get out there," Rawley threw the words over his shoulder, disappearing into his quarters, door slamming.

Lacy *spissed* at Rooster, her hand quickly motioned him toward her. When he stood in front of her she asked quietly. "What did the bodies look like, Rooster?" Rooster hesitated. "I know it was gruesome, but tell me about it," she prodded gently.

"Well...they'd been shot and their throats slit."

"The Dillard brothers," Lacy whispered. "Look, Rooster. I've been tailing those sum-bitches for over a year. You've got to let me out," she said, reaching through the bars, trying to grab his shirt.

Rooster pulled back. "Oh no, miss, ah can't. Rawley'd have ma hide."

"I'm an undercover federal marshal, Rooster," Lacy lied. "My job is to bring those bastards to justice."

55

Rooster's eyes popped. "You an undercover marshal?"

"Yes," she lied again. "Now open this door."

Hustling for the keys, Rooster unlocked the cell door.

Rushing out Lacy picked up her gear then stopped and gave Rooster a peck on the cheek. "Thanks Rooster. I owe you one," she said hurriedly. Heading for the door she slid to a stop, turning and asked, "Rooster, whereabouts do the Clancys live?"

"Five miles northwest, toward Kirby's Knob," he replied.

"Thanks, Rooster." She didn't bother to ask for more details since she remembered the landmark.

Following, Rooster stood in the doorway and watched the girl run across the street to the stables. He touched his cheek where she had kissed him. Smiling to himself, "Mighty fine filly, that one," he said. A few moments later he saw her tear out of the livery, riding low across the neck of her horse. The tattoo of hoof-beats echoed against the buildings. Scratching his head, Rooster surveyed the mess in the office, then begin setting things right and sweeping the floor.

A door opened, causing Rooster to pause in his cleanup. Walking briskly, Rawley unlocked the gun case, retrieving his favorite rifle, a Henry that held sixteen rim-fire brass cartridges. Those confederate boys hated that Yankee rifle, their muzzle loaders no match for the new Henry. *Load it on Sunday, and fire all week,* they said. Next he took a box of shells for the Henry, powder, lead and percussion caps along with extra cylinders for his Navy Colt out of the desk. Lifting the flap on the saddlebags, he dropped the items inside. Rawley looked up then at Rooster.

"Thanks Rooster, I owe you one," Rawley said, picking his coat and slicker off the peg, heading for the door.

"That's what the girl told me too, when I let her out." Head swiveled as Rawley stared into the now empty cell. "You what?"

"Well Rawley," Rooster began, leaning on the broom, "She said she was an undercover federal marshal, been tracking those killers for over a year."

A jaw clenched and eyes hardened in anger, "She is not, Rooster, I would have known about it!" Throwing the words over his shoulder as one heel hit the walk, the other boot reaching for the street, "She's probably a damn bounty hunter!"

Tossing his saddle on the bay, Rawley realized everything was beginning to make sense now; the secrecy, carrying a Sharps rifle, knowing how to protect herself. *Sunshine is a bounty hunter, a damn bounty hunter.* Rawley dug his heels hard into the bay's ribs, forcing a grunt and speed in the horse's gait as he followed a copperheaded spitfire.

Chapter Ten

LACY TROTTED FANCY to within thirty feet of the porch, *Hopefully this is the Clancy home,* she thought, never having been here before. She saw the door standing wide open causing her body to automatically tense, putting her on guard. A hand wrapped around the grip of her gun and rested there. Her eyes swept the layout of the homestead - a small, clean looking board and batten home with a porch running the length of the front. A couple of slat-backed rockers sat on one side of the door with two wooden buckets under the window on the other side of the door. Steps led off the porch on the three sides. Deep wash pans hung on the side of the house facing the barn. Wooden framework surrounded the well. Hanging from the center wooden brace was a metal pulley with a rope tied off to a wooden hook. The barn appeared medium size with corral and stock pens. A line of trees shadowed the far edge of the yard.

No human sounds, Lacy noticed. Fancy kept dancing from one foot to the other, showing her impatience. Lacy relaxed her hold on the reins while one hand rubbed and patted her silky neck, settling the big grey down. Fancy lifted her head up, shook it and blew. Her bit gave a slight jingle.

Lacy tuned her ears to listen harder. A soft breeze carried noises of the farm animals toward her, soft clucking from a few chickens scratching around in the yard. The milk cow's tail swished along its back while the one horse kept shaking its head and stamping at the flies. She heard rooting and snuffling coming from a few hogs out of sight behind the barn. Squirrels were chattering from the edge of the trees.

She saw what seemed to be four sets of hoof-prints. Lacy

threw her leg over the pommel and hopped down. Her knees cracked when she squatted, causing her to wince as she surveyed the ground. One set of hoof-prints headed toward town, *Rooster,* she thought. The other three sets looked to be traveling toward the hills.

As Lacy stood and looked around, she saw old wagon tracks heading to the barn, along with a set of boot prints and a woman's shoe prints with smaller prints made by children. Four sets of large boot prints covered the previous imprints in front of the porch, meaning they were the last ones to ride out of here.

Lacy dropped Fancy's reins and walked around to the side of the porch. Stepping up, she walked quietly to the door, her nose catching the strong odor of blood and the fading scent of black powder. The scent intensified when she stepped over the threshold. Lacy felt as if she had been sucking on copper pennies like candy.

Kneeling by the first body she came to, Lacy noticed the woman had been shot at close range. Her throat was slit from ear to ear. Lacy picked up a hand that was still warm to her touch. Turning over the woman's hand, her eyes settled on the gold wedding band on the woman's third finger. Tearing her eyes away from the ring, she saw the hair, skin and blood under the fingernails. Lacy was glad the woman had put up a fight. *One or more of the brothers will have scratch marks on their faces.* This hadn't been done too long ago either – a good sign. With the tracks outside, Lacy would be able to pick up their trail quickly.

As fast approaching hoof-beats met her ears, Lacy ducked and moved quickly to a wall by the window. Pulling her weapon with one hand, the other hand pushed the curtain aside just a tad as she eased a peek through the glass panes. She heaved a sigh of relief. It was only the marshal. Stepping through the door, she walked to the edge of the porch.

Rawley slid his horse to a stop next to Fancy. "Damn it! Sunshine, you're contaminating evidence," he yelled, swinging off

59

his horse.

Lacy could see his anger. She yelled back, "No, I'm not! But you will, if you come any closer." Her hand gestured to the ground in front of the porch. "Leads, clear ones too. Leave your horse there," she ordered. "Walk around to the side here. I have something to show you." When he walked up beside her, he gave her a look of pure boiling rage. Keeping her face flat and cocking a dark red-gold brow at the marshal, Lacy led the way to the death and devastation inside the house.

Rawley smelled the scent of blood and black powder as he stepped up on the porch. Seeing Lacy here first made him even angrier. She was a bounty hunter, she had no business here. *That's my job!* he thought angrily.

Following Lacy in, he stopped first at Martha Clancy's feet. Eyes roaming the room he found the little girl lying by the cook stove. He walked over and knelt by Hanah. His hand softly brushed her cheek and gently smoothed the white blond hair from her face. Resting an elbow on his knee, fingers pressed the tears back into his eyes. *She won't be playing checkers with me anymore,* Rawley thought sadly. His hand dropped as he looked up and stared blankly at the wall. He blinked furiously, trying to keep the moisture at bay. When that had passed, he swept his eyes around the room. He saw the open doorway to his right. Standing, Rawley already knew and dreaded what he would find; he heaved in air and held it as he steeled himself. The baby not more than four months old, had a bullet hole in its little chest. The tiny throat slit, the bedclothes drenched with blood. He swallowed the bile that rose up in his throat.

Lacy hung back, chewing on a corner of her bottom lip, her thumbs tucked into her britches' back pockets as she watched the marshal make the brutal discoveries. He probably knew these people; it would hit him harder than it would her. She had seen the Dillards' brutal killings before, but the marshal had not.

Rawley turned and saw Lacy analyzing him with detached,

unemotional eyes. Spotting Pat, the lawman pushed past her, his heels rang hollow with angry strides across the floor disturbing the thick silence. They had made Pat kneel on the floor with his hands tied behind his back. A small bullet hole in the back of his head had caused his body to fall forward. His head was resting on the floor with a string of dried blood that had wound its way along Pat's neck disappearing into his shirt. He had been killed execution style.

Lacy followed him. She watched his face display a mosaic of emotions as he struggled to comprehend the brutality of the situation.

Catching her level gaze, Rawley's grim face glared back with barely controlled rage.

Lacy moved closer speaking softly, she asked, "You ready to hear what I have to say about these bastards?"

Breathing in deeply and slowly, the marshal just nodded in response.

"Let's step outside for some air first," she said, leading the way to the porch rail. Placing her forearms on it, she leaned over the rail, hands clasped lightly in front of her.

Rawley followed, placing his hands on the rail with his head down. He took in more slow, deep breaths. He finally looked up, gazing across the yard to the trees on the far side.

"No matter how many times you work a gruesome scene like this, you never get used to the death, destruction and loss of life. You wonder sometimes what their futures might have been. What kind of people the children would have grown up to be," Lacy breathed out quietly.

Surprised at the girl's caring comments, Rawley slowly turned his head to stare at this copper-headed bounty hunter who, only a couple of hours ago, dumped a table of food on him and tried to bring him down with a knee to his crotch.

The girl continued to stare out across the yard.

"You run across this a lot?" He asked simply.

61

"Depends," she said, giving a shrug. "These boys are butchers, slaughtering butchers," Lacy gritted through clenched teeth.

Knitting his brow, Rawley inquired, "Why are you doing this kind of work?"

"Justice. Justice for the victims," Lacy replied softly.

"But you're a…," he began then trailed off.

"A woman?" Lacy answered scornfully. "What you really mean is…why am I not blubbering, becoming a hysterical female, losing my head, carrying on like most women would do?"

Rawley shrugged a shoulder, answering quietly, "Yeah, I guess that's one way to put it."

"You learn to shut yourself down and concentrate on the clues they leave behind…how they killed their victims. Each death scene has a signature. It's my job to figure it out, going after the ones who did it."

The marshal was finally getting some answers to his questions. He realized she was more than just a bounty hunter. She acted like a detective. He asked, "Who do you work for?"

Lacy straightened up. "Myself," she answered flatly.

She turned to the marshal and placed a hand lightly on his shoulder as she spoke softly, "I'm so sorry about your friends. I know this is hard for you. I've seen their work before, you haven't. But now, we have a job to do." Her eyes turned aloof and cold again as she left and re-entered the house.

The marshal watched the girl walk back to the scene of death. He returned to the door and standing in the opening, he tucked thumbs in his hip pockets as he watched her.

Lacy had a cold, calculating and methodical way of going through evidence. Showing no emotion, all business, *She's been doing this for a while,* Rawley surmised

After walking through the room, looking for more clues and not finding much, Lacy walked back over to Mrs. Clancy. Kneeling down, she glanced back at the marshal who still stood in the doorway. "The Dillard boys shoot their victims at close range."

She pointed, "See, powder burns on the clothing. Then, to make sure there are no witnesses to their heinous crimes, they slit their throats. That way they bleed out, in case they happen to survive the bullet," she explained.

Lifting the woman's skirts, Lacy saw that she had been repeatedly raped. Taking a big breath, she added, "They also like to rape the women." She moved to the little girl, lifting her skirts. Lacy let go of the air she was holding. "And the little girls too, but not this time."

Rawley heaved a sigh of relief too, folding his arms and asking quietly, "How long you been after them?"

"Year and a half. This is the closest I've come on a fresh killing of theirs."

Holding up the woman's hand, Lacy gestured with it at the marshal, "She put up a fight, blood, hair and skin under her fingernails. Someone will have some real good scratches on his face and neck."

Rawley suddenly realized something was missing, the boy, little Howie. "The boy, where's the little boy?" he asked, suddenly standing erect, worried now. "Where's Howie?"

"What?" Lacy looked up quickly, giving him her full attention.

"Pat and Martha had three kids, two girls and a boy. The boy is not here."

Lacy jumped up, moving quickly toward the Marshal. She grabbed his shirt with both hands. "Oh, God! We've got to find him!" yanking on his shirt as her eyes filled with horror. "They don't take hostages. When they do, it's only to sell them as slaves across the border!"

Rawley peeled her hands from his shirt, but continued to hold them. "Howie liked to play hide 'n seek. Was...er...is a devil at it. Maybe he's hiding someplace," he offered.

"Okay, I'll check the barn. You check the rest of the places," Lacy ordered as she tried to pull away from the marshal.

"Simmer down, Sunshine," he said, holding tight to her small but strong hands. "The boy doesn't need to see how upset we are," he stated calmly.

Lacy stared at those big paws engulfing her hands in a warm, gentle embrace. It had been years since she had let a man touch her, not even Sam. She tensed. Rawley felt the change and released her. Lacy hastily shied away; whirling, she hopped off the porch.

Calling for Howie in the barn, she became more frantic when she didn't hear any response. Up in the loft, Lacy shifted the hay, but found no little boy. She could hear the marshal calling in the distance.

Lacy met Rawley by the front porch, their eyes mirroring what each felt inside.

Rawley raked knuckles across the beginnings of dark stubble. "They invited me out for dinner one night. Howie was hiding; we couldn't find him. He finally came out from under the house. Guess I'll crawl under. Hopefully, he's there," Rawley said as he knelt to do a belly crawl.

Lacy's fingers bit into the marshal's muscular upper arm, "No. You'll get stuck, I'll go."

The marshal watched as the girl quickly disappeared under the porch, softly calling for the boy.

Lacy crawled into the darkness, her hand swatting the dangling spider webs out of the way. She called out, "Howie, its Lacy. I'm a friend of Marshal Rawley. It's okay to come out now." Crawling further into the darkness, she *spiffed,* as a web caught her in the mouth. Hearing a whimper from far back under the house, Lacy urged softly, "Howie, it's okay now. Come to Lacy. Marshal Rawley is waiting for you." She heard the rustling coming closer, "That's it Howie, come to Lacy."

Rawley listened to Lacy persuade the boy to crawl out, *That husky voice would melt butter.* When needed, the girl could be soft as a feather despite all the hardness she pretended to exhibit.

So she does have a heart, not a block of ice as he had thought earlier.

Seeing a blonde head poking from under the porch, he squatted down and pulled the little tyke out the rest of the way. He stood him up and brushed the dirt and spider webs off him.

Lacy crawled out next.

Rawley helped her up, repeating the process with the copperheaded girl.

Reaching down, Lacy took the boy's hand and sat on the steps. She pulled him onto her lap and held him tightly as she began rocking him.

Watching this scene play out before him made Rawley push his hat back on his head, puzzled. One brow quirked up as he watched the redhead, *The girl might actually be human after all,* he decided.

The boy with his face in Lacy's neck whimpered, "I want my Mama."

"I know, honey," Lacy whispered, holding him even tighter as she rocked. She took a big breath before saying the first thing that came into her mind, "The angels came for your Mama."

"Why?"

Lacy closed her eyes. *God, what am I going to tell him now?* Her mind grasped at the air for an answer. She finally whispered, "They need her in heaven to…to help with…with things."

The little boy nodded into Lacy's neck, he mumbled, "Thiffy?"

"Your sister is with your mama and the angels."

"Papa?"

Lacy looked up at the marshal, her eyes speaking volumes to him. *How do you tell a little boy he's lost his whole family?*

Rawley squatted in front of the them, he placed a gentle palm on the child's back. The towhead peeked around at his big friend, tears making tracks through dirt smudged cheeks.

Rawley's eyes softened, "Your papa is there with the angels, too," he stopped, not knowing what else to say.

The boy reached out for his big friend. Rawley took him in his arms as he stood.

Howie had a death grip around Rawley's neck with his little legs clamped tightly around the marshal's narrow waist. Rawley looked at Lacy, his eyes asking, *Now what?*

Lacy rose, returning the marshal's gaze. The boy reminded her of a stick-tight on the lawman's clothes. The sight made the corners of Lacy's mouth twitch up a little.

Rawley, seeing that ghost of a smile appearing, smiled back.

"Well…I need to get on those boys' trail," Lacy said, glancing over her shoulder. "By the sign, they are heading for the hills into the mountains…gonna be cold with snow up there."

"Now you just wait a minute, Sunshine! That's my job. You take the boy back to town and make sure Doc checks him out."

"No!" Flashes of anger lit the dark depths of her eyes as an irate arm flew out, pointing toward the mountains. "That's fifteen hundred dollars heading to the high country!" Lacy said crossly, poking herself in the chest with her thumb. "I've been tracking them far too long to let someone else do my job." Angry passion fueled her next words. "They've been jamming their thumbs in my eyes for over a year. That money's mine!"

She whirled around as her boots angrily chewed up dirt, moving toward her horse. She stopped abruptly to look at something in the dirt. "Hey, one horse has a broken shoe, that may cause the horse to go lame, which will make trackin' easier," she said as her eyes followed the prints.

Rawley moved to Lacy's side. He breathed angrily, "You blood sucking little bounty hunter!"

Lacy stood slowly and turned even more slowly to face Rawley Lovett.

White fire continued to erupt from blue eyes as dark ones stood their ground. Her's not flinching a lick.

"Call me whatever. They killed your friends," she replied

66

quietly. "I plan to bring them in once and for all, cold or warm, slung on a saddle or dragging them. I don't care which. After you take care of the boy, catch up with me," she ordered as she continued on to Fancy picking up the reins. She turned to face the lawman once more. "I'm sure your Cheyenne blood will lead you right to me," she said tartly. Lacy swung into the saddle and whirled the big grey around following the tracks toward the hills.

"Damn you, Sunshine. Damn you," Rawley whispered.

Chapter Eleven

THE MARSHAL REINED up in front of the Ladies Millinery &
Apparel Shoppe, he dismounted and quietly carried the sleeping
child up the steps to Doc's office. Rawley stopped on the stoop
and turn to look down on his little community. It felt like a month
had passed since the last time he'd been in town. In truth, it had
only been a few hours as he gazed at the midday traffic. He
turned again, his hand opening the door and stepped into Doc's
office.

Doc rose from his desk, putting down the medical journal he
had been reading. Taking off his specs, he motioned for Rawley
to put the boy in the girl's old room.

Rawley expelled a vast lungful of air after laying the youngster on the bed. It felt like he had been holding his breath for
hours. "Guess you heard what happened."

Doc nodded.

The marshal continued, "Lacy found him under the house,
the only one alive."

"Lacy Carrigan?"

"Don't know. I just know her first name. Listen. Doc. I've
got a hot trail. Don't know how long I'll be gone," he said, taking
another deep breath. "You'll look after the boy?"

"Liv and I will."

"Thanks," he said turning, going back into the outer room.
When his palm wrapped around the crystal knob to the outside
door, he stopped and stared at his hand holding the knob, quietly
asking. "You'll see to the bodies?" Blue eyes sadly looked back
at Doc, "It's not pretty. Oh…and there's some stock out there that
needs tending to," he added.

Doc nodded, "I'll get some folks together…take care of things. You just make sure you catch them sum-bitches… 'fore they kill someone else around here," he said.

Rawley acknowledged Doc's words, closing the door softly, his boots setting a hurried cadence down the steps. His normally languid gate had an urgency to it as Rawley cut across the street to Ezra's for more supplies and blankets. If Lacy was right, it would get mighty cold up there. He loaded up his horse, swung into the saddle and rode off to find the trail and Lacy.

Chapter Twelve

Making slow progress, Lacy knew the Dillard brothers would be in no hurry. They always picked out-of-the way places to go on a killing bender, giving them a week or longer head start. This time was a fluke this time. Maybe there was a God after all. Maybe God wanted them caught. Maybe the Clancy family would be the last ones the Dillards ever killed, and if she had her way, Lacy would make sure *that* family got the justice they deserved!

Howie sure is a cutie pie, Lacy reminisced as she guided Fancy along. White blonde hair framed his little heart shaped face. He wore little corded britches held up by miniature suspenders. Lacy would never forget those big blue eyes, staring at the marshal with such trust. Trust that the marshal would make everything all right in his little world again. Well, Lacy determined, she'd make damn sure one lawman made it right with that little boy.

***

THE TRAIL LED into deep evergreen, hardwood and boulder strewn terrain. The sharp scent of pine filled her nostrils. Snow had already fallen in the upper elevations. Lacy could see her breath and Fancy's in the dusky twilight. Finding a sheltered spot against a small bluff of rocks out of the wind, she set about making camp. The marshal would show up, Lacy knew that; without a doubt he would be there soon.

A wolf disturbed the deep quiet of the forest, his howl echoing against the granite sides of the mountains. Lacy sipped her coffee, her ears alert for sounds that did not belong within the forest boundaries. An owl began a short cadence, answered by another one not far away. Lacy sat up straighter. One hand sat the cup down, while the other picked up the Sharps. Fancy nickered, announcing another horse.

Wood smoke teased Rawley's nose. Allowing that to be his guide, he eased the bay closer to the camp. Dismounting some ten yards out, he moved forward, ground cover crackled beneath his boots and shod hooves pinged on overlaying shale announcing his arrival. Stopping, his penetrating blue gaze surveyed the scene through some scrub, but he didn't see Lacy. *Probably ready to bushwhack me,* Rawley decided as he walked into the firelight.

Hearing a couple of rocks clatter, he moved into a half crouch and pulled his weapon with the muzzle aimed at the sound. He caught sight of Lacy coming from around the boulder, aiming that damn buffalo gun at his gut. Expelling air, the marshal relaxed and holstered his gun. He held his mount's reins while he waited to see what kind of reception the girl would give him.

Lacy smiled to herself as she observed the marshal re-holstering his gun. Going over to the fire she sat and picked up her coffee. "You're losing your touch…half-breed," she quipped, resting the carbine against the log next to her, "Thought you'd be quieter."

Rawley's eyes narrowed at her reference to him, "Didn't want you taking any pot shots at me."

Lacy raised red eyebrows, acknowledging his reply. She asked, "Where's the boy?"

"With Doc," he said. Coming further into the firelight, he asked abruptly, "How'd you know I was part Cheyenne?"

Lacy stalled on purpose but she finally answered, "Oh…I have my sources. By the way, are we gonna have a visit from

70

your cousins or any of your other relatives?"

"What the hell is that supposed to mean?"

Her mouth formed a big 'O', as she thought about her answer, "Well...you may have some hostile relatives out there that jumped the reservations. I just wondered if we were gonna have to fight them, too?"

"Not likely..." snapped Rawley. "...My relatives, as you so snippily put it, would be in the lower elevations this time of year *if* ..." his voice emphasized the word if, "...they jumped the reservation...they're not gonna come into the high country until summer...if then..."

Lacy spoke loftily, "Well...I just wondered...but if we happen across any of your cousins, I guess I could just send you out as a peace offering, you knowing their language and all."

"Sunshine, you got one sharp-fanged little mouth."

"I've got my hands full trying to catch up with the Dillard brothers," Lacy defended her words, "I don't need more trouble. I just want to be sure I don't have to go running or hiding, or have to fight your cousins to survive...that's all," she explained

Silence.

Lacy shrugged and broke the quiet, "Might as well unload and get comfortable. There's hot coffee and some beans." She looked at him, then added, "Gonna get cold tonight."

Razzing me about my cousins...hell! thought Rawley. He would bet his bottom dollar she was Lacy Carrigan. He turned to his horse and his fingers nimbly released the half-hitches holding the gear bag to the saddle horn. The sack whispered through the air when he threw it across the fire at Lacy. It landed with a dull thud next to her legs, its contents clinking.

She looked up quickly, her mouth opening in surprise. Closing it, she gave him one nasty, black look.

"Picked up a few more supplies, got a feeling we'll be on a long trek. Split that between us, so's the ponies aren't carrying such a load," he said, ordering her. He untied her new coat, and

71

threw that at her, too.

Lacy's eyes were enormous now. The firelight was reflected in them as she gave him a flabbergasted look.

Rawley spoke brusquely, "You'll need that too, if we're going where I think we're going." Her freckles stood out in the glow of yellow and orange flames flickering across her face but her dark eyes were hostile. Rawley waited for the spitfire to say something. She didn't.

The marshal turned and sauntered back to his horse. He unsaddled the gelding and led him over next to Fancy, picketing it. He dropped his saddle and bags by the fire where they landed with a dull thud. Rustling noises filled the air as he dug out his cup. Lacy listened to the sound of liquid being poured into the tin, mingling with the popping and crackling of the fire. She kept quiet. Rawley sat and leaned back against the leather, it creaked as he settled comfortably into its curve. He watched the girl as he sipped the hot brew, waiting to see what would transpire next.

Silence permeated the circle of campfire light except for the snapping, crackling and popping as flames licked at old tree sap.

Rawley kept his eyes on Lacy's face, noting she wouldn't look at him. She had the darkest eyes he'd ever seen on a body, *dark, like burnt coffee,* he thought as he continued to watch her while she drew patterns in the dirt with a stick. He racked his brain on how to get more information out of her. Not letting her get by with just a *yes* or *no*. "Well Lacy Carrigan, want to tell me some more about the Dillard brothers?"

Hearing her real name for the first time in nine years, Lacy's eyes widened, and then grew cold. She smoothly answered, "Watson, the name is Lacy Watson." Even Sam Luebker only knew her as Watson. If he suspected otherwise, he never let on.

Rawley knew by the expression on her face that he had hit home. Shrewd and smooth, the girl had been playing the part for so long, the lie slipped out naturally.

Opening one side of his saddlebag, he dug out his plate and a fork. Rawley scooted across to the fire and piled some beans on his plate. He was hungry, with breakfast ending up *on* him, instead of *in* him. Looking across the flames at the girl, a log fell sending orange sparks sprinkling into the air. He noticed Lacy continued to stare at him, carefully analyzing him again.

As Rawley scooted back to rest on his saddle, he stretched out long legs, crossing his feet. He took a fork full of beans and smelled them first, then shoveled them into his mouth. *Not half bad,* Rawley thought as he chewed, they had a nice smoky flavor. He'd been afraid she couldn't cook, as thin as she was when he first brought her to Doc. He looked up, gesturing to his plate, "Not bad," he said.

Lacy's eyes followed every move he made; she was conducting a persistent examination of this hunk of masculinity sprawled comfortably across from her, stuffing his belly.

He'd been quick, as Sam said. Figured out who I am, but she had edged around it giving him the name Lacy Watson.

He'd tracked her quick today, just as she figured he would with that Indian blood coursing through his veins. *He is one the best-looking men I have run into, in, well...forever.* For being such a big moose, he was gentle too, *Handling little Howie today, why...he'd be a natural father.* Heaving a silent sigh, she dropped her eyes. She was staring at him too much. Lacy concentrated on playing with a stick.

Rawley watched her as much as she, him. Slowly he began to piece things together about her. *She is Lacy Carrigan, been on the run for nine years. Let's see, that'd make her about 23. Became a bounty hunter or a detective, or both, making her daring, determined and smart. She had a temper that wouldn't quit sometimes. She didn't like men, that's for sure. That brick wall she has built around her heart crumbled just a little when she helped four-year old Howie.*

The girl is good at masking her emotions. What had happened at Carrigan Ranch that made her shut down, going dead

73

inside? I've run across that, usually when a woman has been..., Rawley paused in his thinking. His glanced shrewdly at the girl while his brain clicked parts of the puzzle into place. *Raped. Nah...she would have only been 13 or 14 when it had happened.* But that was the only explanation he could come up with, the reason for her hatred of men. Rawley wanted to be wrong, but his gut told him otherwise.

More and more pieces were falling into place. The girl had turned her rage into justice for victims, becoming a bounty hunter or a detective. He cleared his throat making Lacy jump, "Kinda quiet tonight, aren't cha?" he said, breaking the thick silence.

Lacy looked up quickly, she shrugged a shoulder as her eyes dropped back down. She continued her silence. The stick began drawing in the dirt again.

Rawley frowned at her response, asking in his soft baritone, "You feel up to telling me about the Dillard brothers now?"

Damn! That voice of his is like warm caramel...soothing. Bet it could melt a woman's insides. And I'm sure he's broken a lot of hearts, too! Lacy threw him a look across the flames, her dark eyes squinting through the smoky haze. *He could pull stunts like that with other women, but not me, no siree, not me.*

Lacy squared her shoulders and moved, reaching for the coffee pot. The sound of liquid hitting an empty tin cup mingled with the backdrop of a fire crackling. She sat down, cross-legged this time with her back against the log.

Taking a deep breath, she began, "The Dillard Brothers are probably the worst kind of killers I have ever run across." She picked up the stick and stabbed the ground with it, hard, for emphasis. "They kill for the sheer joy of killing. Sometimes I swear they kill just so's they can drink the blood of their victims." Lacy stopped and looked across the smoky air at the marshal to see how her statements were going down, firelight flickering across his angular face made it even more rugged looking, making it harder to read. His hat pulled down low also made his eyes difficult to read in the shadow.

Stabbing the ground once again, she continued, "They're like a pack of wolves with the taste of blood in their jaws, wanting more and more. They're Satan's own boys. There's no rhyme or reason to their killings. They have wiped out whole families, like your friends, or killed singly. They have raped women, little girls. Then if they are still alive, they sell them across the border as slaves, the boys, too. The men they kill, as they did with your friend. The signature is always the same. They butcher each victim the same way, always picking an out-of-the way homestead or a passing traveler. I think they sometimes hang around a town to watch and choose a victim, then follow them home and do their dirty work. Most times the deaths aren't found out for a week or more, making tracking harder. Today was a fluke. Maybe there is a God after all," Lacy finished up quietly.

Rawley had been watching Lacy's facial features intently while she filled him in. Her listless expression imitated a marble bust. Firelight flickered and zigzagged across a million freckles; her voice becoming soft and flat as she exhibited no emotion whatsoever.

The marshal spoke quietly, "I've known some renegades who killed in a similar fashion."

Lacy deep in her thoughts, continued, "You know that little boy trusts you. Trusts you to make his world all right again," she said glancing up at Rawley. "How do you plan to do that?"

Rawley was taken by surprise at her shift in conversation.

"That little boy trusts you so much he'd follow you to the ends of the earth. How do you plan to make his world right again?" Lacy paused, "Well? How do you plan to help him grow into a normal human being? Someone who will be proud of himself, not afraid, not filled with hate and rage. How do you plan to accomplish that?"

Listening to Lacy's spiel about the little boy, Rawley suddenly understood. It wasn't the boy she was talking about, but herself. He reached for the pot; again, the sound of coffee pouring into a tin cup filled the cold air. A metallic click sounded as the pot settled back on the rock by the flames. The marshal's brows fused together over his eyes while they penetrated the smoky air surrounding the fire, noticing how the flames accented the red-gold of Lacy's hair.

She's hurting deep down, has been for a long time. She probably doesn't realize how bad she's been aching all these years. Rawley took a sip of coffee, answering quietly, "I don't know, Lacy. I really don't know." Swilling the brew around in his cup, he looked up, "Maybe we can figure it out together, after this is all over."

Lacy's teeth clamped down on her lower lip. She just nodded. Stabbing the stick into the ground once more, she stood and shook herself, "Well I've given you a lot to think about. I'm gonna hit the sack. We've got a hard day tomorrow." She went to her saddle and carried it over to where she had been sitting all night and dropped it, the dull thud piercing the quiet. A soft rustling filled the air as she put the new coat on over her old one. *It'll be cold in the morning,* she knew. Removing her hardware, she laid it next to her saddle within hand's reach. Making her bed, she crawled in. Lacy was tired, but she couldn't go to sleep. Finally, she drifted off.

Rawley kept waking and replenishing the wood on the fire. He covered her with another blanket, all the while thinking of what Lacy had revealed to him about the Dillards' sick rampages. But what bothered him the most, in speaking about the boy, Lacy had told him how much she had been hurting all these years. He'd always had a knack for figuring folks out; that gift had served him well in the past and continued with the freckled copper-head. Lacy had given him a hell of a lot more information than she realized. He crawled back under the covers, trying to get warm. Finally, he rolled over, slipping into a light doze.

Chapter Thirteen

IT HAD GOTTEN colder during the night with the wind shifting, now out of the northwest. It was beginning to build and whistle through the tall forest growth. Thick low clouds hung like a shroud over the mountains, covering them in its smoky fog. Rawley sniffed the air, it held the promise of a storm that included snow. *Not exactly something to look forward to,* he thought.

Taking his coffee, the marshal strode over to Lacy and kicked the bottoms of her boots, "Up and at 'em, Sunshine. We've got a long haul today." Nothing moved under the blankets, so he kicked the boots again. "Let's go, Sunshine. You're the one all hot and bothered about that bounty money. You want it? Hop to it," he said, kicking her boots harder.

A muffled response came from under the cocoon of blankets.

As he squatted next to her, a smile began to play around his lips, "You say something, Sunshine?"

A hand reached out to pull down a smidgen of the blanket, just enough to expose freckled lids still heavy with sleep and a small upturned nose with a mouth already in a frown. Lacy grumbled, "You always so happy this early in the morning?"

He chuckled at her question, "Sourpuss in the mornings, huh?" She pulled the covers back over her head, making him smile. Taking a corner of the blanket by her feet, Rawley yanked it off Lacy.

"Hey!" she protested as she sat up. "Damn you, you half breed!" she muttered scrambling up. "I was all nice and toasty and you had to go and ruin it," she said, giving him a shove.

Laughing a little harder, the marshal's grin expanded at her response.

77

Lacy realized at that moment that he just liked getting a rise out of her. "You get some kind of pleasure out of making me mad?"

"Who, me? Naw…," Rawley deadpanned.

Instead of slugging him like she really wanted to do, Lacy reached for the empty water canteens. Her footsteps angrily ground into the frozen turf as she moved toward the horses. She released them from their pickets and headed toward the stream.

"Hey!" Rawley called after her. "Don't you want your coffee first?"

Lacy stopped and slowly faced the marshal, she snarled, "Men! The only thing you're good for is target practice!" She gave him one last black look and turned around, continued toward the stream, towing the two horses.

Grinning even more, Rawley pushed his hat back on his head. Still couldn't get a smile out of that girl. He had to admit though, she sure is fun to get a rise out of. *Never know what her reaction might be,* he mused. Returning to the fire, he dished up a plate of leftover beans for himself.

Lacy brought the horses back, dropping the canteens by the marshal. He gave her a quick look when she did. She walked over to her saddlebag and dug out her knife, attaching that to her britches' belt. Picking up her hardware she put that back on. Feeling Rawley's eyes boring holes into her back, she snipped, "Now what?"

The marshal gestured toward her knife with the fork, swallowing the food before speaking, "That's a hunting knife."

She picked up a plate and filled it, "So?" Plopping down next to him, she began to eat.

Handing her a cup of coffee, Rawley quizzed, "Know how to use it?"

Giving him a look that should have singed his eyebrows, Lacy snapped, "I wouldn't have one if I didn't know how to use it!" Looking around as she chewed her breakfast, she pointed to a tree about ten yards away. Swallowing, she said, "See that tree? Throw your knife at that tree."

The marshal didn't respond.

Lacy threw out a challenge, "Well...go on, throw it! I *dare* you."

Rawley's masculinity wouldn't let him resist that. Standing, he pulled his out of its sheath. Aiming it, he sent the knife singing through the air, sinking into tree bark with a *thunk.*

Lacy's eyes popped, "Not bad, not bad for a half-breed."

The marshal threw the girl a dirty look when she said *half-breed.* He knelt pouring himself more coffee. A thunk vibrated through the air reaching his ears; his head swung looking at the tree, his brow creased. *I didn't even hear her throw it.* Striding up to it, he saw the hilt of Lacy's knife resting against his, her blade in the same cut his had made. Pulling both knives from the bark, Rawley turned and ambled back to Lacy, thinking. *She threw left-handed. Not too many whites could handle a knife like that, but she did. Even better than I can.*

He bounced the hilt in his hand, returning the knife back to her, "How many hours did you have to practice to achieve that?"

Lacy took the knife and slid it into the sheath, ignoring the marshal's question.

"Satisfied now?" she taunted him instead.

One dark brow rose, amusement shinning from his eyes, "Reckon so."

Lacy noted *He's got those woman-killer blue eyes.* For the first time, she wondered why he wasn't married. *Must be something women don't like once they get to know him.* Tossing her thoughts aside, she said, "Good, we need to get moving."

Chapter Fourteen

THE SNOW BEGAN coming down about mid-morning. It fell lightly at first in big soft flakes then increased in intensity, covering the ground quickly as the wind picked up. Pretty soon they plowed through six inches then eight plus of the white stuff.

The marshal reined in alongside Lacy; she had stopped to survey the terrain. Heading up they were approaching more evergreens, though a few hardwoods still dotted the landscape, with roots grabbing hold in the underlying rocky surface. Evergreens were beginning to hold onto the white flakes coming down. The snow began to balance on the bare branches of hardwoods.

"You lost the trail before it started snowing, didn't you?" he asked.

Whipping her head around Lacy retorted, "I did not!"

"Know where you're going?"

"Up there."

Lovett followed Lacy's gaze, "You really think they'd go way up there?"

"Yep."

"I think you're wrong. Only fools would try to winter up there."

"That's right. They're not expecting someone to be tailing them, either. We have the element of surprise on our side. We're pressing on," Lacy finished firmly, nudging Fancy forward.

Rawley cocked his brow at that. The spitfire had a point, he had to give her that much. Clicking his tongue, he moved his mount forward following the girl.

The wind increased in intensity, turning the forest into a howling, shrieking banshee. Trees bent to the will of the wind.

Conditions kept changing, first snow then back to sleet. His hat pounded with the hard pellets ricocheting off the brim and bouncing to his coat and beyond. Rawley pulled his collar up closer around his ears.

With their heads down, the horses plowed with difficulty through the wind and snow. Curly icicles decorated manes and tails as steam rose off their rumps from the exertion of the climb.

Two figures astride their mounts assumed the appearance of white flour sacks with the whipping sleet and snow sticking to them like glue. The marshal's breath froze, clinging to his dark beard around his mouth, resembling salt.

"Lacy!" Rawley hollered into the wind, "Rein up! We need to find a place to hole up!"

She glanced over her shoulder at him, shouting. "No! We press on!"

"You cantankerous female!" the marshal bellowed, "I said, rein up! We need to find shelter!"

"No! We keep moving!" Lacy hollered back.

"That does it!" Rawley muttered. Taking the rope off his saddle, he swung it around his head a few times then let go. It sailed through the air to settle over Lacy's shoulders with precision learned long ago. Giving a yank, he pulled her backwards out of the saddle then watched her flounder in the snow like a trout flopping on land.

His actions took Lacy by surprise. She stood, falling and thrashing about against the whipping wind. Finally, she braced herself with a wide stance. Her hands struggling with the rope, she finally pulled it over her head and angrily tossed it aside. Lacy plowed through the snow toward the marshal, *I'm gonna kill him,* her mind said.

"That knock some sense back into that brain of yours?" he yelled against the wind, coiling the rope back up while watching her out of the corner of his eye. He draped the coil over his horn. He wanted his hands free. His gut told him to anticipate a burst of

81

fury from the copper-headed girl.

Flames shot from beneath red-gold lashes, eyes hot enough to melt the snow pellets landing on them. Lacy made a quick move to take Rawley's gun.

Ready for her this time, Rawley grabbed her wrist and twisted her arm pulling it upward, making the little copper-head stand on her toes against his horse.

Lacy wasn't done though, quickly brandishing her knife, but only able to slice air as Rawley caught that wrist too, making her drop the knife. "You gonna listen to me?" He shouted.

"No! We keep moving!" she yelled back.

He twisted her arms harder, causing her to wince in pain, "Now you gonna listen?"

For a split-second fear laced dark eyes, then disappeared.

Rawley saw the raw emotion, but just as quick her veiled look returned concealing what he had seen in her eyes.

"We're wasting valuable time! We keep moving, going as far as we can, then hole up, you bastard!" Lacy snapped hotly. Feeling the marshal loosen his grip on her, she jerked her wrists out of his grasp hard enough to tumble herself back into the snow. Standing once again, she retrieved her knife and slid it back into its holder. "One of these days lawman," she shouted. "You and I are gonna have a knock-down, drag-out and I'm going to win!" Lacy retreated further, her freckled cheeks flaming not with cold but anger.

Taking the coiled rope off the horn, he slid the strap through the coil, re-attaching it back to the saddle. Rawley glanced at the wildcat. "I doubt it, Sunshine," he said. "I seriously doubt it."

Lacy stepped up into the saddle, her heart pounding against her chest. The marshal had scared her. She knew he was stronger than she was, as big as he was, but his quickness surprised and frightened her. It had been a long time since someone had scared her. Lacy knew he was right about holing up, but she wanted to go as far up the mountain as they could, then they'd wait out the blizzard that was bearing down on them.

A few hours later, Lacy found what she was looking for. At first, she rode past it due to almost whiteout conditions. Realizing that, she had backtracked. Lacy led the way into a crevasse that held a shallow cave. It was big enough to accommodate her, Rawley, and both horses.

Lacy had found the cave when she had first run away. She had stayed there a few days to get her thoughts together, then headed to the cabin where she spent the rest of the winter.

Dismounting, she stared into the dimly lit cave. All that firewood she had gathered back then was still here. At least they'd have heat. The marshal ducked as he rode in. Stepping down off his saddle, he began pulling the rigging off the bay. Rawley carried the saddle and the gear bag to the cave's back wall, dumping them.

Lacy did like-wise.

The wind roared and whistled across the entrance, blowing fine, dry pellets into the shallow cave.

Lacy loosely hobbled the two horses. It wouldn't do to be stranded on foot in the snow within these mountains. She patted both of them and walked away.

Laying the makings and starting the fire, Rawley watched the girl taking care of the horses before herself. No wonder that mare doted on her. His eyes followed her as she made her bed, taking the coffee pot outside and packing it with snow.

Without a word, Lacy handed it to Rawley. She went to her bedroll and sat down cross-legged. She kept her eyes focused on the dirt floor while her fingers played with a loose string on her corded britches.

Gazing at the fire as it began to crackle and pop, the flames ignited the dry wood. Rawley didn't exactly know what to do with the girl. Lacy had an argumentative way about her, besides being hot-tempered. An independent cuss for a girl, well, really a woman. He knew he'd scared her; he'd seen it in her face. That fear being the only other emotion he'd witnessed so far from her, besides anger and then compassion for the little boy.

Adding more wood to the fire, the flames began throwing dancing shadows of light against the back wall of the cave. Finally producing the much-welcomed heat, the ice began dripping from his beard. He took a gloved hand and swiped it across his stubble attempting to dry it.

Rawley addressed Lacy, "You know Sunshine, you'd better get a handle on that temper of yours," he said, taking off his gloves and laying them next to the fire to dry. "Or you'll find yourself tangling with more'n you can handle."

Lacy clamped her lips tight as she threw him a dirty look. Taking off her hat, she laid it down next to her. Jamming hands into the pockets of her coat, she scooted back against her saddle.

Outside, the wind whistled and raged through the spruce and fir. Inside, sounds of the fire crackled as it ate the wood. Two horses continued stamping and shaking themselves, disturbing frozen icicles, tinkling when they fell. Those sounds bounced against the backdrop of the cave. Breathing the frosty air, two humans chose to ignore each other.

Taking the soot blackened pot that Lacy had filled with snow he poured store ground coffee inside. As his thumb flipped the lid shut with a short metal click he ground a level place in the dry dirt settling it close to the flames. Rawley made up his bed, jockeying the saddle around into the position he liked best and scooted down on his saddle blanket. Covering his shoulders with another blanket, he placed his hat over his face and fell into a light doze.

Chapter Fifteen

EXHAUSTED, LACY HAD dozed off, but the cold woke her; she had forgotten to cover herself with a blanket. Then it hit her. *I've got to pee, bad.* She wondered how she was going to accomplish that with the marshal here and a blizzard outside. Lacy stood and gingerly stepped over Rawley's long legs, walking toward the entrance of the cave.

"Going somewhere, Sunshine?"

Lacy jerked at the sound of his voice. Glancing back over her shoulder, she said, "Quit calling me that! I'm not your Sunshine!"

Removing his hat, Rawley grinned.

"Um...I've got to...um...you know..." she didn't quite know how to tell him she had to go pee.

Realizing what she was talking about, "Don't go too far, I don't want to come rescue you out in this mess." Seeing she still had on her pistol, he added, "Fire three shots in the air if you get lost."

Lacy gave a short nod and disappeared into the swirling snow.

Rawley noticed that some of the stuffing seemed to have gone out of the girl since he'd scared her. Grinning, he got up and poured himself some coffee.

Lacy struggled against the wind, pulling up her coat collar. She squinted into the whirling mess and tried to get her bearings. She headed to her left, stopped and finished her business. Turning to go back to the cave, she stepped off into thin air.

When Lacy landed, she lay deep in the snow, trying to get the wind back in her lungs. As she took a deep breath, pain shot through her mid-section. Grabbing her middle with her arms, she lay there untill the pain subsided. *Now I've gone and done it!* Stubborn pride kept her from firing her pistol.

Turning on her side, her eyes followed the tracks her tumble had made. The bluff wasn't too high, she could make it back up. The pain in her side made moving difficult as she slipped and clambered to find foot and handholds under the snow. Finally reaching the top, she rolled on her back, closed her eyes, trying to catch her breath. The snow quickly filled her eye cavities, nose and mouth, creating a ghostly appearance. Lacy spit out the snow as a hand swiped at her eyes. "Boy, you really blew it this time," Lacy muttered. Sitting up, she flopped back in pain. Rolling over on her belly, she squinted into the swirling white mess. Finding her previous prints now almost totally obscured by the blowing snow, she rose to her knees and crawled back to the cave opening.

Lovett began getting concerned. Lacy had been gone just a tad too long. "Dad-gum hard-headed female!" he muttered disgustedly. Standing at the entrance of the cave, he listened for gun shots but didn't hear any. She may be lying unconscious somewhere. He'd wait a few moments longer and then see if he could find her tracks.

Lacy found the entrance of the cave and hauled herself up by holding on to the rock face. She had to walk in like nothing happened. "I must've busted a couple of ribs the way this hurts," she mumbled through chattering teeth. "Lovett is gonna laugh his fool head off, when he finds out what a stupid thing I did." Lacy straightened and tried to walk normally as she entered the cave.

Rawley looked up as a snow-covered figure walked by him. A silly grin began to peek out from under blue eyes. He watched as Lacy slowly made her way to her bed. Easing herself down gently, she sighed closing her eyes.

"Well, what happened to you? I was beginning to worry."

Her eyes still closed, she gripped her mid-section. "I decided to see how a human snowball felt." As Lacy expected, Rawley began laughing. Her ears pricked up listening to the warm bari-

86

tone, thinking how nice it sounded. She groaned inwardly. *I won't be around much longer, I'll be moving on again once these sumbitches are caught,* she thought.

Rawley couldn't keep the grin from spreading rapidly, "Is that why you look like a snowman?"

For once, Lacy kept her mouth shut. It hurt every time she tried to breathe.

The marshal, noticing the difference in her demeanor, scooted over next to her and touched her arm lightly. This time she didn't jerk away. He asked quietly, "You hurt, Sunshine?"

At first, she shook her head no, and then whispered, "I don't know, I…I just hurt." Lacy fastened her jaw tight, trying to keep her chattering teeth quiet.

"Where?"

"My, my, ribs, I…I think," she chattered.

Kneeling next to her, Rawley gently moved her arms and began unbuttoning her two coats.

Lacy's eyes flew open. She used all of her to strength fight the big lawman. He grunted at the girl's sudden fury.

She cried out, "Don't touch me, mister!" Her arms, fists and boots flailed at him.

Rawley had his hands full trying to grab those quick moving fists and feet. Finally sitting on her, pinning her arms to her sides, he yelled, "Lacy, will you just cut it out! I'm not going to hurt you." The girl stilled suddenly. He looked into two pain-filled and scared brown eyes. Lacy stared back at him like a cornered doe facing its killer.

Lovett decided to press her to see if what his gut had been telling him was on its mark. Taking a breath, he took the plunge, "Sunshine, I know who you are," he said, quietly. "You're heiress to one of the biggest spreads in the territory."

Lacy's eyes darted away from his face.

"I know something happened out at Carrigan Ranch, nine, ten years ago. I know your mama committed suicide."

Lacy cut him a quick glance, then her eyes darted away once again, but not before Rawley saw the quick glistening of tears. "I know you ran away not long after, been on the run ever since." Taking in another breath, Rawley added, "I know you've been raped, by whom I don't know yet." All the stuffing seemed to melt out of her at his last statement. Lacy wouldn't look at him; she kept her eyes focused on the cave wall. Rawley relaxed his hold on her. Lacy cut a hasty look in his direction when he did. His eyes were glowing with a softness and warmth, confusing her.

Rawley sat back on his heels, "I do know that I don't care to tangle with the Dillard boys by myself. My partner doesn't need to be hurt going after them, won't do me any good," he said. "I need someone to make sure my back is covered and I've got her back, so what will it be, Sunshine? You gonna let me see how bad you're hurt or do we saddle up and go back to town after this storm is over? It's up to you."

"No!" Lacy croaked, "We keep going!"

Hearing the spit and vinegar come back into her voice, the marshal grinned at her words, "Okay." He finished unbuttoning her two coats, then his hand reached for the buckle on Lacy's hardware.

She stopped him, "No!"

"Aw right, you do it," he said, backing off.

"No, it stays."

"You're worse than a mule. I'm trying to help you…"

"I don't need your help," Lacy interrupted, spitting out the words, "Why don't you just leave? I can handle the Dillards' by myself."

The marshal pushed his hat back on his head and stared at her.

Lacy glared back, then flitted her eyes away from his face.

Damn, she's stubborn. "Sunshine, you're beginning to get my dander up."

Lacy swung her eyes back to him as she retorted, "As you do mine, half-breed!"

"Well...now that we finally agree on something, take the hardware off or I'll have to manhandle you again. Maybe tie you up, so you quit hurting yourself."

Folding her arms across her stomach, Lacy squeezed her eyes shut. Clenching her jaw, she knew he would do what he threatened. Finally, she did as he requested, laying the rig not far from her hand. Lacy moved her arms to cover her eyes, leaving only her mouth showing.

Seeing the fists form, Rawley knew Lacy would be white knuckling it while he touched her. As he began pulling her shirts out of her britches, he heard the girl gasp. Raising the shirts to her breasts, he once again heard her suck in more air. Trying to make light of the situation he said, "Why, even your tummy has freckles."

Lacy shot him a one-eyed snarl from under her arms.

Rawley grinned again. The discoloration began on her right side he examined that first.

When the marshal's rough, calloused fingers touched her skin, goose bumps popped out and Lacy whistled in more air. His thumbs sliding over her ribs made her shiver.

"I know it's cold. I'll be done in a second."

Keeping her eyes tightly shut under her arms Lacy thought, *That's not the reason you numbskull.* She hadn't allowed another person to touch her since her grandfather, not even to get a hug from Sam's wife, Sally. Feeling those fingers slide over her ribs scared her. Twice today, the marshal had scared her. He was gentle and that scared her, too.

Pulling her shirts down, Rawley backed off, "I don't think anything is broken. You're bruised and you'll be sore."

Lacy peeked out from under her arms.

The girl's look made his mouth curve upward. "You'll live," he said. Moving back toward the fire, Rawley poured Lacy some coffee. Then he knelt beside her and helped her to sit up, handing the cup over.

Lacy cast a glance up at his face as she took the cup in both hands, then she fixed her eyes back on the warm liquid.

Rawley knew her emotions had been doing battle within her. He had felt that heart just a thumping against her ribs. *Thank goodness nothing is broken.*

Lacy spoke so softly, Rawley could barely hear her, "How did you know?"

"Oh…I just kept putting two and two together, 'till I had the right answers," he replied lightly.

"Sam said…," Lacy began, then stopped.

"What?"

"Nuthin'…you gonna tell?" Lacy questioned softly, puckering up her face as she waited on the bad news.

Rawley saw the girl bracing for what she figured would be his answer, "No…your secret is safe with me."

Relief washed over Lacy like a waterfall.

"That's your business. Far as I'm concerned, you're Lacy Watson, though we both know it ain't true."

Lacy gave a slight nod.

He asked softly, "Did Vern know?"

Another silent nod.

Rawley gave her time, waiting on her reply. Seeing her shivering, he placed a blanket around Lacy's shoulders.

The marshal's tenderness had her glancing at him in surprise. Lacy quietly answered, "He…he wanted me to press charges, but, but, I couldn't"

Anger flared, "Why the hell not? That man raped you!"

Lacy's head spun, she looked at the big lawman with such a deep sadness in those dark depths, causing Rawley to catch his breath. He closed his mouth tightly and waited again.

"That man as you call him, is my grandfather," Lacy whispered. She ducked her head quickly, so he wouldn't see the tears.

90

It had been over nine years since she had told anyone what had happened. Vern had been the only one who knew, until now.

Rawley grew hot with anger, "That bastard!"

"I don't want to talk anymore," she said, placing the cup in the dirt. Lacy slid down, closing her eyes.

"Sunshine," he said as he squatted back on his heels, "Maybe one of these days, you'll trust me enough to tell me the whole story."

"I won't be around," she whispered rolling onto her side. "Ow", the pain made her return to her back.

Rawley reached for his saddlebag, digging around inside the leather as he finally pulled out a small pouch. Opening it, he poured some powder into a cup and added water, stirring it with his finger. He handed the cup to Lacy, "Here...I want you to drink this. It'll ease the pain and help you relax."

Lacy shook her head no.

"You need something. I don't carry whiskey."

"No...I have to keep my wits..." she began then trailed off.

"What? You think I'm gonna assault you? Dream on, Sunshine, you're not my type."

"Quit calling me, Sunshine..." she groused, then stared at the murky water in the cup, she asked, "...What is it?"

"Something Doc made, he uses a lot of medicinal herbs and whatnot," he explained.

Furrowing her brow, "It'll help?"

Rawley nodded.

Lacy swallowed the liquid and gagged as the bitter taste filled her mouth. "Ugh! That's awful," she said sputtering as she threw Rawley a dirty look. "It had better work, tasting that bad."

Taking the cup from Lacy's hand, he said, "Lay back and let the powder go to work."

Lacy nodded. Pretty soon she felt kind of floaty. The next thing she knew, her world went black.

Chapter Sixteen

WATCHING AS THE tension flowed from the girl's face and body, Rawley knew what Lacy had told him just touched the surface of her pain. As he drank another cup of coffee, he kept glancing at her, noticing as her face softened as she fell into a deep sleep.

What was it she had asked him last night? 'How did he plan on helping the boy grow up to be proud of himself and not afraid, not filled with hate and rage?' "Yeah, that was it," Rawley muttered to himself.

He walked to the entrance of the cave and stared out at the swirling snow.

Rawley began running over every moment through his head since he had first seen her in the saloon. Lacy had disguised herself as a boy, an undercover ploy he figured. She had gotten herself shot. He didn't even know the story on that yet, either. Girl kept her mouth locked tighter then the Denver Mint, throwing away the key in the process.

He contemplated what else he'd figured out about her. The girl had turned to the only thing she felt worthy of, flushing fugitives out of the brush. A fugitive herself, running from her past. That thought curved his mouth into a slight grimace. Of course, if he was to mention that to Lacy, she'd come swinging at him. That thought allowed a tight smile to grace his rugged features.

Rawley sobered as another thought filtered through his brain. He recalled again what Lacy had said the night before, not afraid. The girl used that temper of hers to cover up her fear, a fear so great, it made Lacy run constantly from the memories, not able to face them. Now, it had become normal for her to chase fugitives, to be running, moving on to the next case, just chasing and running in a never-ending circle.

He turned, walking back to the fire. He threw more wood on the flames and watched the sparks fly. Lacy had been on the run for over nine years. He doubted she would even know how to begin living a normal life.

Carrying that burden all those years, it's a wonder it hadn't burned a hole in her gut. Only Vern had known through the years. "I bet it tore at his gut too, keeping that kind of secret. Now Vern is dead and I'm the only one left holding the secret," Rawley whispered to himself.

He slid his saddle and bed closer to Lacy, knowing they needed to sleep together to stay warm. Rawley scooted in next to Lacy and pulled her close arranging the blankets to cover them both. Lacy began to whimper, surprising him.

"No, no, please not again. Please no, not again."

The bastard raped her more than once! His anger produced red dots swimming before his eyes as Lacy's hands clenched into fists. "Shh, shh Sunshine," he said, trying to quiet her fears. "It's me, Rawley. I'm not gonna hurt you. Shh, you're safe now. Hush, honey." Even in her sleep Lacy still fought her past. What a way to live, he thought.

Holding her tighter, his hand softly brushed the red gold tendrils from her face. His forefinger smoothed the tension puckered across her forehead. He finally felt her relax. Rawley relaxed too, eventually dozing off.

Chapter Seventeen

OPENING HER EYES, Lacy blinked and tried to bring her eyes into focus. Her brain felt thick. She closed her eyes again and dozed off. Waking later, she sat up and noticed that she wasn't as sore today. Scrambling to her feet, she stumbled outside. After taking care of her business, Lacy knelt in front of the cave and scrubbed her face with the cold snow, trying to clear her foggy brain. Wiping her face with the sleeve of her coat, she walked back inside.

"There's a towel in my saddle bag," Rawley offered.

Finding it, Lacy finished drying her face then stumbled back toward the fire. She poured a cup of coffee and sat down gingerly on the log. She stared into nothing, not even noticing the storm. Sipping at the hot brew, she blinked as she tried to focus. She poured herself more coffee. The hot brew felt good trickling down to her stomach.

Rawley observed all this with wry amusement, knowing Lacy had slept so hard it would take her a while to wake up. He went back to his whittling and blew the shavings out of the whistle he was making for the boy.

"What kind of horse is Fancy?" He asked out of the blue, then waited on her answer. Rawley glanced up when he got none, "Hey, sleepyhead."

That got a response. Lacy blinked, giving him a wide-eyed empty stare as she continued blinking. "What kinda horse is Fancy?" Rawley asked again.

"A cross blue-blood."

"A what?"

"Sire and Dam came from Kentucky and Virginia."

"A race horse?"

Lacy tilted her head looking over Fancy's lines, "Umm, could be or brood mare, her lineage is good enough."

"Those kinds of horses cost money. How'd you end up with a race horse?"

Lacy looked down at the cup. "She was my thirteenth birthday present," she explained softly. Rising quickly to avoid more questions, she announced, "I can't wake up. I'm going back to bed." Lacy curled into her blankets.

Rawley watched the girl lying there with her back to him. Returning to his whittling, he realized he had touched another nerve with Lacy by being curious about her. All he wanted was a little information.

Maybe if he handled her with some patience and understanding and if she'd just quit fighting him all the time, he might be able to help her face the hurt of all those memories. *Why would I want to do that?* He asked himself. *I haven't got a clue, but I do know she's not my type.* Rawley liked soft women, feminine ones, who liked to wear dresses. Not a hell-fire and brimstone, freckle faced, gun-toting copper-headed spitfire. He asked himself again, *Why do I want to help her then?* Shaking his head, he concluded, *I ain't got a clue.*

Rawley blew more shavings out of the whistle as he continued to contemplate the girl. He'd known people, well, didn't know them personally, but had heard of people so traumatized by something in their past, they'd changed their whole personality. They would take a new name, pick up an accent, drink heavily and heaven knows what else to forget. Rawley figured Vern had told her to change her name so her grandfather couldn't trace her. As for her personality, he didn't know what she'd been like before. All he had to go on was the spitfire image she had portrayed so far.

Lacy had mentioned a Sam the day before, Rawley remembered as he continued working on the whistle. He knew a few fel-

95

lows named Sam, but there was only one they possibly both knew, Sam Luebker. Rawley's hands stilled as he stared into the fire. Come to think if it, Lacy's detecting methods were a lot like the ones Sam used. His brow wrinkled as he glanced again at the still figure. That's probably how she knew he had Cheyenne blood running through his veins.

Lacy Carrigan remained one complicated girl, well, woman. Every time he thought he might have her figured out, something else always popped up to blow his theory out of the water, like getting a race horse for her thirteenth birthday.

Rawley shook his head grinning, then sobered as another thought dawned on him. The grandfather had been buying Lacy's silence after molesting her, a bribe to keep her quiet. Justin Carrigan knew what he did had been wrong, so he bought Lacy's silence with the horse.

Puzzlement etched across Rawley's robust features. He couldn't for the life of him figure out why her mother and father hadn't put a stop to the sick sum-bitch. Unless Lacy never revealed to them what her grandfather had been doing to her.

Rawley put up his whittling, knelt, and poured himself more coffee, then strolled over to the cave entrance. The wind and snow had begun to die down. Rawley thought they might be able to move out tomorrow and catch these monsters who had butchered his friends.

Whenever Pat and Martha came to town, little Howie and his big sister Hanah would come find him and they'd play checkers until it was time for them to leave. A sad smile graced his face as Rawley remembered. He would put Howie on his lap and they would play against Hanah. Hanah would let Howie win just enough times to keep the little towhead happy.

I'm going to miss them. He had felt the closest to that couple than to any other friends he had made since coming to White River. Well, besides Doc and Miss Liv. Now all that was left of that family was a little four-year old boy.

He poured his coffee out, the liquid hissing in the frigid air as it hit the snow. He piled more wood on the fire, and crawled in next to Lacy. He pulled her tight against him, and covered both of them with the blankets. Rawley noticed how nicely Lacy fit into his body. He wondered what it would be like to make love to her, wake up like this every day, and make love again. *Don't even go there, she's not my type,* he gave himself a mental shake before closing his eyes.

Chapter Eighteen

SOMETHING PLEASANT TEASED her nose. Lacy stirred and stretched under the warm blankets. Her ears caught the early morning rustlings from Lovett. A freckled nose picked up the scent of fresh brewed coffee. Lacy cracked an eye open as bright sunshine peeked into the cave entrance; the storm had moved on. Lacy watched the Marshal as he flipped something in a pan. Red-gold brows squeezed together as she got up and walked over to him. She stared at the pan, then at him. The batter sizzling in the pan teased Lacy's nose and ears some more.

Rawley glanced up, "Made some flapjacks this morning. You haven't eaten in a few days, figured this might hold you for a while."

"Flapjacks here?" Lacy's mouth dropped then closed as she recovered. She grabbed her cup as she poured herself some coffee.

"Sure, why not?" he said, putting one on a tin plate. He sprinkled it with sugar and cinnamon, and then handed it to her, "Roll it up. Try it."

Lacy did as instructed, taking a tentative bite. Her eyes widened as the flavors hit her tongue. "Umm, that's good." Her brow puckered as she chewed, "Where'd you learn that?"

He smiled, "Had a real good cook on a trail drive once. He taught me that trick." He handed Lacy another one and fixed his own, and then ate.

Lacy ate four to Rawley's five.

Warm eyes observed Lacy guzzling her fourth cup of coffee. Rawley asked, "Feel better now? You had a good sleep and your tummy's full; are you ready to ride today?"

Lacy silently nodded. Picking up the plates and cups, she washed them in the snow, then packed them in the gear bag.

She picked up her saddle and flung it on Fancy's back. Next, she rolled up her bedroll and ground cloth tying it behind the cantle. Leading the mare out, Lacy waited on the marshal. Standing by Fancy's head, she gazed into the horse's eyes the color of dark heartwood. "Fancy, we're not that far from the cabin now," Lacy whispered. She swung into the saddle, patting the grey's long neck.

Rawley rode up alongside Lacy, his eyes looking in the same direction as hers. They refocused on a face, cute as a speckled pup, the cold making her cheeks rosy. "You know these mountains pretty well, don't you?"

Lacy pinched her bottom lip with her teeth and gave her customary short nod as her heels tapped Fancy's ribs. The rider and horse moved out without a word. Rawley sighed inwardly, *Gotta be the quietest damn female I've ever met,* gently nudging his bay's sides as he followed the mare and the bundled-up figure riding her.

Chapter Nineteen

LATE THAT AFTERNOON she reined up Fancy giving her a short breather. Lacy's nose detected something floating on the wind. When Rawley drew alongside of her, she asked, "Smell that?" Her eyes brightened while a hint of a smile tweaked rosy cheeks.

He had also caught the faint whiff drifting on the breeze, "Wood smoke."

"That's right," she agreed. Lacy pointed across in front of him, "Northwest wind blowing it down this way, the cabin's that-a-way," clucking the big grey forward.

Rawley grabbed the sleeve of her coat, "Wait a minute. You've been here before? The same with the cave, haven't you? That's why you were so sure they'd be up here. You hid out here before, didn't you?" he asked.

Lacy fastened her lips tight while her eyes became sharp. She jerked her arm out of the lawman's big hand, refusing to give him a direct answer, "C'mon. We need to get there before dark, check out the place."

The girl sure ain't gonna answer my questions, he thought, pursing his own lips while he watched Lacy and Fancy pull ahead.

Thirty yards from the cabin, they both dismounted and surveyed the terrain. Smoke curled from the rock chimney built onto the back of a one room cabin. In the growing dusk, the glow of a coal oil lamp shed light on a small square of snow from one window built into the west side wall. Another square of light illuminated the porch from the south window, placed next to the one door. The small barn that had been built nestled between granite walls on the southeastern side. Thick undergrowth and tall ever-greens sheltered the small cabin to the south, west and north. Lacy checked her pistol one last time. She looked up at the marshal, and in a soft whisper asked, "Ready?"

"I am if you are," Rawley replied as he looked at Lacy.

Expelling the breath she had been holding, "Okay, let's go." Lacy's heart hammered in her chest. She dragged in more air for her starved lungs. *It's almost over. Finally. I hope,* she thought.

Ten yards or so from the lighted cabin, they stopped and squatted behind thick cover. Their warm breath mingled like puffs from a steam engine swirling above a smokestack as they peered through the bushes, the fog melting into the brisk air, only to return with each breath.

Looking over at the girl, Rawley quietly asked, "You scared?"

Lacy's head swiveled, "Of course I'm scared, you nitwit!" She paused, taking a deep breath then repeated his question back to him, "You scared?"

"Yep!" He grinned

There's something reassuring about his smile, she noticed. Lacy hauled in more air as she flung that thought out of her head, "Good. That means we'll be on our toes."

"Any other doors in or out of this place?" Rawley asked.

Lacy shook her head, "No."

"Aw…right," he began to formulate a plan in his head, but he wanted to hear what Lacy had to say, too. *Probably some cock-a-mamie scheme, knowing her,* "Got any ideas on how we're gonna tackle this situation?" he whispered.

Shrugging, she whispered tartly back, "You're the one with all the relatives who tricked Custer, so…you tell me!"

Rawley gave Lacy one of his own dirty looks. "I swear, Sunshine. Sometimes you come up with the damndst' things."

Ignoring the Marshal, she whispered, "I've got to get closer…" as she began edging around him.

Rawley grabbed the back of her coat, yanking her towards him. She landed in the snow at his knees.

Her neck swiveled to look up at him as a husky whisper growled, "What 'da go and do that for?"

"You stay put. I'm goin."

Venom spat from her dark depths.

Rawley blinked. He would have sworn on a stack of Bibles he could actually see Lacy bristling up like a porcupine ready to throw its quills.

"Like I said, you stay put," he said again.

The venom disappeared. "No, I'm goin'. You're too big. I can hide better," she said, rising quickly and scrambling for the back of the cabin. The marshal grabbed at thin air this time as she dodged out of his reach.

Rawley whispered, "Sunshine, you're impossible." He watched as Lacy flattened herself against the cabin wall, her body edging towards the window. He waited, his rifle ready.

Just as she was about to peek in the window, Lacy heard the door creak open and laughter filled the cold night air.

Boot heels thumped on the cold wood that creaked with his weight. "Now you two don't go peekin' at my cards," a voice said, "I gotta go take a whizz. Be right back." A hurried cadence thumped across the porch toward Lacy, silencing as his boots hit the snow.

Lacy's eyes went wide as her tongue glued itself to the roof of her mouth. She flattened herself tighter against the cabin wall, the moonless night helping to conceal her.

The brother hurried over to the bushes and began watering them. Steam rose as the liquid melted the snow then refroze immediately

Lacy watched from the shadows, all the while holding her breath thinking, *Not seven feet away, right in front of me!*

Rawley, seeing what had transpired, cursed, "Aw shee-yut!"

Lacy's right hand reached for a log on top of the pile next to her. The snow muffled her steps as she made her move. Swinging the log, it went *thwack* against the man's head. She watched him crumple at her feet without making a sound. Lacy gave a start when the marshal showed up suddenly standing next to her.

"You okay?" he asked, puffs of fog accenting his words.

Lacy nodded, "Pick 'em up, we'll haul 'em to the barn." She helped Rawley put the man on his shoulder. As she led him around to the back of the barn, their boots squeaked against dry snow, the only sound that broke the stillness. Opening the door, rusty hinges let loose with a squeal. Soft knickers came from within the barn. Two humans stopped dead in their tracks, their breath at a standstill. Their ears were tuned to listened, but they heard nothing except the horses. Lacy gently eased the door open further. Rawley entered and stopped to let his eyes adjust to the darker recesses of the inside of the barn. His eyes swept the interior and making out a post, Rawley walked over to it, dropping the unconscious man with a thud next to it. Kneeling by the body, the marshal straightened it up against the post, its head flopping over to the side. Rawley pulled limp arms behind the post and then looked around for the girl.

Fumbling around in the dark, Lacy found some rope hanging on a wall. Walking over, she tossed it to Rawley. "Tie him up, tight," she ordered in a loud whisper as she dug out her bandana gagging the man with it. She waited on the marshal to finish. "One down, two more to go," she whispered. "They're gonna come looking for him soon," she said, grabbing his sleeve and pulling, "C'mon! Let's move!"

Just as Rawley and Lacy came up beside the cabin window again, they heard the door open.

"Aubrey? Hey boy, where are you? We need to finish this game." Boot heels clunked against the wood coming closer to the edge of the porch and then stopped. The voice called again, "Aubrey? Where the hell are you?" The boots stepped into the snow.

Rawley slammed his rifle butt onto the second brother's

103

head, catching him as he went down and then slinging him over his shoulder. He spoke quietly to Lacy, "I'll put him with the other one."

Lacy nodded, watching the big marshal carry his load and disappear around the back of the cabin. Lacy plastered herself against the wall once again. She took a slow deep breath. Her heart hammered so hard it made her ears ring. *This one is gonna be real suspicious now,* Lacy told herself.

Sure enough, the door opened and the third brother walked out to the edge of the porch, calling, "Aubrey? Keller? Where the hell are you two? C'mon boys. That's enough playing games. Where are you two?"

Ed! Lacy thought.

Calling again, Ed stepped off the porch into the snow, his eyes keenly searching the shadows looking for his brothers. Ed stood not six feet away from Lacy.

Pulling her weapon, Lacy eased away from the darkness of the cabin wall. She stated in that low husky voice of hers, "The game is over, Ed. Drop your weapon. Easy…now."

Ed turned slowly to his right facing the quiet voice. He spied a small figure standing a short distance away, hat shadowing the face, "Who 'r *you?*"

Ignoring him, Lacy told him, "You've got a choice, Ed. You can come peaceably with me sitting upright in the saddle or slung over it belly down. What's it gonna be, Ed?" Transferring her weight to the balls of her feet, her body became rigid with anticipation.

It's just kid standing in front of me, a damn kid! His mouth shifted, creating a twisted look.

From her viewpoint, the light from the window highlighted only the lower part of his face. Lacy didn't like that; she preferred watching the eyes. They revealed a lot more then faces did, she'd learned over the years.

Suddenly his pistol appeared out of nowhere, flames bright in

104

the darkness as they shot out of the muzzle. During that split-second Lacy had already hit the snow rolling. Landing in a prone position, elbows resting in the snow, one hand steadying the butt of her pistol, the heel of the other slammed down hard cocking back the hammer of the single-action colt, simultaneously her finger pulled the trigger. Fire breathed from the barrel. The deafening sound crashed over Ed as he staggered back. The pea-sized piece of lead plunged deep into his flesh. His eyes bulged and saliva mingled with the blood from his mouth. Creating a red string that slowly slid down his chin dripping, staining the snow. *I'm hit, that damn kid, kilt me!* Ed wobbled, his hand shook trying to aim at the figure lying in the snow. Dying reflexes made his finger jerk the trigger, gun firing harmlessly into the air as he folded into himself, dropping to the snow - dead.

Hearing guns shots, Rawley flew out of the barn and raced toward the cabin. He spotted two figures lying in the snow off to the side of the porch. Checking the first figure, Rawley pushed him over on his back. There in the faint light, he saw a wound easing blood. His hand felt for a pulse and found none. His attention then turned toward the second person. He noticed Lacy had sat up on her knees, still holding her gun and gasping for air.

The marshal knelt by her, placing a palm on her shoulder making her look at him, "Sunshine…you hit?"

Lacy blinked and shook her head no. Returning her attention back to the gun she still held in her hands, she took in another ragged breath.

Rawley hauled the girl to her feet, his eyes tracking across her body, looking for blood, "You sure, you're all right?"

Lacy wrinkled her forehead and nodded again. She stumbled forward, catching herself she continued towards the body. "Help me get him to the barn, will you?"

Dragging Ed between them, they entered the wooden structure. Looking around, Rawley found a lantern. Taking a glove off, he unbuttoned his coat and dug in his shirt pocket for a match.

The globe handle screeched from lack of use as he pulled it down lifting the globe. Using his thumbnail, Rawley scratched it across the surface of the match, the sound of the phosphorous flaring cutting into the cold silence of the barn. Lighting the wick, he closed the globe. Looking around, he found another and repeated the process.

Soft light filled the barn while he peered around, noting the three horses watching him with mild interest. There were three doors in the stable; the one behind him and the one on the opposite wall as well as a single sliding door with a smaller one next to that. Turning slowly, he took a good look at the Dillard brothers. The three boys looked to be in their late teens to middle twenties, maybe a little older with lanky to husky builds. Rawley had seen nasty looking hombres before, but these boys looked like sod busters, not killers. Turning, he spoke to Lacy, "You sure these are the Dillard brothers?"

Lacy nodded, pointing to the first one they'd brought in the barn, "That's Aubrey, the youngest. That one is the middle brother. Name's Keller. The dead one is the oldest, Ed."

"Where they from? They look like sod busters."

"They are…were…from Missouri. They've killed in every territory, well…almost every territory west of the Mississippi. Satan's own spawn," Lacy told him, her lips pressing together in a tense line.

Hearing a groan, they both turned toward the sound. Aubrey was beginning to recover.

Anger began a slow burn deep inside of Lacy. She walked over to the boy and stared at the two-legged monster. This one had the scratches on his face from the Clancy woman. That made Lacy's rage rise further.

Aubrey looked up to see the *purtiest l'il gal* he'd seen in a while, flaming hair and big brown eyes you could melt into. He could feel himself rising.

Lacy's anger continued to grow as did the bulge in his pants.

106

She knew exactly what he was thinking.

Her flaming temper overrode whatever sense Lacy did have. Standing alongside the boy in case he struck out with his legs, she whipped out her knife. Bending over, she stuck it against the boy's throbbing neck. His eyes quickly went from lust to fear, afraid to move.

Lacy whispered with deadly calm, "How 'bout I do you like you did your last victim?" Sliding the knife lightly across his throat, drawing blood. The boy blanched with fear. "Or better yet…" she began, brandishing the knife at the fly on his britches. She used it to pop off the buttons. She watched the boy wiggle against the post. "How 'bout I just slice off your…," her hand laid the edge of the blade across his bulge, then lightly sawed the blade back and forth, its edge beginning to cut through the material. The bulge suddenly wilted. He looked at the knife, then back at her. The boy's eyes wide with fear, he mumbled something against the bandana, shaking his head vigorously. Lacy's eyes, cold and hard swept over his face as she added, "So you can't play no more." She whisked the knife away only to continue her threatening attack on his torso. "How 'bout…" she sliced the buttons off his shirt and slit his long handles, exposing his skin to the cold air. He shivered. "How 'bout…" she began as she slowly and lightly, sliced his skin upward, "I gut you like a hog at killing time, but I'll leave *you* alive. Take your innards out," dark eyes never left the boy's face as Lacy's arm waved at the barn rafters, "Throw them up over those beams there, so you can watch your guts swinging from the rafters, like sausages hanging from the beams of a smokehouse. How 'bout that?" Lacy finished quietly.

Shocked at what he was witnessing, Rawley couldn't move. His boots were rooted to the dirt floor like a large oak. He'd never seen a female act like that before. Regaining focus, his ground eating stride placed him at Lacy's side in seconds. He grabbed her wrist and swung her around as he wrenched the knife out of her hand. Lacy had traveled to somewhere deep within her soul, he

107

noticed. Moments later, her eyes came back into focus, fixing a blank deadly stare on him.

"That's enough, Sunshine! I'm the law here. From now on you'll do as I say!"

Freckled cheeks scorched with anger, she blasted the law-man, "I ought to whittle your ears off for that! 'Sides, you ain't the only law around," she told him through clenched teeth. Push-ing around him, she moved toward the two boys, angrily tearing the guns out of their scabbards. She shoved the pistols into the marshal's belly when she walked past him. Rawley caught them, barely. He watched Lacy as she struggled to slide open the barn door. He didn't even bother to help, she'd pissed him off. The door continued protesting as the rusty wheels screeched from lack of use along its track. At last it slid open and she disappeared into the darkness.

Rawley expelled a huge breath of air. *That girl is one hard...* he thought, *Thank goodness, I'm one of the good guys, I'd sure of hated to 'ave been in the boots of any of those other fugitives she'd captured in the past.*

Turning around he looked at Aubrey. Rawley narrowed his eyes at what Lacy had done to the lad. The blood from his wounds was drying. Lacy didn't cut him bad, just scared him enough to pee on himself. Laying the pistols on top of a feed bin along with her knife, he took his hat off and slapped it hard against his thigh. The other hand combed his hair back in frustra-tion. The girl's tactics had to stop, at least until they got the boys back to the fort, *Then, she can go her way and I'll go mine,* he thought, jamming his hat back on.

The barn door protested again as Lacy pushed the door wid-er, accommodating the two horses. Leading their mounts in, Lacy placed them in a stall. She stripped off their rigging and threw the saddles over the stall wall. The stirrups banged against the wood partition angrily. Releasing her rope from her saddle, she tossed it at the marshal, "Better tie up their feet. They may get nasty.

Don't want either of us to get hurt."

Rawley gave Lacy one of his own blistering looks as he knelt by Aubrey's feet. Quickly, the boy drew his knees up, his boots landing hard against the marshal's chest. Rawley grunted in surprise as his body flew back. He'd let his guard down. *That's not like me. Damn girl's got my head screwed on backwards.*

Lacy hastily pulled her rifle from its boot. Running over, she slammed the butt into Aubrey's cheek. Bones crunched, he yelled then slumped unconscious against the ropes. Lacy smiled as she whispered, "Well…that took care of him for a while."

Rawley scrambled up, ripping the carbine out of her hands. Lacy's eyes grew round at his interference. "Damn it, Sunshine! An inch higher and you could've killed him!"

"So? Good riddance…the bounty's the same dead or alive. Besides, he kicked you," she answered, reaching for her rifle.

Raising the Sharps up out of her reach, Rawley said, "This case has got you all messed up in the head! You can't keep going around being a one-man vigilante committee! You're not standing back, looking at this case objectively! You're too emotionally involved!"

Color flamed across a million freckles, "You haven't seen what I have."

"I observed their work," he stated quietly.

Lacy held up one finger, "Once! I've seen it over and over and over!" An irate hand kept flipping in a circle, accenting angry words, "Now give me my rifle!" she demanded.

"No."

Her fist rammed hard into his gut, hopefully surprising him enough to drop the weapon.

She'd caught him off guard, but he managed to keep the rifle out of her reach.

"Dammit! Lovett! These are my prisoners! Give me my rifle!"

Rawley cocked his head at the venomous copper-head and

wondered, *If I were to light a match and hold it close to her ears, would they explode from the angry fumes I just know are perkin' around in there?* He blinked, not knowing where in the hell that came from. Tossing that train of thought aside, he asked instead, "You gonna butt-crack anyone else?"

Lacy pressed her lips together again and looked at the dirt floor as she jammed her hands into the pockets of her thick coat. She took a deep breath then exhaled slowly as she shook her head. "No," she finally answered.

"Can I trust you?"

Lacy's head jerked up. "Trust me? You're an ass, Lovett!" she said disgustedly. "What do you think?"

"It doesn't matter what I think. I want to hear you say it, that I can trust you."

Dark eyes darted away from Rawley's hard scrutiny, then darted back. She exhaled noisily, "You can trust me."

"I hope so," he said, giving the girl one last hard look before handing over the Sharps.

Rifle in hand, Lacy marched to the feed bin and plopped herself up on top of it. She pushed the pistols off and they landed in the dirt with a dull clank. Replacing her knife back in its holder, she scooted back to rest against the wall. Lacy squeezed her lips into a thin line, focusing her eyes on the beams above, ignoring the marshal.

Deciding to let the freckled vixen cool off some, Rawley walked over to his gear, releasing his saddlebags from the saddle. Throwing them over his shoulder they banged against his chest and back with a thud. Rawley said. "I'm going to the cabin, see if there is anything to eat."

Lacy continued to stare at the beams. He slowly shook his head, thinking *Damn kid!* He closed the big door, still protesting at its use.

Entering the cabin, Rawley closed the door as he gazed around the small room. Looking behind him, he saw a small window next to the door. Beside the window, pegs stuck into the wall for coats and rigs with a shelf hung above that. A big fireplace took up almost the whole back wall with a bunk just a few feet to the left of it and another window above the bunk. The table centered the room with three chairs around it. Coal oil lamp and a half-full bottle of whiskey and three glasses with amber liquid in them along with cards and money littered the tabletop. As Rawley's eyes continued to sweep the room, he found the boys' supplies in the corner to his right of the hearth. *Seems Lacy was right again. Looks like the boys were going to be here for the winter, hiding out and letting the heat ease off.* Above the supplies, he saw a shelf loaded with books. *Books?* Rawley took off his hat and reaching behind him, he hooked it on a peg, shaking his head at the oddity of having a shelf full of books way out here.

He threw a couple of logs on the fire and watched the flames begin to take hold. One thumb found a back pocket and tucked itself into it. He rested an elbow on the mantle as his fingers rubbed his thick stubble, thinking about the situation that freckled face girl had put him in. His fist suddenly slammed into the mantel, crunching his knuckles. Lacy was frustrating the hell out of him. *Normal?* That word didn't even figure into the girl's composition. She had developed into a ruthless, reckless, and dangerous female, worse than hot tempered and just toeing the line of the law. *One of these days she'll cross that line. When that happens, she'll be the one who is hunted.*

Rawley looked at the bottle of whiskey. Picking it up, he gave the bottle a hard stare. A chiseled jaw became more defined with anger. Turning, his arm slung the bottle into the fire. It exploded, releasing what he had been feeling inside. He'd never known anyone like her before. No telling what she would have done to those boys if he hadn't been there. No telling what she had done to her prisoners in the past, either.

This bounty hunting was screwing up her head. He wondered what Vern and Sam would say if they could see her now. This vengeance against what her grandfather did to her was getting out of hand.

Making a fresh pot of coffee, Rawley slumped in a chair, gazing into the sizzling, crackling fire as his thoughts turned elsewhere. *If Lacy couldn't keep a cool head, then it's up to me to do so.* Mentally shaking himself, he found a plate and dished up some of the venison stew that the boys had in a pot on the swing arm. Glasses clinked when he pushed them out of the way, followed by a raspy sound as his hand slid the cards and money to one side of the table. Straddling the chair, Rawley sat and ate.

He should've realized Lacy would be trouble the minute he first laid eyes on her, riding into town as a boy. But he had let the fact that she'd been hurt and a girl get in the way of his common sense. He could kick himself for getting involved. *If I knew then, what I know now...* he shook his head.

His chair scraped against the wood floor as he rose and fixed a plate for Lacy. Heaving in air, he exhaling it noisily; he did not feel overly excited at the prospect of seeing the spitfire again. Rawley reluctantly headed for the barn.

Hearing the latch jiggle, Lacy hopped off the feed bin and dropped prone on the dirt floor. Propping herself up on her elbows, she aimed the Sharps at the door, ready and waiting.

Rawley pushed open the door and stepped inside. He stared down the top of that long rifle barrel and traveled the length of it until they rested on a freckled face with two dark eyes holding a steady bead on him. His eyes narrowed. "You always shoot from your belly?" he asked, the heel of his boot tapping the door shut.

Rolling her eyes as she stood up, "Less of a target, my aim's steadier." She then went back to the feed bin and resumed her perch.

"Brought you some food and coffee," he said. Steam rose in the cold air as Rawley poured coffee into the tin cup. Within the quiet confines of the barn, it seemed to echo loudly. He handed that to her as he sat down and leaned against the wall. A hand pushed the plate toward her leg. Rawley poured another cup and took a sip saying, "Go on, eat."

Lacy shook her head no, followed by a sip of coffee.

His eyes tapered, "You haven't eaten since this morning. You need to eat."

A shrug was her answer.

"You like this every time you flush fugitives out of the brush or is it just with these three?"

One shoulder rose to her ear.

"You gonna eat this?"

The copperhead remained silent.

"Okay, I will. I'm still hungry." *That got a response.* Lacy cut him a swift glance, causing a smile to pop out as his mouth surrounded a forkful of food.

Finishing his second plate of stew, Rawley told Lacy, "Why don't you go back to the cabin, eat, and get some sleep. I'll take first shift, tho' I doubt they'll be going anywhere," he said as he nodded at the tied-up boys.

Lacy shook her head "No. I'll pull first shift. You go get some rest."

Giving the girl a cock-eyed look, Rawley said, "Possessive 'bout your prisoners, ain't cha?" He continued looking at that freckled profile, noticing a cute, turned-up-nose for the first time. "Alright, I'll come relieve you in a few hours." He really didn't feel like arguing with her anymore, that temper of hers had begun to wear on him. He slid off the feed bin, the utensils clinked and pinged as he gathered them together. Picking up the pot, he left without further comment.

Dark eyes drew closer as Lacy stared at Rawley's broad back in stony silence as he ambled through the barn door. She almost bit her tongue in half thinking. *That marshal is interfering with my job!* Telling her he was the law here, *hell*, she knew the law. She'd worked for Sam. *I know the law. That stupid lawman drew a busted flush. He had no clue as to how evil these boys really were. I'm protecting him, keeping both of us alive.* Lacy tried to justify her actions. *The quicker I let my prisoners know who is boss, the less problems I'll have.*

The events of the day finally caught up with her. Sliding down to the dirt floor, she pressed her back against the feed bin. Blinking to stay awake, it didn't work. Her eyes drooped. Finally, Lacy fell over, sound asleep, still gripping the rifle.

Chapter Twenty

SOMETHING JERKED RAWLEY awake. His ears perked up listening while his eyes bounced around as he tried to get his bearings. The fire was the only sound he heard; coals sizzling, licking at old sap in the wood. He'd slept hard those few short hours.

Trying to stay on top of Lacy's furious temper and then keeping his own under control had been taxing, to say the least. Rolling off the bunk, he stretched, fingertips able to touch the beams crossing the ceiling. Pouring himself some coffee, he carried the cup in one hand, while the other whisked his hat off the peg, settling it on his head.

Opening the door, Rawley stepped out into the darkness, the extreme cold taking his breath away. Boots thumped to the end of the porch then became silent except for the occasional squeaking his boots made against the snow. He continued toward the barn to relieve the meanest, hottest tempered copperhead he'd ever known.

Rusty hinges announced his arrival. Seeing Lacy sprawled on the floor, he quickly checked the boys, realizing they were still tied up. He quietly walked over to the freckled redhead, squatting down as he grinned. *She's out cold.* He softly brushed the hair out of her face thinking, *Sleeping like a little angel. Wished she'd stay that way.* He eased the rifle out of her grip, leaning it against the feed box out of her reach. Then he shook her shoulder, "Lacy. Lacy…hon. Time to wake up." He shook her again, "Lacy, hon. Lacy…wake up. It's my turn. You can wake up now," jiggling her shoulder again. A fist came out of nowhere, slamming into his chest. Rawley recoiled in surprise. "Hey!"

Lacy shot up, ready to fight, "Oh, it's you," she sighed, rubbing her eyes with the heels of her hands. "I'm awake. I'm awake."

"Uh-huh," he said. "Go on back to the cabin and finish your nap. I'll take over now."

Lacy rose and stumbled out of the barn.

Rawley watched the girl wobble through the door, still half asleep. *Damn kid,* his mind said as he rubbed his chest.

Memories washed over her when Lacy entered the cabin. Closing the door softly, she leaned against it and sighed heavily. Tired eyes roamed across familiar walls and objects. Her mind remembered the time she had spent here; a winter alone in this cabin after she had first run away. She had whiled away the time learning to shoot, practicing till she hit her mark six out of six times. She taught herself that drop and roll and how to use a knife. *Enough memories,* she told herself. Flopping onto the bunk, she immediately fell back asleep.

***

DAYBREAK HADN'T COME soon enough as far as Rawley was concerned. Leaving the prisoners – a hot cup of coffee the only thing on his agenda for the moment, he slogged through the bitter cold headed to the cabin. He couldn't wait to warm his bones by some welcome heat. Stamping his boots on the wooden porch, a gloved paw opened and shut the door softly. Seeing that the fire had become mostly coals, he threw more wood on. Rawley removed his gloves, laying them on the mantel and took the poker, stirring the coals and igniting a flame. As his eyes swept the room, they landed on the figure lying in the bunk. Lacy, sleeping on her belly, little sounds escaping from her open mouth. One arm dangling off the bed completed the picture. *Girl's gonna be the death of me yet,* he sighed, rubbing tired eyes. Rawley set about making a fresh pot of coffee.

He had seen the deer hanging out back last night. Returning

116

to the frosty morning air, he sliced off a slab of frozen venison to cook, along with some quick biscuits.

Squatting next to Lacy, ready to duck if an irate fist should fly toward him, Rawley spoke, "Sunshine…wake up, breakfast is ready. Sunshine…it's breakfast time."

Lacy cracked open one eye, focusing on the marshal's face, *He's right easy on the eyes early in the morning, 'specially with that woman killer look of his,* her mind said, then added, *Don't even go there.* Rolling over, she covered her eyes and groaned, "Is it morning already?"

"Yep, afraid so," he said. Rawley was surprised a fist hadn't come flying through the air at him.

"Ugh," she whispered. Lacy sat on the edge of the bunk and stared at her boots. *Damn, I'm tired. But soon it will be over and then I can rest.* She mentally shook the tiredness from her body and her first thoughts of the marshal out of her head. *Don't even go there,* she reminded herself again. Rising, she walked to the table, and stared at the food which made her stomach churn, then flip over. "I'm not hungry. I'll just saddle up the horses," she said as she headed for the door. She lifted the latch and pulled open the door. A blast of cold air swirled around her, making her catch her breath.

Rawley surprised her by ripping the latch out of her hand and slamming the door shut. "Oh no you don't, Sunshine! You're gonna eat today."

Facing all that brawn and muscle the thought crossed her mind, *He makes me nervous.* Lacy tried to hide her thoughts by standing a little taller, giving him one of her best blistering looks. "I told you! I'm not hungry!" Lacy argued as she reached for the latch, again.

Rawley gently took her by the shoulders and led Lacy to a chair and forced her to sit down, "I want you to eat today. Won't do me any good, you start passing out on me."

"I'm not gonna pass out on you!" she hissed. "It's just

117

that…uh…the food's turning my stomach," Lacy finally admitted.

"That's because you're too hungry. Now eat small bites at first."

No, I won't! He makes me too nervous to eat. Trying to hide her thoughts again, Lacy put her chin in her hand, giving the marshal a dirty look. Soon a big yawn split her face.

Up went one dark brow when Rawley saw the yawn. A fork full of food continued on its way into his mouth. "Better eat. We got a long haul today," he said, talking around the food.

Lacy bounced up. "That's right. We do," she said, rushing out the door.

He rolled his eyes as he shook his head and sighed. *Girl is about as hardheaded as they come.*

Outside, Rawley cut more meat off the deer, then cut down the remainder for the wolves. Next, he packed up and headed for the barn.

Lacy had saddled the five mounts, then tied Aubrey and Keller to drag or walk behind the horses.

Rawley's eyes turned the color of a polished pistol barrel. He continued striding toward the barn. He did not like what he saw, but kept his mouth shut as he loaded up Ed. Walking over to Aubrey, his hand grabbed a handful of hair, pulling up the boy's head. Rawley looked into a purple and black swollen face. He was in no condition to walk. The boy needed to ride.

Lacy turned in her saddle to address the lawman, "Mount up. We got a good three days' ride."

Rawley advanced toward the girl, his anger flaring from beneath his black lashes. "What the hell do you think you're doing? Aubrey can't walk! He's too badly hurt thanks to you! He needs to ride!"

Lacy leaned down toward the marshal, her eyes narrowing into slits, color brightening freckled cheeks in anger. "You listen to me good, Lovett. I'm not all brawn and muscle like you, so…," taking a finger and tapping her head, "I have to use my l'il pea-picking brain. Making my prisoners walk fifteen to twenty miles a day leaves them too tuckered out to argue with me at night, allowing me a little sleep. Keeping the food and water away, makes 'em real tame. Now, mount up!"

"That's sadistic!"

"Is it? I call it self-preservation. No one gets killed. No one gets hurt and we all arrive alive! Mount up!"

"You can't keep taking your anger and your hatred out on the fugitives you catch just because you don't have the guts to confront your grandfather for what he did to you!" His eyes, already frosty with anger, turned to diamond chips. "How many times do you have to kill your grandfather before you give it up?"

Gasping from his verbal onslaught, Lacy recoiled as if she had been slapped.

"You have all the warmth and welcome of smallpox when it comes riding into town! You know that?" he snapped. "I don't know where you were in line when they passed out hearts, but you sure as hell didn't receive one!"

He saw Lacy drop her hooded look back into place, hiding her emotions once again.

Rawley spun angrily, walking back to Aubrey. Cutting enough rope to tie the boy in the saddle, he helped him up and eased him over to the horse, supporting him as he mounted. "I'll get you to a doctor soon as I can, son," Rawley stated as he finished tying the boy in the saddle.

Hearing the metallic click of a hammer being pulled back, Rawley stiffened.

"The boy walks."

"No. He rides." Rawley's deep voice dropped lower, "Go ahead. Shoot me in the back. You do, I'll see you hang."

It seemed like ages before he heard the hammer ease down with a soft click, a gun whispering back into its holster and leather creaking as horses moved off. Turning his head, his eyes followed the girl as she rode out. Keller, his hands tied by a rope half-hitched to Lacy's saddle horn, struggled to remain on his feet as he was pulled along. Rawley slowly expelled the breath he had been holding, "Damn kid. I've had enough," he muttered. Whipping out his knife, he ran over to Keller and cleanly sliced the rope. The boy fell with the sudden slack. Feeling the taunt rope go slack, Lacy spun around in the saddle and yelled, "Lovett! You bastard!" Whirling Fancy around, she aimed the big grey on a collision course with the marshal. At the last second, Fancy swerved, throwing Lacy out of the saddle. She landed on top of Rawley, knocking both into the snow. Keller saw his chance. Scrambling up, he ran toward the nearest horse, his teeth chewing on the rope tying his hands. At last the knots loosened enough to where he could slide out his hands. Grabbing the reins, he mounted the big grey. Kicking heels into her ribs, he rode past the two still thrashing about in the snow.

"You damn little…she-devil!" Rawley grunted, taking another blow to his ribs. Lacy scrambled out of his grasp. Standing, she locked both hands together, straightened her arms and swung, like an ax aiming at a large tree. The movement caught Rawley across his back, surprising him and driving him to his knees. "That does it," he mumbled, rising again. Lacy had whirled, watching Keller ride off on her horse. Taking a few running steps, she suddenly landed face first in the snow. After tripping her, Rawley quickly grabbed both ankles, lifting them up so the little hellion didn't have any leverage. Lacy twisted, turning and flopping like a hundred and fifteen pound catfish. "Lovett! I'll kill you for this! I swear…I'll kill you!" She yelled. Rawley dragged her sliding on her belly, pulling snow with her, like a plow, over to where Keller had dropped the rope. Bending down, he picked it up. Kneeling, he not so gently put a knee in her back. "Oww! You bastard! That hurt!" He trussed up her ankles, bending legs at the knees. Lacy kept twisting, squirming, her body digging a hole in the snow as she struggled to break the grip he had on her. Holding her kicking legs down with one hand, Rawley's other hand caught an irate arm and pulled that behind her, adding that to the ankles. Catching the other wrist, he added that to the three, making a foursome. Breathing hard, he stood and surveyed his handiwork. Lacy twisted her neck, seeing nothing but snow-covered boots and pants. Rolling on her side, she gave him the dirtiest look she could muster, "Lovett, you're an ass! You let Keller get away!" She declared hotly.

The marshal heaved in more breath for his air starved lungs. *Damn kid is quick.* It had taken everything he had to subdue her. His fingers brushed his hair out of his eyes while he said, "Maybe that cold snow will cool down your temper some, Sunshine."

Turning, he walked over to his hat and picked it up. He brushed the snow off before resetting it back on his head. Rawley threw one more look at the trussed-up girl, then mounted. Two fingers brushed the brim of his hat as he nodded toward the girl, riding past her, heading off down the hill after Keller.

"Lovett?" Lacy yelled. "Where do you think you're going? You can't leave me like this! Lovett? Lovett...," dragging his name out to four or five syllables instead of the two. His name echoed against the granite of the mountains.

Aubrey still remained on his horse. His one good eye had watched the fracas that had just transpired in front of him. Too hurt to follow his brother, he just stared at the girl.

Lacy's eyes followed the marshal until he dipped out of sight below the rise. She struggled against the knots he'd tied, but she couldn't budge them. Her head flopped back into the snow. *Damn, you Lovett!* He hadn't scared her this time, just made her mad, fighting mad, letting one of her prisoners escape. Lacy struggled some more, then gave up. She felt someone staring, it was Aubrey. "What are you staring at, you sick little rat?" She snapped.

Aubrey shrugged, sending the pain ricocheting in his swollen cheek pulsing into his brain.

121

Fifty yards down the hill, Rawley saw Fancy standing by a small grouping of spruce with no rider. Reining up the bay, he quietly slid the rifle out of its boot. Slipping off the leather, he dropped the reins and moved toward some cover. Rawley scanned the area thinking, *What the hell happened to Keller?* Moving closer to Fancy, he still saw nothing except her. The horse kept ogling him, watching his movement. As she nickered softly, the lawman flinched. Easing closer, the only sound he heard were his own footsteps squeaking in the snow and Fancy blowing every now and then. The forest remained still. He looked at the evergreens and snow laden branches of the numerous trees, nothing moved. A fog enveloped his head as he breathed. *Where in the hell is Keller?* Rawley kept his crouched position as he slowly made his way to the grey. Coming alongside, he rubbed her neck. She butted and nuzzled his chest. His eyes continued to sweep the terrain. Then he saw it, a disturbance marking the pristine surface of the snow. Following it, Rawley came to the edge of a bluff. Looking down, he saw the busted up remains of Keller Dillard. Limbs askew, neck twisted at an odd angle. Noticing the churned-up snow at the edge, he figured Fancy had dumped Keller over the rim. Going back to his horse, he replaced the rifle in its boot then released the rope from the saddle.

Slogging back to the edge of the cliff, he tied the rope around the nearest evergreen, threw the rope down and began the descent to the body. Dropping the last few feet into wind-blown thigh deep snow, Rawley plowed his way to the boy. Taking off one glove, he began to examine the body. No pulse, his neck broken from the fall. Looking back up the ragged face of the cliff, and noting the disturbed snow along the way, he surmised the boy must have hit every jagged edge on the way down. Slogging back to the rope, the lawman jumped, grabbing the rope. He began the hand over hand slow ascent back to the top. Pulling himself up over the edge, he crawled toward the evergreen. Standing, Rawley released the rope. Picking up Fancy's reins he pulled her along toward his horse. Recoiling the rope, he returned it to the saddle. Mounting, he headed back to the little firebrand; hopefully the copperhead would have spit out some of that venom by now.

Lacy lifted her head, hearing snow muffled hooves coming toward her. Rawley rode past the trussed-up girl, not saying a word. His peripheral vision caught her eyes going wide in a freckled face and jaw dropping as she watched him.

"Where's Keller?" Lacy demanded. "Lovett, what the hell did you do with Keller?"

Rawley slowly dismounted and ambled over to stand alongside Lacy, staring at the tied up girl.

Color began flooding across her face as her eyes became hostile. She snapped, "Damn it, Lovett! Where the hell is Keller?"

He continued gazing at his handiwork while asking, "You always sprinkle your conversation with swear words?"

"Pffttt..." she replied. "...Untie me. I can't feel my hands or my legs." Lacy waited; when he didn't move she hissed, "Damn it! Untie me, you jackass!"

Rawley just moved into the barn and looked around. Finding what he needed, he walked back outside. Rolling the girl back on her belly, he placed a knee between her shoulder blades, holding her down. "Hey! What the hell do you think you're doing?" Lacy shouted, trying to squirm. Taking the pole he'd found in the barn, he slid that under the knots holding her feet and hands. Rising, hands gripped the pole about a foot each way from the knots. He lifted the pole with the girl attached, chest high. Lacy squealed, thrashing around, "Damn it, Lovett! Put me down! This ain't funny!"

"Yep! That'll work," he said.

Lacy stilled, twisting her head. "What'll work?"

"Tying the pole between two horses."

Lacy gasped, "You wouldn't dare. Put me down, you big galoot!"

Rawley grinned, "Pretty please…"

"No!"

"Alright, have it your way," he said moving toward the horses.

"Wait," she cried.

Rawley stopped, ears tuned waiting on Lacy's next words.

Lacy gritted her teeth and mumbled like she had a mouthful of marbles, "Pretty please."

He grinned, "Beg your pardon, Sunshine?"

She gritted as she spoke a little louder, "I said, pretty please!"

His hands let go of the pole and Lacy landed with a whumph. "You bastard!"

Squatting next to her shoulder, Rawley pushed his hat back on his head and then said calmly, "Your temper has delayed this little trek back down the mountain by several hours. You gonna behave so we can get moving?" *The girl's temper seemed to shake the air around her like warning rattles on a snake.*

Lacy cast her eyes down.

Several long moments passed, while he continued to wait. The girl nodded at last. Rawley sighed with relief and began to untie his handiwork. He hadn't liked trussing Lacy up this way, but it was the only thing he could think of to calm her down. Lacy moaned, trying to get the feeling back in her limbs. Rawley pulled the girl to her feet. She sagged back into the snow, so he swung her into his arms. Lacy gave him a dirty look, but didn't try to fight him.

"Where's Keller?" she asked, when he came alongside Fancy.

"Dead," he replied, hoisting her up in the saddle.

"You kill him jus' so's you could get $500 in bounty money?"

Blue eyes gave her a withering look, "No. Fancy did. So…the money's still yours, Sunshine."

"I need the body as proof…" she began.

"He's down at the bottom of a ravine."

"Well...I still need the body," she insisted.

Rawley draped an arm over Fancy's neck as he gave Lacy a tired look, "No need. I'll vouch for you."

Straightening in the saddle, her eyes narrowed as Lacy snipped, "Really now...Mister Lovett? You'd do that for me?"

The skin around his eyes tightened. "Don't push me, Sunshine," Rawley told her. "You just found out what I can do to you, when I get mad. Unless you're just dying to be trussed up like a hog again, don't push me," he warned. Adding as an after-thought, "The last thing I want to do is hurt you, but it's still on my agenda if you push me, Sunshine."

Backing Fancy up, Lacy scowled at the Marshal. Rawley dropped his arm from the animal's neck. She exhaled into the air as she reined the grey around and headed toward the rise and down the mountain.

Rawley let a lung full of air escape as he swung into his sad-dle. Resettling his hat, he sighed again thinking, *Never, never, in my born days have I ever met a female like her.* Clucking his tongue, he moved the bay into motion. Pulling Aubrey's horse, he began following the rigid back on the slight figure riding the grey.

Chapter Twenty-One

DARKNESS HAD SETTLED in when Rawley reined in alongside Lacy, "We stop here for the night."

"No, we keep going," she said, as her eyes continued to focus forward.

"Aubrey needs some powder for his pain. Thanks to you," he added sarcastically, "We stop here." Lacy kept riding. "Do as I say…" Rawley warned, nudging his bay to keep pace with the grey.

"No! We keep moving!"

For the second time that day, his anger rose to its limits. Rawley grabbed her oversized coat under her chin and gave a yank, hauling Lacy half out of her saddle.

She gasped.

Pulling her to within inches of his grim face, jaw tight with anger, he growled, "You sick little witch! You'll do as I say! We stop here!" Her eyes widened as surprise flooded her face. An angry look continued to threaten her. Finally, Rawley shoved her away from him, his strength almost tumbling her out of the saddle.

***

LACY SAT HUDDLED close to the fire, trying to warm herself. The dancing flames mesmerized her, having a hypnotic effect. Her mind blocked out all sounds of Lovett removing saddles and taking care of Aubrey, digging around in his gear bag, retrieving cups. The sound of water was soon heard being poured from the canteen into the coffee pot. More rustlings were heard as grounds were added to the pot, then clinking noises as the lid was closed and it was set near the flame. Later the scent of brewing coffee filled the surrounding air.

Her mind reflected on what the marshal had said to her that morning and again a little while ago, telling her she didn't have the guts to face her grandfather, tying her up like a hog ready for the spit and then calling her a sick little witch. *Maybe it is time to get out of this business,* but this was the only trade she knew.

Realization hit, *I'm not normal*, Lacy thought as tears bit the backs of her eyes and made her nose run. She sniffled. *I can't do all those normal things most women can do. No, I'm not normal.* Lacy sniffled again as she made up her bed, laying the ground cloth and her saddle blanket flapping the air when she shook it. Picking up the heavy leather saddle, she dumped it at one end of the blanket. Lacy upended the saddle, so the fleece padding would be her pillow. She crawled in, pulling the blanket up to her chin. She hadn't cried in nine years and she sure as hell wasn't going to allow those emotions to take over now.

Rawley had watched Lacy start the fire and then just sit there with her dark eyes reflecting the flames. Not eating once again, he watched her crawl into her bedroll without a sound, except for the sniffling.

Rawley knew he'd been hard on her about why she treated her prisoners so harshly. And about her grandfather too, but sometimes you needed to hurt to help. Sometimes things like that, needed to be said. *And I sure didn't like trussing her up like some animal. But hell, she fought me like a man, I had to do something.* Firelight continued to flicker across his chiseled features as he too sat and stared into the fire, listening to her sniffling. Maybe his words had finally sunk in.

Chapter Twenty-Two

The traveling party had been riding through the frozen terrain for four days. Five horses and three riders rode into the post, one of the few remaining after the Indian wars. The post had maybe thirty-five to fifty men stationed there. Tubes of smoke rose from chimneys in the cold still air. The yard was pretty much deserted except for those soldiers who had to pull duty in the icy environment.

Shod hooves clipped against the frozen turf within the confines of the post's yard. A rope attached to Rawley's saddle pulled Aubrey's horse along as Lacy pulled the other two horses. The Marshal and Lacy riding abreast of each other, reined up as one in front of the commander's headquarters. Rawley swung out of the saddle stiffly as he threw a look at the girl. Lacy hadn't spoken one word after that last fiasco at the cabin. He hadn't even tried to make conversation with the copperhead, not wanting the verbal tussle that always seemed to ensue.

Walking up the steps, the marshal stopped. His tired eyes swept over the young soldier as innocent eyes looked back at Rawley from under the brim of the boy's cap. Rawley thought, *Probably joined up looking for adventure after Custer's big blunder.* A heavy sky-blue kersey wool cape covered most of his uniform. A lemon-yellow stripe ran down the outside of his light blue wool pants, denoting his rank - private. Rifle resting on his shoulder had moved into both hands as Rawley mounted the steps, eyes watchful. Stopping in front of the private, the marshal thumbed at the door, "I need to see the commander." The soldier nodded and walked to the door, knocked and opened it, saying, "Sir...someone to see you, sir."

The commander pushed his chair back, causing it to scrape against the wooden floor. He pulled his thickset build to a standing position. Tilting his head, he looked at the scruffy man who had entered his office. Eyes traveling further up the face, he took in the tired bright blue eyes. Recognition finally flitted across the commander's face.

"Well...well, if it ain't Rawley Lovett. Long time, no see," he said, eliciting a big smile as he shook Rawley's hand, "What brings you way out here?" Jovial eyes disguised the horror he'd lived through during the Indian wars. Sandy blond hair mingled with grey at the sides, blonde beard filled with streaks of grey surrounded a wide smile. Epaulets decorated the shoulders of his dark kersey wool coat, sky-blue pants with a darker yellow stripe that marked him as an officer ran down the outside of his leg.

"Got a prisoner for your stockade. He'll need medical attention. There were two more. One's dead, another dead at the bottom of a ravine."

"Who?"

"The Dillard brothers."

"You caught those nasty polecats by yourself?"

"Uh...no. Me and my partner."

"What? You got a new deputy now?"

"Uh no, it's a bounty hunter."

Not believing his ears, he strode around the lawman. The commander's heels drummed across the planked wood. When he opened the door, he discovered a girl astride a big grey. His eyes popped.

Lacy had leaned slightly forward when the door opened, her forearms resting lightly on the saddle horn while her gloved hands loosely held the grey's reins. A coppery braid dripped over one shoulder, and a big hat partially shadowed a pale freckled face. She returned the commander's stare.

The commander looked back around at Rawley in surprise, "A girl?"

129

"Uh-huh…that's Lacy Car…" he caught himself. "Uh…Lacy Watson."

"Lacy Watson?" The commander repeated swiveling his head back around. His boots made a hurried thumping noise across the porch and clattered down the steps, stopping next to the mare. "Young lady, it is a pleasure to finally meet you," he said, taking her hand in his and giving a gentle squeeze, "The Pinkerton's and the Wells Fargo boys speak very highly of you."

Color rose in Lacy's face as she whispered, "Thank you, sir." Looking up towards Rawley, she saw the look of surprise on his face as he stood in the doorway. She licked her cold dry lips, dropping her gaze to her hands.

The commander walked around the two prisoners, and peeked at the one slung over a saddle, dead. Eyes traveled to the boy, his face grotesquely swollen. Speaking to the soldiers in the yard, he said, pointing, "Take that one to medical. And I want around the clock guard on him! You got that, Sergeant?"

"Yes, sir. What about the body, sir?"

"Stash it in the livery. It'll keep in this weather."

"Yes sir."

Climbing the steps, the commander stopped alongside the tall lawman, asking, "You said one body is at the bottom of a ravine?

Rawley nodded.

"Guess you want a voucher for the three?"

"Yes sir,"

The commander nodded, leading the marshal inside.

Finishing the paperwork, he handed it to Rawley.

Rawley took it asking, "How'd you know Lacy worked for those companies?"

"You didn't know?"

Rawley gave a shrug, "I've just known her a short while. She doesn't talk much."

"You must not be in the right circles, Rawley," the commander said, grinning at him.

"Must not be," Rawley returned with a slight smile.

"From what I've heard, they give her the tough cases their boys can't crack."

"They do?"

"That's what I hear."

"Well…" Rawley said, moving toward the door, brushing two fingers along the brim of his hat, "Thanks, commander." He closed the door softly behind him and stood staring at the girl in the saddle. Rawley studied her from the porch, his eyes shrewd as silent questions flitted across his dynamic features. Lacy pressed her lips together, squinting dark eyes back. He's finding out more about her then she wanted. *Another of my secrets exposed. Damn!* Straightening up in the saddle, Lacy slowly turned Fancy toward the gate and White River.

Moments later, riding quietly alongside each other, Rawley once again contemplated this girl. She was more complicated and secretive than he first thought, besides fighting like a man. His mind wondered what else she had been keeping secret.

Rawley like to talk. He enjoyed the exchange of banter with people. Lacy had to be the quietest female he had ever run across, well…except when her temper flared. But even then, afterwards, she would clam up on him. Most women he'd known couldn't keep their tongues in their heads. With this one, he felt as he was talking to himself most of the time. Rawley doubted an earthquake could jar that tongue loose from the roof of her mouth. *Hum…* thinking, he glanced slyly at the figure riding next to him.

He offered up, "Well Miss Freckled Sunshine, what's nex…" Something flew out of nowhere, the sound of knuckles cracking in the cold air when they made contact, slamming him hard in his jaw. That sent him sailing out of the saddle, his large frame hitting the frozen ground with a solid thud. A slight figure seemed to take wing and fly across his horse, the full weight of her body slammed into his chest. He exhaled heartily as irate fists punched him, accompanied with grunts in the midst of each vigorous blow.

131

His arms rose, "Damn you, you little hellcat!" Rawley managed to feint off the rapid-fire maneuvers that seem to be coming from every which way. His strength finally over powering her, he wrestled Lacy's legs in a scissors lock with his. At last, he caught her flailing arms and pulled them in a cross-hold tight against her chest. He rolled over, pinning her beneath him as he yelled, "Damn it! Lacy Carrigan, cut it out!" Her ears rang with his explosion of anger.

Both breathing hard from the exertion of yet another fight, their faces ended up only inches from each other.

"I'm tired of your shenanigans! Tired of you fighting me like a man! You're a woman! For Gawd's sake! You ain't 'sposed to do that!" He bellowed.

Lacy flinched as copper tendrils flew off her forehead in the gust of wind. She blinked at his fury.

"I'm tired of you being mad at the world and taking it out on me! Tired of you not speaking to me. Tired of you keeping secrets from me! Tired of you fighting me all the time! From now on, you will be civil to me," he warned. He shook her demanding, "Do you understand?" Shaking her again, he repeated, "Do you understand me?"

Speechless, she didn't even try to struggle against the man whose body pressed her into the frozen ground. At last finding her voice, Lacy rasped out, "You started it! Now get off me! You're heavy!"

Rawley tilted his head; big round burnt coffee eyes and a million freckles gazed back at him warily. He could feel her heart beating a rapid drum roll against her ribs. Suddenly, he wanted to kiss this hard-nosed female. Rawley leaned in closer and saw her eyes grow rounder. His lips met Lacy's resistance, but allowed his kiss to linger. Then finally, he pulled back and asked softly, "There now, isn't that better then fighting all the time?"

Lacy's face puckered up, a loose hand covered her mouth as silent sobs began to shake her body. She turned her head to the side so he wouldn't see her cry. She gasped for air as she tried to quell the tears, the sobs beginning anew.

Rawley could have kicked himself. Seeing the tears dribble across that little freckled nose and coursing down her cheek, he spoke softly, "Sunshine, if anyone has a reason to cry, you do."

Lacy just cried harder.

Exasperation crossed his face, "Look, you need to talk about it. Get it off your chest. It's eating you up inside!"

Lacy shook her head, taking a deep breath as she tried to calm her emotions.

"I'm a good listener," Rawley said, inviting a response.

Shaking her head once again, she took another deep breath, whispering, "Let me go. Let me go…please. Just let me go."

Rawley released her.

She scrambled up so fast he thought she had been stabbed with a red-hot poker. Lacy wiped her face with the sleeve of her coat, smearing dirt and tears together, hurrying toward Fancy.

Rawley stood up and dusted dead grass off himself, taking steps and following her, "You know Sunshine, you pack quite a wallop," he said, touching his soon to be sore jaw. *The damn girl had lightening reflexes.* "But that's not exactly the way a lady would behave."

Lacy hesitated. She kept her eyes focused on Fancy's neck as she spoke quietly, "I'm not a lady and never will be one, either." She swung into her saddle and turned Fancy toward town.

Rawley watched that straight back of Lacy's as she rode off. He felt like a heel. But if those tears meant anything, it was the fact that she was beginning to feel again by allowing those emotions to rise to the surface releasing the pain and grief. Dusting off his hat, Rawley jammed it back on his head, stepped into his saddle and followed the girl towards home.

Chapter Twenty-Three

WHEN HE REACHED the livery, Rawley dismounted and led his horse inside. Turning when she didn't follow him, he questioned the girl, "You not coming?"

After the incident outside the fort, Lacy didn't know how to react. She darted her eyes all around, gazing up and down the street. She sighed inwardly, at last bringing brown eyes back and focusing on his face. She shook her head asking instead, "Um, where's Cotton Top staying?"

"Who?"

"Cotton T… I mean Howie…Howie Clancy. Do you know where he's staying?"

"Why? You wanna go visit?"

Lacy nodded slightly.

Rawley reached into his saddlebag and pulled out the whistle he had carved. Handing it to her, he smiled saying, "Give him this for me, will you? But tell him not to blow it in the house. Miss Livy will box his ears." He pointed southwest toward the edge of town.

Lacy followed the direction of his finger.

"Last house on the left, painted a pretty, soft yellow. Can't miss it."

Not returning his smile, Lacy reined Fancy around and trotted down the street toward the house.

His eyes followed the girl, then he shook his head tiredly and sighed. Lacy had worn him out physically fighting him during most of the trip. All he wanted to do after taking care of his horse…Number one, get cleaned up…two, eat, and three…sleep.

Rawley usually remained a pretty laid-back person with an

easy going personality, but this fiery redhead sure as hell had kept him on his toes. He yawned, calling out to the stable owner, Luke, that he'd see him later.

Lacy approached a pretty, yellow clapboard home. Scanning it, she noticed its neat appearance. Flower boxes under the windows and across the edge of the porch were filled with dried dead stalks due to the cold. A porch swing hung from the ceiling, just biding time until warmer weather. A rocker and table sat near the swing, both painted yellow to match the house, creating an inviting conversation alcove for warm summer evenings.

Even though Lacy didn't voice her thoughts to the marshal, she had been desperate to find out if Cotton Top was okay. Lacy knew how it felt to lose your family. Her family had become dead to her, too. *Cotton Top and me are just two orphans drifting on the wind,* she thought. Easing out of the saddle, she looped Fancy's reins around the railing. Taking a big breath, she exhaled it slowly, climbing the steps. Lacy rapped knuckles on the door, then hearing footsteps on the other side, she waited.

The door opened, causing Lacy to silently gasp as she stared into the face of her old teacher, Olivia Johnston. *Damn, I knew I should've never come back to this town,* Lacy realized. *Olivia Johnston is still pretty as ever.* In the past, Lacy had always admired the way the woman had carried herself. Dark blond hair, now with a tinge of grey at the temples, still pulled back into a neat little bun at the base of her neck. Her oval face displayed a pretty mouth that always had a ready smile for her pupils and light grey, kind, intelligent eyes that never missed a trick with her students. These eyes contained a question.

Olivia spied a bedraggled female who looked somehow familiar standing on her porch in an overgrown coat and a big hat that shadowed a face filled with dirty smudges and a million freckles. Red gold tendrils of hair framed the freckles and dark eyes. A braid draped over her shoulder that reached almost to the front pocket of her dirty coat. "Yes?" she inquired.

The voice brought Lacy back to earth, "Uh…I'm Lacy Watson," she began, "Is Howie Clancy staying here?"

"Why…yes, he is," she said, opening the door wider allowing Lacy to enter. She turned and called out, "Howie…there's someone here to see you."

Taking off the hat, her fingers twirled it nervously in her hands as Lacy's eyes swept the familiar room. Nothing had changed in nine years. *Mama and me used to come here and have tea, sitting on that flowered print chesterfield sofa, all prim and proper, dressed up in pretty clothes with other girls and their mamas at Miss Olivia's.* Happy memories. She tossed them back into the dark recesses of her mind when she heard the pitter-pat of little feet running.

"Miff Wafy! Miff Wafy!"

Lacy squatted and grabbed the towheaded tyke in a bear hug, "Cotton Top! I sure did miss you!" She pushed him back and looked the boy over. Blue eyes peeked out at her from that shock of white blond hair. Perfect little teeth smiled and his rosy cheeks lit up his heart shaped face. A new flannel shirt was tucked into corded britches, still held up by miniature suspenders. Lacy glanced down; Cotton had on shiny new shoes, too.

"Miff you thoo, Miff Wafy!" he said. Then he took her hand, pulling her into the overly warm kitchen.

The heat felt good to Lacy's cold cheeks and body.

"Come…" said Howie. "Gama Wivy's making cookies for da…" he paused and looked back at Olivia.

"The bazaar."

Nodding, "Da' zaar. Come on."

Lacy gave a sigh of relief, laying her hat on the table. *Cotton is going to be okay.* She sat as he pushed the plate of cookies toward her, jabbering all the while.

Olivia poured Lacy a glass of milk while racking her brain, trying to figure out where she should know this woman from.

Lacy took a bite of cookie and closed her eyes as the sweet

goodness hit her tongue. Looking up at her old teacher, she commented, "Good. Real good." Lacy helped herself to several more. It had been days since she had eaten.

As she pulled another sheet of cookies out of the oven, Olivia was still trying to figure out how she knew this woman. *All those freckles,* her thoughts paused. *That's it! She had to be Lacy Carrigan!* Doc had told her, a girl named Lacy had found Howie. She must have been with Rawley tracking the Clancy family's murderers. Glancing back at the woman, she asked, "Lacy, do you mind staying with Howie? I've got to get some more baking supplies."

Lacy looked up and then nodded.

"Be back in a jiffy," Olivia said. Picking up a basket, bonnet and heavy cape, she hurried out the door. She made a beeline for Rawley's.

Entering the marshal's office and closing the door behind her with a soft click, Olivia set the basket on the table.

The lawman hearing the door open and shut, called out, "Be with you in a few minutes."

Moving toward his quarters, Olivia stood in the doorway with hands on her hips, staring at the handsome rogue who stood in front of the looking glass, his chest bare, with a towel draped over one shoulder, shaving off the heavy stubble. "If I was thirty years younger, Rawley Lovett, I'd have already sunk my claws into you," she teased, rolling grey eyes upward as she fanned herself with her hand as if a heat wave had suddenly blown in.

Turning at the voice, Rawley flashed that smile of his, "And if I was thirty years older, we would've already been married!"

"Humph! Well, hurry up. I've got something important I want to talk to you about," she said, taking a seat at the table.

A few moments later, Rawley came out, buttoning his shirt then tucking it into his britches. "Well?" He inquired.

"Well...I have a visitor at my house."

"Ahh..." he said, nodding, "Lacy Watson."

Olivia gave him one of her best teacher looks, daring him to lie to her, "You sure?"

Rawley flinched from the look Olivia gave him, warily asking, "Why?"

"She's Lacy Carrigan, isn't she?"

"What makes you think so?" he asked, jamming thumbs into back pockets.

"Humph!" she imitated Doc. "I'd know those freckles anywhere. She's Lacy Carrigan isn't she?" Olivia demanded again.

Rawley sighed, "I promised I wouldn't tell."

"Well, I know you're a man of your word. I won't press you."

Relief washed over his face.

"What do you know about her?" Olivia asked.

Rawley shrugged, "Not much. She's a bounty hunter. Got a temper that won't quit sometimes. Can handle a gun, herself, and a horse. She doesn't talk much."

"My...my...I see, a bounty hunter..." Olivia said, slowly shaking her head. She gestured at the chair on the other side of the table. "Sit down. I want to tell you about the Lacy Carrigan I once knew."

Rawley moved to the table and eased himself into the chair, resting his forearms on the table and lightly clasped his hands together.

Olivia looked up at the ceiling, her mind going back in time. "Lacy was a happy go-lucky child, always smiling and laughing. A chatterbox really."

Rawley cocked a brow at the word 'chatterbox'.

Olivia continued, "A smart, inquisitive girl. She had the most beautiful auburn hair with red-gold highlights I had ever seen on a child." Olivia focused her eyes back on the marshal, "Then, overnight, something changed. I thought she was getting sick. When I tried to feel her forehead, she shrunk away from me. From then on, she stayed by herself, wouldn't play with the other children. Her attendance at school became sporadic. Then she quit coming at all. I tried to visit her at home once, but was turned away. Later I heard Marie took her own life. I guess Lacy disappeared not long after that," Olivia finished quietly.

"When you noticed the change how old..." he faltered, dreading the answer.

"About twelve and a-half."

Rawley clenched his hands so hard the knuckles turned white.

"She is Lacy Carrigan, isn't she?" Olivia asked softly.

Rawley nodded slightly.

"I see. Well as far as I'm concerned, we didn't have this conversation," she assured him.

He gave her a look of gratitude.

Olivia placed a soft hand over his "Be careful with her, Rawley. She's vulnerable and fragile."

Jerking his head up, he let loose, "Fragile? Hell! You know how many times she whupped up on me out there?" Rising and pacing the floor then whirling around, he marched over to Olivia and the table slamming both palms down hard.

Olivia jumped.

"And almost beat me? She's almost as strong as I am and twice as quick! Fragile? Hell!"

"Is that how you got that bruise on your face?"

Rawley fingered his jaw, "Yeah...that was the last time she slugged me."

Olivia rose and walked over to him. "Rawley...you men can be so dense sometimes. I don't mean physically," she said, patting the front of her dress, "I mean emotionally, inside." Tilting her head, she watched the emotions play across Rawley's face at what she had just revealed. "Well...I need to get those supplies...before those two send out a posse after me." Picking up her basket, Olivia turned and faced him. "I do know this, Rawley Lovett. If there is anyone who can give us back the old Lacy, it would be you," she smiled. Giving her signature three finger wave, Olivia left the office.

Rawley gazed out the window watching Liv walk across the street going into Ezra's store. He muttered to himself, "Twelve and a-half when that old man began having his way with Lacy." His mind buzzing, he swung around, slamming his fist into the wall making the coffee cups rattle. Rawley sighed. The trip had exhausted him, causing him to lose his temper too quickly. He needed to eat and then sleep. Grabbing his hat and coat, he jerked the door open, then slammed it behind him. Rawley heard the windows rattle as his boot heels angrily chewed up the wood planks on his way to Maddie's.

***

"I'M BACK," SHE called out to the two in the kitchen. Olivia heard the patter of little feet running towards her; she bent down to see what Howie had in his hands.

"Thee! Thee! What Miffer Rawwee made me? A wiffle! A real wiffle!"

"How wonderful," she replied, smiling at the glee in the little boy's eyes.

"Miff Wafy thaid I can't bow in da house. I have thoo bow outhide."

"That's right," Olivia agreed, tousling the boy's hair. She walked into the kitchen to find Lacy sound asleep, her head resting on her arms. She placed the basket on the table and walked over to Lacy, shaking her shoulder, "Lacy...Lacy...I'm back."

Lacy jumped up, her chair crashing backwards against the floor and pulled her weapon on the teacher. Olivia reached for Howie, shoving him behind her skirts. The two continued to retreat toward the door. Realizing how badly she had scared Olivia and little Howie, her cheeks flared red across a million freckles. She stammered, "I'm...I'm so sorry, Miss Liv. I...I fell asleep." The pistol whispered quickly back into its holster. Lacy righted the chair and collapsed on the seat. Her forehead dropped into her hand. She repeated, "I'm sorry. I didn't mean to do that." then added quickly, "I need to be going." Her fingers coaxed the boy over to her, giving Howie another hug. "I'll see you soon, okay?" Looking into those innocent blue eyes, her hands tousled the baby fine white hair. "Thanks for the cookies," Lacy said, throwing the words over her shoulder as she half ran out the door. Jumping over the steps, she quickly mounted Fancy saying, "Let's get out of here, Fancy Girl. Then we'll rest some."

Lacy suddenly realized how exhausted she was, *Pulling my pistol on a teacher and little boy.* The thought made her neck and face grow warm as she pulled the rigging off Fancy. Tangling with that Marshal all week had worn her out mentally and physically. She hauled her gear to the back of the stall after bedding Fancy down in the town's livery. Untying her bed roll, laying the ground cover followed by the saddle blanket, she upended her saddle. Flopping down, she fell asleep instantly.

Chapter Twenty-Four

LUKE WALKED OVER to the mare. He patted her neck as his eyes traveled over the grey's nice lines. Rawley had told him to be expecting the big horse back as a boarder, but he wasn't expecting a girl sleeping in back of the stall. *Rawley picked up another saddle tramp, big moose has got a heart as big as a washtub,* he thought.

A small wiry lightweight frame sat on legs bowed from too many hours in the saddle long ago, one leg shorter than the other, causing a hobbled step, more 'n likely because of the leg being broken too many times. Luke Castleberry had been a saddle tramp, oh…must be, pert near twenty years ago, when he had wandered into a little place that didn't even have a name back then. Just a few buildings with a few folks that hung around and formed the township of White River, named after that beast flowing not too far from the edge of town. The little spit-in-the-dust community had survived the Indian wars, floods, droughts and disease that became part of everyday life out here. Luke wrangled the wild mustangs so prevalent on the prairies, breaking them and then selling them to the army for remounts during the Indian uprisings. He had built himself up quite a little nest egg which enabled him to start his own business, the livery. It was built with the sturdy logs hauled down from the mountains with blacksmithing on the side. He understood horses and knew the grey had other blood running through her veins, besides the Spanish blooded mustangs running wild on the prairies.

Walking across the street, Luke thought about the big marshal. He liked Rawley. The man had an easygoing, laid back, calming effect on situations that occurred in and around White

River, showing a maturity far beyond his years. Oh, he'd liked Vern, too. But with Rawley's commanding size and presence and sharp, intelligent blue eyes. Luke knew that when Rawley used a certain tone in his voice, assuming an air of authority that was almost scary like, you didn't mess with the lawman. White River remained in good hands with Rawley Lovett around.

Looking up from his mail as the door to his office opened, Rawley smiled his greeting. "Hey Luke…have a seat…"

"Howdy…Rawley." He remained standing, his feet fuss-fiddling impatiently.

Rawley frowned, "What's itching your britches, Luke?"

"Uh…I's got sumtin' I want ya ta see ober ta my place, see what ya make of it."

"You do, huh. Well let's go see what it is," he said as he grabbed his hat. Slipping on his coat, he followed Luke out the door.

Reaching the stable, Luke hung back and pointed, "There."

Rawley saw the big mare, walked to the stall wall and rubbed her neck. "Hey, Fancy Girl," he spoke softly. Turning back towards Luke. "It's just Fancy," giving the stable owner a confused look as to what he wanted him to see.

"Not the harse, ya numbskull!" he griped, looking at the marshal like he had peas for brains. "Look back ah tha stall."

Rawley leaned over the partition and saw the figure huddled in her blanket, sound asleep. A big smile creased his face, "It's okay, Luke. It's the girl who helped catch the Clancys' murderers," he whispered, "Got another blanket?"

Luke nodded and went to get it.

Covering Lacy, Rawley patted the mare as he stepped out of the stall, "Don't step on her now, Fancy Girl." Facing Luke, he said, "Just let her sleep. She gets a little testy if you wake her up suddenly. Don't want you to get your head blown off. Come and get me when she's up. Night and thanks, Luke."

Walking back to his office, Rawley looked up at the sky to

see clouds scudding across the moon. He sniffed the air, commenting to himself, "Change coming. Wouldn't be surprised winter showed up early this year." He stepped into his office and more welcomed sleep.

Chapter Twenty-Five

FINDING RAWLEY A little after noon the next day, Luke told him the girl was awake and now grooming her horse.

Walking quietly into the stables, Rawley leaned on the stall wall, listening to the raspy sound of a brush being pulled across Fancy's coat.

"Afternoon…Sunshine…"

The raspy sound stopped. Lacy ducked under Fancy's neck and twisted her head upwards. Glimpsing the marshal, she sighed inwardly. Then she disappeared behind the horse. Rising slowly, she peeped warily at him over Fancy's withers.

The lawman's mouth twitched, trying to keep a smile from busting out as he watched a redhead, two big eyes, dark as coffee along with a dirty face smothered in freckles, peek at him from across the back of her horse. *Even with a dirty face she's still cute as a speckled pup.*

"Wind's turned. Getting colder, wouldn't be surprised if we get some snow tonight. Got a warm office and hot water for you to get cleaned up, then we can get something to eat." Getting no response, Rawley offered again, "Well…how 'bout it, Sunshine?"

Continuing to stare back, her eyes roamed the face of the handsome man who had given her so much trouble the last week. Lacy couldn't make up her mind. She wanted to say no and she wanted to run, but her feet remained rooted to the livery floor.

Rawley waited patiently.

After a few more moments of thinking how hungry and cold she was, she decided to take him up on his offer. She slowly gave that short, hesitant nod of hers.

"Grab your gear and c'mon then," he said as he ambled back

across the street to his office.

Lacy hurriedly picked up her things and trotted after the lawman. Saddlebags bumped against her legs and her hand carried the buffalo gun. Lacy had to wait as a wagon rumbled across the street in front of her. She picked up her pace and entered the office on the marshal's heels. Rawley instructed her and pointed, "Coat, gun belt and hat on those pegs there. The rest of your gear you can put on my bed." He opened the door to his quarters, then stood back. Rawley leaned against the doorjamb and folded his arms across that expanse of chest. He waited to see what Lacy would do.

She just stood there, her eyes bouncing everywhere except at him.

He moved to the pot-bellied stove and pulled the bandana out of his back pocket. Rawley wrapped the cloth around the handle of the metal bucket he had heating the water. Lifting it, he walked into his quarters and set the bucket on the floor.

Watching his fluid movement, Lacy remained rooted to the floor once again. She couldn't believe how a big man like him could move so smoothly, gracefully, like a cat. *Must be that Indian blood,* she figured.

Coming back into the office and nodding into his room, he told her, "Better get a move on 'fore the water cools off."

She leaned the big carbine against the wall and hung her hat on one peg. Unbuttoning the two coats, those followed the hat. Her hands hesitated before unbuckling her rig. She shrugged and the soft leather whispered when she pulled the strap from the belt's loop, and hung that up, too. Picking her saddlebags off the back of a chair, Lacy edged past the lawman, heading into his quarters and closing the door softly.

Rawley grinned, *The girl still ain't gonna talk.* Lacy would need some fresh clothes again, so he headed to Ezra's store. Sorting through the shirts, he spied a pretty green, thick flannel one. He held it up and decided it would look nice with her coloring.

146

He bought the shirt, underwear, wool socks and pants.

Lacy had stripped out of her dirty clothes and stood naked in front of the looking glass. Leaning closer, she touched her face. *I do have a lot of freckles*, she realized. It had been a long time since she had even bothered to gaze at herself in a looking glass. She began washing up. As she finished her hair, she heard a soft knock at the door. She quickly grabbed the towel and wrapped herself in it.

A package sailed through the air and landed on the bed. "Got you some fresh clothes, bring out your dirty ones and we'll take 'em to the laundry on the way to eat," a voice announced. Then the door closed softly.

Lacy swallowed, exhaling in relief that he hadn't come in this time. She plopped herself on the bed and opened the package. She held up a green shirt and stared at the door, then back at the shirt. Her mama always said she looked best in blues and greens. *How would he know that?* She wondered. Hurriedly dressing, Lacy opened the door.

Hearing that, Rawley swiveled in his chair as it squeaked. He rose and took the dirty clothes from Lacy, placing them with his. He stood back, his thumbs hooked into back pockets, studying her. *The girl's plumb tuckered out.* Her freckles were the only color on a pale face, she had dark circles like bruises under hollow, brooding eyes. His eyes trailed down her figure, stopped at Lacy's waist. He smiled, "Looks like we got to put the nose bag on you for a few days."

Lacy threw him a quizzical look.

Rawley pointed at her waist, "Your belt. It's in the last notch."

Glancing down at her waist, Lacy then looked up and shrugged.

Helping her with her coat, Rawley said softly, "You look nice in green," as his hands smoothed the garment over her shoulders.

147

Lacy stiffened when he did that.

Picking up on her subtle reaction to his touch, Rawley dropped his hands and opened the door for her.

Lacy hesitated; she didn't know what to do with all this politeness being shown to her. *Especially with all that fighting we did on the mountain and the plains. I thought he'd still be mad at me.* Her eyes bounced to his face then to his shoulder and back again.

"Well, I don't know 'bout you, but I'm starving," he said, trying to get the girl movimg.

When she finally decided to slide past the Marshal, Lacy turned sideways to avoid bodily contact with the man, making Rawley grin. Stopping on the edge of the planked walk, she waited as he closed the door and then had to skip a little to keep up with his long strides.

At the laundry, Lacy listened to the conversation outside the door the lawman was having with the owner. She looked over her old hometown. It had grown – more people and businesses. Too many people would know her as Lacy Carrigan; *But I'm not her anymore, I'm Lacy Watson. I need to saddle up and leave tonight, before anyone recognizes me.* Rawley exited the laundry and Lacy, dropping her thoughts, had to run, skip, run, just to keep up with his long strides as they walked toward the *Blue Bird Café.*

Chapter Twenty-Six

RAWLEY OPENED THE door for her once again. Stepping into the warm room, Lacy took note of the fragrant odors wafting across her nose, making her stomach grumble. She took in the bright, colorful room. *I don't remember this place,* she thought, as her eyes swept the dining area with its whitewashed bead board covering the lower half of the walls. Robin's egg blue painted the upper half of the walls, offering a soft warm welcome. White shelves dotted across the expanse of blue. Trinkets and various teapots sat on the shelves. Two windows, set into the wall on each side of the door, looked out onto the street. Crisp blue and white checkered curtains hung at the top of the windows and door. These curtains were pulled back and tied with a darker blue ribbon for a draped effect, creating an inviting entrance to the little café. Continuing the theme, blue and white checkered tablecloths draped over the eight or so tables in the room.

Lacy heard the chatter ease up as she and the Marshal entered the café. Her eyes hardened as she allowed her gaze to drift over the patrons. Embarrassed, folks quickly dropped their stares, continuing with their meals, the buzz beginning to grow again with silverware clinking against plates.

Rawley cocked his brow at the girl, his Wyoming sky blue eyes continuing to crinkle with merriment. The girl had been chasing outlaws for so long he knew she had to be cataloging those faces into her brain. Leading the way toward a table, he pulled out a chair for her. Lacy hesitated, stunned at all this politeness. Rawley gestured for her to sit, which she did, reluctantly, causing a half smile to break out again. Hanging his coat on the back of his chair, Rawley straddled it and sat down across the table from Lacy. Her eyes kept darting around the room as she avoided looking at him. Finally, her eyes came back to rest on the bruise marking his jaw. "Look, I'm sorry I slugged you out there, but…but you made me mad!"

Rawley grinned, "So's I noticed."

"I'll pay you back for the clothes too, once I get some money in…" Lacy offered as she looked down and began fiddling with the silverware.

"I know you will, Sunshine," Rawley answered softly. "I sent off the vouchers, should be getting a bank draft out of Cheyenne in fifteen to thirty days."

Lacy groaned out loud, slumping back in her chair, thinking, *I've got to stay in this town a month*?

"What?" Rawley asked

Lacy shook her head slightly, "Nuthin'…I was jus' gonna leave…"

He feigned surprise. "Leaving town so soon? Why you just got here? What about Cotton Top?"

She pressed her lips into a thin line. Inhaling deeply, she cut a harsh look back at the marshal. His penetrating look had Lacy dropping her eyes and gazing at her hands.

"Being a bounty hunter's kind of a lonely business. Don't have much chance for conversation out there by yourself. You never know who your friends or your enemies might be…" the marshal stated quietly.

Lacy gave him a surprised look, "How'd you know about that?"

"Been one before. Didn't like the fact I'd soon be a sittin' duck, if I kept it up." Rawley tilted his head and fixed a steady gaze on Lacy, "Same thing's gonna happen to you, if you keep it up, Sunshine," he finished softly.

She leaned towards him and hissed. "Quit calling me Sunshine."

"Why? It suits your sunny disposition…" he countered dryly.

150

Lacy rolled her eyes in response, but she knew he was telling the truth. She'd heard what happened to some bounty hunters. So far, she'd been lucky but she knew her luck would run out some day.

"Aye, laddie, me boy! Where ye bein'? Missed ye at dinner!" A bold voice interrupted.

Lacy's head swiveled toward the booming sound. She allowed her gaze to travel over a well built, husky frame of a woman. She saw rosy cherubic cheeks, the focus in a round face with green eyes twinkling under a wildly disheveled mess of curly reddish-brown hair and woven with threads of silver. The woman wore a blue frock with a white collar at the neck and the crisp white apron that covered her ample figure was tied smartly in the back with a large bow. *Must like eating her own cooking,* Lacy thought not so nicely.

Rawley rose and gave the matronly woman a big hug, "Been busy, but I'm here now and *starving!"*

"Ach! Ye do me proud, laddie, wit' ye a liking me cooking so well."

Maddie then allowed her eyes to focus on Lacy, appraising her, "Aye laddie! Chust, what ye brung me here? A wee purty lass to set me eye's a green wit' envy now, 'eh?"

Rawley draped an arm across Maddie's shoulders and made the introductions, "Lacy, I'd like you to meet Madeline Campbell. More affectionately known as Maddie and this is Lacy Car...," stopping himself when he caught Lacy's black look, "Uh...Lacy Watson."

"Aye, Rawley Lovett! Ye've got an eye fer ye women, that's fer sure. Ye 'no how tae pick 'em!" Maddie squinted again, evaluating the copper headed girl. A green flannel shirt highlighted the girl's coloring, peeking out from under the large coat she wore. A sour, pinched looking mouth gave way to tired, hooded eyes surrounded by a million freckles. *The wee lass could be pretty, if she worked at it. Bet'cha, she'll have me laddie turned on his ear, a fore too long. Ya, I kin feel it in me bones already,* Maddie voiced part of what she had been thinking, looking at Rawley, "Aye...ye chust may have met yer match in thiss wee lass...me boy."

Lacy, embarrassed by the conversation swirling above her head, focused dark eyes on her hands. Listening to the cheerful banter between these two friends made Lacy realize they had things she would never have, laughter, friends, smiles, love and a home.

A pebble seemed to lodge itself in her throat, causing a lump and making it hard to swallow. Tears began to burn the back of her lids. Lacy blinked hard and fast, trying to keep the tears from spilling over and dribbling down her cheeks. She didn't know what was wrong with her; she'd cried more in the last few days then she had in ages.

Her destiny had already been laid out for her, no turning back, just her and Fancy chasing fugitives. Lacy's nose began to run, making her sniffle. Suddenly, a big hand reached across and gently rested on hers, making her look up quickly.

Surprise flitted across Rawley's face at the big tears welling up in those dark eyes, threatening to overflow.

Lacy jumped up and hurried to the door. Her hand reached out quickly and jerked it open. She scurried out, slamming it in her wake. Curtains fluttered in the sudden gust of wind. Picking up her pace after looking up and down the street for evening traffic, she ran to the stables and buried her face in Fancy's neck, wetting it with her tears.

Rawley picked his coat off the chair and threw words over his shoulder, heading toward the door, "Be right back, Maddie."

"Aye, lad...ye've met yore match in thet wee lassie...fer sure," Maddie replied as she placed hands on her generous hips. "Aye, ye've met yer match...me boy," she repeated softly.

***

152

RAWLEY LOOKED BOTH ways up and down the street, as he slid his arms into his bulky coat before sprinting across. He pulled open a side door with well-oiled hinges and quietly stepped inside the dimly lit interior.

Hearing hay rustling beneath boots, Lacy moved to the back of the stall behind Fancy. She sniffled and wiped her face with the sleeve of her coat, taking in deep breaths of air as she tried to gain control over her emotions.

Rawley patted Fancy's neck as he came alongside the mare and observed Lacy huddled against the wall. He pulled a blade of hay from the rack and stuck it in his mouth and ambled toward the back of the stall and Lacy. One hand tucked itself into the pocket of his coat, while the other continued holding the blade of hay chewing on the stem. Tilting his head, he looked down into a million freckles covered with tears. Removing the blade from his mouth, he asked softly, "What got you so emotional back there, Sunshine?"

Taking a deep breath, Lacy shook her head, "Nuthin'…" then whirled toward him as she spoke bitterly, "I loved and trusted someone once and they took that love and trust and…and betrayed me with it! I'll never be trapped like that again!" she announced as her eyes trailed down Rawley's virile chest to rest on three shirt buttons.

Bafflement crossed the marshal's features at Lacy's statement. *Now where the hell did that come from?* Rawley wondered. "That still don't answer my question, Sunshine."

Gazing at his shirt, Lacy suddenly realized that she was attracted to this big moose! Pulling her gaze from the buttons back to his face, she thought, *I've never been attracted to anyone before, ever.* Her mouth dropped open at the sudden realization. It caused her to stammer, "Well…well, that's the only answer you're gonna get," she rattled off quickly, shoving past the marshal on her way out of the stable, her boots scuffling through the hay strewn floor.

153

Rawley frowned at her odd response as he watched Lacy trounce through the doors. Throwing an arm over Fancy's neck, he asked, "What are we gonna do with that girl, huh Fancy?" The horse shook her head as if to say, *I don't know.* Chuckling, he tossed the blade of hay aside and followed Lacy outside.

Furious at herself for being so emotional lately, Lacy had grabbed the pump handle, jerking it as hard as she could. Catching the marshal out of the corner of her eye coming through the doors after her, she groaned. Lacy's frustration made her pump harder, the water gushing into the horse trough.

When she saw him standing quietly on the other side of the water, gazing intently at her as if he were trying to get a look-see into her mind, she grumbled, "Why do you keep dogging me all the time? Pestering me…asking stupid questions! Why can't you just leave me alone?" She bent down and splashed icy water on her hot face.

"Guess you could say I'm curious as to what makes you tick."

Lacy rose, water dripping off her nose and chin, "What makes me ti…" She stopped and wiped her face with her coat sleeve, replying hotly, "You moron! I'm not some clock that needs to be wound every seven days!"

Digging into his back pocket, Rawley pulled out his handkerchief and handed it to her. "No…I think you're wound tight enough as it is, Sunshine…tight enough to bust a spring."

Lacy grabbed it and finished drying her face. She returned smartly, "I am not." She shoved the piece of cloth back into his belly. Then she spun on her toes, legs traveling fast, back to the barn.

Grinning, Rawley caught up with Lacy, catching her.

She whirled, raising and twisting her arm, trying to break his hold.

"No…you don't, Sunshine," he said, tightening his grip, "Maddie's waiting supper for us. She gets a little testy if she has

154

to throw out good food," he added, giving the girl a long look and finally released Lacy's arm. He started back across the street. Halfway there, he stopped and looked over his shoulder, giving the girl an annoyed glance as he asked, "Well, you comin' or not?" Not receiving an answer, he turned on his toes, continuing toward the little diner.

Lacy inhaled, filling her lungs with the crisp air, and then exhaled noisily as she rolled her eyes. Throwing her arms in the air, she gave up, following after the marshal.

Marching through the door after him, Lacy's chair angrily scraped across the floor as she jerked it away from the table, then plopped heavily into her seat.

After draping his coat on the back of his chair, Rawley settled again across from the girl, merriment glinting in his eyes, "You can take your coat off and stay a while Sunshine…"

Lacy's feathers continued to ruffle at his words, the spark of anger still flashing from beneath her red-gold lashes. In the end, Lacy shed the coat as her eyes traveled over the décor, "She kinda likes blue and white, doesn't she?"

"Yeah," he smiled, gazing around himself.

Maddie approached, giving them both a disgusted look as she propped fists on her generous hips. "Well? Ye two…aboot a done wit' ye fussin'?"

Rawley and Lacy quickly glanced at each other. Settling back in his chair, Rawley answered, "I guess. For now," playing with the fork as he cut Lacy a long look, her eyes narrowed in response. He grinned.

"Humph! Lassie, what will ye have tae drink?"

"Uh milk, please. If you have it?"

"Aye, we have it. Ye…laddie?"

"Milk too, then coffee."

Nodding, she asked, "Lassie, ta eat?" Pulling a pencil out of that bird's nest of a hairdo, she touched the tip to her tongue. Pencil now poised above a pad, she waited.

155

Lacy turned in her seat to read the menu on the wall. *At least she doesn't serve liver soup, good.* She couldn't make up her mind, it all sounded so good. Gesturing with her hand as she turned back around, she said, "I'll just have whatever he's having."

Rawley rattled off his request. "I'll have steak, medium rare, those good fried taters with the onions, and your bread with plenty of butter."

Lacy's eyes grew round as wheel hubs, "You can eat all that?"

Maddie affectionately placed an arm around Rawley's shoulders, her cheek resting against his black hair. "Aye! Me laddie...he's chust a growing boy," she said, laughing softly as she left the pair.

Lacy rolled her eyes at the remark.

Rawley grinned once again, watching Maddie sashay toward the kitchen. Turning his attention to engaging the girl in a conversation, he quickly concluded, *Well...that isn't going to happen.* As a last resort, he explained, "Ya know, a conversation is 'sposed to be an exchange of words," as two fingers gestured between Lacy and himself, "Between two or more people."

Lacy just stared at the big moose, rolling her eyes again for an answer.

Rawley sighed inwardly. Girl still wasn't gonna talk. He gave up.

When the steaming platters of food arrived, Lacy's eyes popped at the mound of food on her plate. She spluttered, "I can't eat all this!" She looked first at Rawley then up at Maddie.

The matronly woman smiled fetchingly, "Lass...if ye can't eat what's on yure plate, chust give it to the lad! 'Member, he's a growing boy," she said sprightly, moving off to take care of a customer at the counter.

Reaching across the table for the salt, her hand stopped. Lacy jerked it back as if bitten. She bent her head for a closer look.

156

Yep! Worms...she has worms in the salt! Icck! Lacy thought. Her eyes cut to the table next to them, she squinted at that salt shaker too. *Worms...worms in all the salt shakers,* drawing her face into a grimace, she suddenly lost her appetite.

Rawley looked up from his meal, Lacy hadn't begun eating. Picking up the salt he passed it to her, "You need some salt?"

Lacy shook her head briskly as if to shake gnats from her hair. Pointing at the bottle and leaning toward Rawley, she whispered, "Worms...the salt has worms in it!"

Giving the girl a cock-eyed glance, he looked at the bottle, turning it around in his hand. *There's no worms in there,* he thought. Then it dawned on him. "That's not worms," he said, "it's rice."

Lacy argued, "It's worms! I'm telling you...it's worms!" Her finger continued to wiggle full throttle at the bottle.

He rolled the shaker with the fingers of one hand before speaking, "You have been out on the trail too long," he said. "Maddie puts rice in all of her salt shakers, it soaks up the moisture." Opening the other palm, he sprinkled salt into his hand, "See...so the salt won't clump up, so it will pour freely. It's not worms, Sunshine," he explained.

She felt the heat begin at the V neckline of her shirt, slowly rising and covering her face. Lacy ducked her head in embarrassment.

"It's okay...a lot of people make the same mistake," he quietly reassured her. "In fact, Maddie caught hell when she first started filling the shakers with rice and salt. Folks were accusing her of wormy salt, too," he further explained. Passing the salt to her, Rawley offered, "You want the salt? You need to eat." Her hand reached out tentatively and taking the shaker she sprinkled some on her meat and potatoes.

Lacy tucked into the first real knife and fork dinner she'd had in a long time. The marshal followed, digging into his own mile high pile.

Rawley smiled as Lacy cleaned her plate, "Thought you said you couldn't eat all that."

Sopping up the last bit of juices with a piece of bread, Lacy glanced up and popping the bite in her mouth, she shrugged as she finished her milk.

Swallowing the last of his coffee, Rawley asked, "You ready?"

Lacy nodded as she stood, pulling on her coat.

"I'll be out, soon's I pay Maddie," he said, watching Lacy walk toward the door.

Outside, Lacy leaned against the porch post and jammed her hands deeply in her pockets, protecting them from the cold as she inhaled the crisp air. She watched the soft flakes swirl down beginning to cover the steps and street. Without realizing it, Lacy automatically proceeded into her old deputy's mode. From her location, she scrutinized every alley, her eyes probing into the dark nooks and crannies of the town's landscape.

The town's grown up, but then so have I, thought Lacy. *A laundry, Olivia Johnston...I never dreamed, Miss Liv would still be here. I need to saddle up and leave tonight, before anyone recognizes me. Forget about the money!*

She straightened and kicked the post with the toe of her boot. Resting her forehead on the cool wood, she sighed. She was tired, so tired.

Rawley laid a bill on the counter.

Maddie took it, and then leaned across toward the marshal. "Laddie, ye've met yer match in thet yon wee lassie," she said, nodding toward the door. "Aye ye kin mark me words, afore ye know, that wee lassie will have ye 'rapped round her l'il finger." Nodding again, she waggled eyebrows at the lawman, eyes twinkling, "Aye...ye kin mark me words, lad."

In turn, he gave Maddie a crooked look that said she was squirrelly. Rawley answered, "You don't know what you're talking about, Maddie! You're as nutty as that fruitcake you bake!

'Sides, she's not my type."

"Aye, may haps me iss…but yon wee lassie will have ye heart so tangled up, ye'll not being a knowing if ye be a-comin' r' a going. Aye, we'll chust be having a wedding here afore too long. Ye mark me words, laddie."

Scoffing at her predictions, Rawley retorted, "Jeepers, creepers! Maddie! Your eyes get crossed staring into that crystal ball of yours?"

"Aye, may haps they iss…that. But ye mark me words. Ye've met yure match with yon wee lassie." Maddie stuck a finger in Rawley's face. He stared at it for a second before his eyes drifted back to cherubic cheeks and Maddie's twinkling eyes. "You hear me good, laddie! Ye hurt that wee lass, ye'll being ah answering ta me! Ye hear me, laddie?"

Taking his change, he stuffed it in his pocket, replying, "That's twice someone said that to me here lately."

"Ya…well, ye heed me words, lad," she warned him again, gazing at the broad back of the lawman as he walked out the door. Coming to stand alongside the counter, folding her arms across her generous bosom, she whispered, "Aye, Rawley Lovett, we'll being a marrying ye off yet. Ye kin mark me words."

Lacy straightened as the door opened. "Took you long enough," she said testily. "What's she bending your ear about? For you to stay away from me, that I'm a bad influence on you?"

Rawley smiled. *Girl sure is touchy*, he thought as he and Lacy walked. One set of heels seemed to take several seconds between steps, accenting his long strides. The other set, quicker, indicating smaller steps. He looked down, "No…just the opposite. Said I was gonna marry you…" he announced dryly.

Stunned, Lacy stopped and reached for his arm. She turned him towards her, "What?"

Rawley looked into a face that remained cute despite her temper. "You heard me."

Recovering a little, Lacy spluttered, "Well….well…she's as

159

nutty as that fruitcake she bakes!"

He grinned at Lacy's words "That's exactly what I told her, too."

"It'll never happen. 'Sides...I'm leaving soon," she finished firmly.

"Uh-huh," he said, not believing a word the girl said. "Well...let's find you a place to sleep in the meantime." Together their boot heels rang in hollow cadence on the wood planks. One set departing with a slow, leisurely pace, the other, maintaining a light pitter-patter, attempting to keep up with his long strides. As they stepped off onto the frozen street, the odd cadence became a scrunch...scrunch, followed by a faster scrunch, scrunch, breaking into the deep nighttime quiet. Their boots picked up their hollow cadence again, when they reached the wood steps in front of the marshal's.

Entering the office, Rawley offered, "I don't have much in the way of accommodations, but you're welcome to my quarters. I'll take a bunk in a cell."

Hanging her coat up, Lacy shook her head. "No. I'll just take a bunk in there," she said, nodding at the cellblock.

"You sure? It won't hurt me to sleep in there."

Lacy shook her head again as she shoved hands deep into the pockets of her britches, clenching them into fists, the material hiding them and her nervousness from the marshal.

"Alright. Well, I've got to go make my rounds," he said opening the door. Glancing back at her, he added, "See ya tomorrow, then."

Lacy looked at him, her tired gaze hooded, she gave him a short nod.

Rawley closed the door softly.

Lacy leaned against the doorjamb. Hands still deep into her pockets, she looked at the bunk beckoning to her.

Puffing out her cheeks, she blew tendrils of coppery hair off her forehead. Lacy knew she needed to saddle up and leave tonight, before folks began figuring out her real name, but she was so tired. Heaving another noisy sigh, which echoed off the log walls in the confines of the cell block, Lacy decided she would leave after she had gotten some sleep. Heading into the cell, she flopped on the bunk and quickly disappeared into the deep abyss of an exhausted sleep.

Chapter Twenty-Seven

WALKING THROUGH TOWN, Rawley continued checking doors. Most folks were holed up out of the cold. Pulling the coat collar tighter around his ears, he shoved his hands deep in the pockets of his coat and leaned against a post watching the soft flakes fall from the sky. Rawley gazed at his warm vapors as they hit the cold night air creating a fog that swirled above him melting into the crisp darkness. He thought again about the girl. He'd been thinking a lot about her lately, too much.

He felt God had brought Lacy back to her hometown for a reason. *Why?* Rawley wasn't sure yet. Tossing ideas around in his head, he concluded it could be to make her come face to face with her past, or to end the Dillards' rampage, which she had done.

Lacy's a survivor, he thought; no doubt about it. She had built a repertoire of survival skills and behaviors which she used to emotionally detach herself from people, sometimes becoming physically aggressive as she did with him. *She's also terribly frightened,* he'd figured out, using her temper to hide her fear. But deep down he realized she remained broken, her insides shattered from past events in her life. Lacy had never recovered from those incidents that had happened so long ago, allowing no one to see her pain or her grief. She continued to hide herself from the world by chasing fugitives. That is, until just a few days ago, when he had forced the issue inside the cave causing her to cry. Rawley knew he turned to mush when tears became part of the equation, but Lacy's tears really tore at his heart.

Liv may be right. Inside the girl could be vulnerable, just plain yearning for affection and understanding. That incident at the cabin? Well…all he could say about that is…folks had better

162

skedaddle for cover when that temper came bubbling up to the surface. But if one were to push all of that aside, a real problem remained. That one of these days she could explode, that temper maybe killing the wrong person but also getting herself killed in the process.

Yeah, God had been shuffling this situation around pretty good by putting Lacy Carrigan in his life. Rawley didn't know exactly how his role in this particular circumstance would play out. He just knew the girl wore him out, mentally and physically. He stamped the snow off his boots and headed for Stewart's.

After brushing the snow from his shoulders, he removed his hat and shook the fluffy white stuff off it, too. Stamping his boots again, he opened the door to Mike's place, then shut it softly, closing out the cold. Fingers raked dark hair back into place while he surveyed the small crowd. *Most folks were playing it smart tonight, staying home.* Rawley saw Doc was having a nightcap.

Doc raised a hand in greeting and Rawley nodded.

Walking over to the bar, he asked Mike for a whiskey.

Mike took one look at the Marshal's haggard face and said, "You look like hell, Rawley," while a hand tapped the bar with a glass.

Giving the barkeep a disgusted look, Rawley said tiredly, "Thanks Mike, I can always count on you to bolster my spirits."

Mike grinned. Pulling the cork out of his better rye, he poured the amber liquid into the glass. Resettling the cork, he said, "Sure am glad you caught those bastards. The Clancys' were a nice family, town is gonna miss them."

"Wasn't me," began Rawley, sliding the glass closer. "That girl has an uncanny knack for flushing outlaws out of the brush," he said, swallowing half the liquid.

Mike refilled the glass, "All the same, I'm glad you caught them sum-bitches."

Rawley nodded, reaching into his pocket for a coin.

The barkeep held up his hand, "On the house tonight, Rawley. On the house."

Nodding his thanks, he picked up his glass and walked towards Doc. Weaving his way through the tables, the few patrons out on this cold night spoke to the marshal, "Nice job Rawley," said one. Another added, "Glad those bastards finally got their due." "Hope they rot in hell,' said the last one.

Rawley just nodded, too tired to answer. His hand grabbed a chair back, legs scraping against the wood floor, interrupting the unusual quiet of the saloon as he pulled it out. Straddling the seat, he sat down with a sigh.

Doc asked, "Tired, son?" A heavy grey wool coat sat on the doctor's shoulders tonight. The thick scarf of bright red wool Liv had made him hung around his neck, dripping across the front of his open coat. His hat rested on the table; had flattened the unruly grey hair leaving its imprint above his ears. Where ever the hat did not reach, hair still stuck out over his ears lending a whimsical look to a superficial stern expression. A salt and pepper mustache that needed trimming covered his upper lip, followed by the ever present grey and black stubble. Tonight, his string tie drooped to one side, hanging loosely as if he had been pulling on it all day.

Hunching shoulders over his arms resting on the table, his fingers wrapped around the glass as Rawley answered, "Yeah." He sipped at his drink.

"Rough trip?"

"Yeah," he repeated. "Specially when you got a female bucking ya the whole way. Never knew dynamite could come in such a small package."

Doc harrumphed, "So…she's staying with you?"

Rawley threw Doc a sharp glance. "How'd you know 'bout that?"

Doc leaned back in his chair, "Oh…word gets around. 'Sides, I knew you wouldn't let her stay in the stable on a night like this."

"Sheesh! For a small town, it sure has got big ears. White

164

River has got to have the best grapevine within a hundred miles. Who needs a telegraph, when we got townsfolk like we got?" Rawley fussed tiredly.

Laughter rumbled, "Liv said Lacy looked exhausted yesterday."

Taking another sip, Rawley swallowed and then said, "Yeah...she is. We both are."

"Pulled her gun on Liv, too, scaring her and Howie half to death when she woke her up," Doc informed him.

"Damn kid!" Rawley exclaimed as he twirled the liquid around, "She's quick and testy if you wake her up out of a sound sleep."

Doc nodded, "Where's she at now?"

"Sleeping...I hope. But I wouldn't put it past her to be snooping through my files."

"Nah, she wouldn't do that now, would she?" Doc asked, grinning.

"Wanna bet?" Rawley returned. Swallowing back the rest of the rye, he asked, "You ready? I need some sleep."

Chairs scraped as they pushed back from the table.

Vocal "Good nights," reached the ears of the crusty older gentleman and the younger one. Silent waves by the two acknowledged the goodbyes.

Stepping into the cold, Doc shivered, "Damn cold! I need to take my practice to a warmer climate."

"Doc...you've been saying that every winter since I've known you. Now you can't be cold with that heavy coat and that pretty red scarf Liv made you," the marshal said.

Doc harrumphed.

"You gonna take Liv with you?" Rawley teased, grinning.

Head spinning, he looked up at the young giant. Doc grumbled, "Hell, no! She likes this dad-blasted weather!"

The marshal's smile cracked wider as their boots walked in timed cadence with each other. Arriving at the lawman's office,

165

the two men said their good nights and parted company.

Inside, Rawley threw more wood in the stove, turning down the damper for the night. He turned, walked over and hung up his coat, rig and hat. Looking in the cell, he noticed Lacy had curled into a tight little ball the way she always slept. Walking in, he gazed at the still figure. Moving forward, Rawley bent down and removed her boots. He whispered to the sleeping girl, "Seems I'm always taking off your boots and covering you up, Sunshine." He covered her with a couple of blankets and then knelt down, his fingers lightly brushing away the burnished copper strands of hair, exposing more of those cute freckles.

Suddenly, he realized he cared about this spunky little red-head. Jerking his hand back as if he'd been stung, Rawley quickly reminded himself, *She's not my type.* Standing, he gave Lacy one last look, then walked out toward his room for some much needed sleep.

Chapter Twenty-Eight

WAKING, LACY ROSE hurriedly and scurried out of the cellblock. The anxious expression on her face told Rawley what she wanted. He pointed toward the back door and said, "Out there."

Stocking feet quickly carried Lacy to the alley. A few minutes later, she burst through the door, huffing, "Why didn't you tell me it snowed last night!" She jerked the chair from alongside his desk, scraping it along. Then picking it up, she slammed it down in front of the stove. Witnessing Lacy's short fit of temper, Rawley's eyes grew big as he watched her plop herself down onto the seat. She held her stocking feet in the air, close to the heat.

"You didn't ask," he grinned.

"Pfffttt…" she replied.

"Coffee's fresh and hot," Rawley offered.

Lacy shook her head, "No. I'm going back to bed."

***

TEN HOURS LATER, Lacy finally emerged from the cell. Stocking feet padded to the shelf holding the earthenware cups. Picking one up, she poured some coffee. Her nose whiffed the delicious aroma. Then she sipped and sighed as the hot liquid flowed into her tummy. She continued looking out the window. Her eyes noted the muddy buckboard tracks crisscrossing the town's main thoroughfare from where the sun had warmed the earth, melting the snow. Ezra had come out, sweeping the blown and melting snow off the walkway and steps in front of his store. Leaning on his broom, he carried on a silent conversation with

167

someone. *Ezra looks as if he hadn't aged a lick,* she thought. Colorful garters still graced his upper arms. She remembered those from her childhood. The dark sleeve protectors kept his white shirt from getting too dirty. His framework was still of medium build. Lacy watched as his head threw itself back in a silent laugh at whatever the man standing in front of Ezra had said. She smiled slightly. Turning from the scene across the street, she placed her cup on Rawley's desk. Sitting, she curled herself in the chair, knees up and an elbow resting on them. Laying her chin in the crook of her elbow, her dark eyes followed the marshal's movement as he cleaned his guns. *He's got awfully big hands, yet they're nimble, sure of themselves, and gentle.* Her mind remembered just how gentle those big hands had been when he'd checked her ribs in the cave.

Rawley kept cutting quick glances at Lacy. He noticed her eyes weren't so hollow looking today, the dark circles almost gone too. The girl dozed off again, jerking herself awake.

"You sure have been sleeping a lot, you feeling okay?" he asked.

Lacy close her eyes again, sighing inwardly. There were a lot of things she'd like to tell the marshal, but couldn't. Lacy replied instead, "The letdown after the chase, I guess."

Pulling a piece of wadding through the split-end of the cleaning rod, Rawley said knowingly, "Uh-huh." Then he plunged the cleaning rod down the barrel of a pistol. Pulling it in and out, he asked, "Give any thought to what you're going to do next?"

Lacy gave a shrug.

"Winter's not exactly the best time for chasing fugitives, lessen you head south."

She just shrugged again.

Giving an exasperated sigh, Rawley laid down the pistol. The chair squeaked as he leaned back and laced his hands across his flat stomach, staring at the girl. "Sunshine...I swear! You've got to be the quietest female I've ever run across. Most women I know can't keep their tongue in their head…" he said, sitting upright in the chair again. It squeaked in response.

Blinking wide, Lacy just stared right back.

"…With you, I feel like I'm talking to myself most of the time. Why here lately, I've even started to answer myself," Rawley said with a grin. Picking up the pistol, he removed the cylinder, "Now, let's start this conversation over again."

Lacy's eyes scanned the beams above, taking in cobwebs that hung from the ceiling over the file cabinets while she listened. Her gaze came back, resting on his face. A glimmer of a smile curved the corners of her lips ever so slightly, allowing dark eyes to smile, too. "Why? You seem to be doing just fine, all by yourself," she observed.

Rawley saw a hint of merriment in her eyes.

Lacy continued, "Besides…I don't like to waste words."

Grinning before answering, Rawley said, "So's I noticed."

Chewing on her bottom lip, she offered up, "Loose lips can get you killed."

His smile going broader, he nodded in agreement, "That's true. So…now we got that all settled…what are your plans?"

Lacy gave another shrug.

Wiggling the cleaning rod at her, Rawley said, "Nah…aah. No, you don't, Sunshine. You answer me with *real* words."

Starting to give another shrug, Lacy stopped and cocked an eyebrow at the marshal. Then she glanced over his shoulder at the file cabinets, saying. "Guess I'll go through Vern's files…" *Oops*, she realized, at Rawley's expression. "I mean your files, see what's there. Maybe…wire some folks. See if they have any cases for me. Ooh…I don't know…" she said, looking down at her stocking toes as she grabbed them with a hand.

"I see…" he said. Laying down the pistol, Rawley pulled open the top left drawer. Wood squeaked against wood. "I have a job here, if you want it." He laid a deputy marshal's badge on the desk top, his long fingers sliding it closer to Lacy while his other hand pushed the drawer back into place. It protested its sudden use again.

Lacy blinked, seeing the familiar object she had worn for two years. She quickly grabbed her bottom lip with her teeth to keep quiet.

From Lacy's expression, Rawley knew he had hit home again, "I can offer you fifteen a month, traveling expenses and found, that includes Fancy," he said as he waited. When he didn't receive an answer, Rawley further explained, "That means a place to sleep, your food, and boarding for Fancy."

Lacy blasted the marshal with an evil black look. She groused back at him, "I know what the hell found means, you jackass!"

Rawley rolled his eyes, *Damn kid! I don't know why I picked her up off that stupid riverbank!* he thought, slowly shaking his head.

Lacy's eyes flitted back to the piece of metal on the desk. Her finger tentatively reached out, lightly tracing the words, *Deputy Marshal.* She licked lips that seemed suddenly dry, chewing on a corner of the bottom one. Her hand gingerly picked up the small piece of metal. Her eyes softened as a slight smile began to glimmer at the memories, *good memories* she'd had with Sam and Sally. Remembering all the things Sam had taught her, she recalled laughing back then too; not much, but some.

"The way you're caressing that thing, I'd say you've been one before," said Rawley, interrupting Lacy's memories jerking her back to reality. He watched as the veil dropped back down in her eyes, hiding the emotions he'd glimpsed only a few seconds ago.

"Why? What happened to your last deputy?"

"Got married. His new wife didn't cotton to him being a lawman. So, to please her, he quit."

Mouth forming an 'O', Lacy nodded, "But why me, you'd hire a girl?"

"Sam hired you. Must've been something he saw in you. I'm willing to take that chance too," he told her, leaning back in his chair. It squeaked again. *Got to put some oil on this damn thing,* he thought while he waited for an explosion.

Lacy gasped, her eyes turning hostile. *Damn, he's quick!* She opened her mouth, ready to deny it all.

Seeing the hostility, he butted in, "Nah…ahh, Sunshine. First thing you're gonna learn working for me is to put a handle on that temper of yours." Rawley paused and then added, "It's still on my agenda, if you push me," he reminded her.

Color rose from the V of her shirt, clear to the roots of her red hair. She thought about how the marshal had trussed her up like a hog at the cabin. Lacy wanted to fan the heated color she knew covered her face, but didn't dare. *It would just mean I have feelings, and I don't…have feelings.* she thought, not realizing how transparent she had become to Rawley.

Well at least the girl's got the decency to blush, he thought. Rawley continued, "You already knew I worked for Sam. So why don't we put his training to good use, working together?" *That color rising like it just did. Why…it made her even cuter!*

Rearranging her legs, Lacy hugged knees to her chest with her chin resting on them and contemplated what the Marshal had offered her. She tilted her head toward him. "Where would I sleep?" she asked, lifting her head and glancing over her shoulder at the cell block. "One of these days, you're going to fill those up."

"Ooh…thought I'd put a bunk in my quarters for you," he said, grinning when Lacy threw one of her blistering looks his way. His chair squeaked again as he rose, "C'mon, I'll show you." Leading the way down the hallway, he pushed open a door, allowing Lacy a peek inside. "This used to be Glenn's quarters. I've just been using it for storage. But we can fix it up for you, if you decide to stay…" he said, leaving his words hanging in the air.

Gazing into the small room, Lacy saw wooden boxes stacked against the far wall. A single bed under a grimy window with an old washstand leaned against the opposite wall. Lacy became torn. She shouldn't be staying in this town as long as her grandfather remained alive. But in truth, she'd been getting mighty tired of the chase. *I've been running for nine years, maybe it is finally time to stop, like Lovett said. Have the guts to face my grandfather.* She turned, giving the marshal a shy glance as she silently exited.

Rawley blinked. *Damn kid! Here I offer her a job, a place to sleep and all she does is walk away!* He sighed as he continued to watch her stocking feet trudge up the hall.

Refilling their coffee cups, Lacy took her perch back in the chair.

Easing back down in his chair, it squeaked again as he swiveled around facing the desk. *Gotta get some oil from Ezra's, stop this infernal squeaking,* Rawley reminded himself again. Picking up the pistol, he resumed cleaning it, asking, "When was the last time you cleaned your guns?"

She shook her head and shrugged one shoulder, "I'm going back to bed. I need more sleep," Lacy said. Putting down her cup, she rose and edged behind Rawley.

The chair squeaked again as Rawley swiveled. His hand reached out lightly touching Lacy's arm, stopping her. She cut a glance at his hand and then settled her gaze on his face.

"Sunshine…why don't you sleep in my bed, it's a lot softer than those hard bunks," he offered.

Lacy looked at the big bed in Rawley's quarters, then back at him, not knowing what to say. She just stood blinking at the lawman. His hand still rested lightly on her arm.

"Lacy?" he began softly, "Did you ever want to stop running long enough to plant your feet somewhere? So's maybe those boots of yours could get a little dusty for a change?"

Lacy looked at her stocking feet, then back at the marshal as she continued to stare at this hunk of masculinity. She couldn't figure out how in the world he seemed to be able to say what she had on her mind all the time, thoughts that she couldn't find the words for. Silently, she turned. Going through to the marshal's quarters, she closed the door just as quietly.

Rawley watched the door close ever so softly. Exhaling, he thought, *I made the offer, now it'll be up to her to make a decision, one way or another.*

Lacy sunk on the soft bed and just sat there, her mind whirling with everything that had transpired. She was still exhausted and even more so after that little exchange out there. Lying back, Lacy rested her head on the marshal's pillow, her nose and lungs filling with his scent. Breathing deeply, it smelled of fresh air, pine and his musky manliness. Lacy snuggled into the pillow, breathing the tantalizing smells as she drifted off.

***

MAYBE IF I FIXED it up for Lacy, she'd stay, he hoped. Rawley began hauling wooden boxes out of Glenn's old room, setting them in the hallway for now. He sneezed once, then again, from all the dust he'd been stirring up. After sliding and moving the bed and small washstand around, he swept the dust bunnies out, sneezing a couple more times. His broom swatted at the cobwebs near the ceiling, sweeping all the dirt and dust out the back door. Blue eyes swept the room once again. *It's missing something.* Rawley decided he needed Maddie's feminine touch and in a few hours, it would actually look like a woman's bedroom, not a storeroom.

Then he did something totally out of character for him. He headed down to Ezra's store and actually bought a gift for a female. Liv and Maddie had been the only ones before, well...except little Hanah, Howie's sister. His eyes saddened, thinking of pretty little Hanah as he laid the appealing comb and brush set on the washstand. *Hanah would have loved the pretty*

173

hair set, he thought moving out of the room and closing the door.

Doc stopped by and Rawley showed him the room. He just harrumphed and said he and Lacy were invited to supper at Liv's. "Be there at six-thirty," he ordered grumpily.

Waking abruptly, Lacy wondered where she was and then she remembered. Padding into the office, she poured a fresh cup of coffee and stood with her back to the heat. Sipping from the cup with her hands wrapped around its warmth, she observed Lovett. *I can't believe he's still cleaning guns.*

"I'm hungry," said Rawley. "We've been invited to Miss Liv's for supper, so get washed up, 'sposed to be there at six-thirty."

Glancing at the clock hanging on the wall next to the cell door, Lacy asked, "Didn't you eat dinner?"

"No. I was busy," he said, rising, as the chair squeaked once again at the sudden movement. "C'mon I'll show you," as his hand beckoned her to follow him.

Reluctantly, Lacy did.

Waiting for her to stop beside him, Rawley then opened the door to the old storage room.

Lacy just stared at the transformation. Blue and white curtains on the window shining brightly now, pulled back with darker blue ribbon gave the curtain a draped effect. A bright coverlet adorned the bed. A rocker sat by the washstand with a humped back trunk at the foot of the bed. Spying the brush and comb set, Lacy walked over to it, fingering it gently. *It's beautiful,* she thought. She glanced over her shoulder at the marshal, asking softly, "Why?"

Hooking his thumbs into back pockets, he replied, "Thought you might want a place to call your own."

"I told you, I'm leaving."

"Uh-huh. Well till you do, you can sleep in here."

Silence continued from Lacy. She didn't know what to say, so she said nothing.

174

"A thank you would do for starters," Rawley reminded her. "Oh, and you need to thank Maddie. Was her...who did most of the fixing up."

Her mouth had gone dry. Lacy licked her lips hoping to stir up some moisture; it didn't work. So, she just clamped them into a tight line, glancing shyly at the marshal as she carefully edged past him.

Sighing, Rawley just rolled his eyes at the ceiling. Her silence was really beginning to grate on his nerves.

Chapter Twenty-Nine

LAUGHTER AND JOVIAL conversation ricocheted off the walls in Olivia Johnston's small dining area. Gazing around, Lacy took in the delighted antics of the marshal and Howie. Rawley and Doc were exchanging light banter, Liv adding her voice to the exchange. Howie was squealing as Rawley tickled the boy. All of this happiness had begun to get on Lacy's nerves, giving her the beginnings of a whopping headache. She kept quiet, not joining in except when spoken to, then she would say her piece and glue her tongue to the roof of her mouth again.

She continued to observe the big lawman with the small tow-head, his eyes lighting with affection for the little boy. Rawley wrapped his long arms around the youngster, hugging him. The little boy hung onto him. *He'd make a good father,* her mind told Lacy. She quickly threw the thought out of her head.

Liv stood up and removed Howie from Rawley's lap. "Time you got ready for bed, young man," she said, sitting the boy down. Her hands shooed him toward his room, "Go on, now. I'll be in to read you a story in just a moment."

Lacy saw her chance for escape. Jumping up, she offered, "I'll do it." *I need to get away from all this happiness anyway.* She quickly followed after the boy.

Liv returned to the kitchen after seeing Lacy and Howie go off hand in hand, the little boy chattering like a magpie.

Doc and Rawley stayed at the table, sipping coffee and having a second helping of Liv's apple pie.

Doc kept his voice low, asking, "Rawley? What do you think the girl will do now?"

Swallowing the pie, Rawley followed that with a sip of coffee. Cocking a dark brow, he shrugged before answering, "Do' no, Doc, can't seem to get many answers out of her, unless you make her mad. She can be an ornery cuss when that happens, and then she doesn't shut-up." Scraping the fork across the now empty plate, gathering flakes of pie crust on the end of his fork. Rawley poked it into his mouth saying, "I showed you Glenn's old room, I'm hoping she'll stay…I offered her the deputy's job…"

"You did what?" Liv interrupted, coming out of the kitchen to sit back down at the table.

Leaning back in his chair, Rawley repeated, "I offered her the deputy's job."

"You can't be serious?" Liv exclaimed.

Raising dark brows, they stared at Olivia, "Yeah…I am."

"That's no job for a woman…it's dangerous!"

"Really? What do you think she's been doing the last nine years? Lacy sure as hell ain't been knitting socks and quilting blankets for the Ladies' Aid Society, Liv!" He reached across the table and poured himself another full cup of coffee. Setting the pot down, he gave Liv a hard look saying, "No. She's been flushing fugitives out of the brush for nine years, and she's good at it. Worked for Sam Luebker, same as me, he taught her the same things he taught me. No. I'd rather have that fire breathing dragon covering my back as anyone else." He sighed inwardly before adding quietly, "I trust her, she's bright, gutsy and daring and…" his mind wandered, searching for the right words. Rawley didn't want to say, *cute as a speckled pup*. He couldn't find it. "Uhh…well, you'd just better watch out when her temper gets rolling…" he finished lamely.

Liv rolled her eyes at Doc as he harrumphed. She gestured with her hands, "Rawley, she's a young lady, maybe if you'd treat her like one…"

He cut her off, "Lady? Lacy even admitted she's no lady, and she said she'd never be one either!"

Giving Rawley yet another dirty look, Liv retorted, "Even

so…that office is no place for a young woman."

"Well…she didn't exactly come with a set of instructions, Liv, when I picked her up off the river bank!" he snapped back angrily.

Liv groaned, muttering, "Men!" Pushing herself away from the table, she left the two men to check on Howie and Lacy.

Soft laughter rumbled from Doc, "I heard tell that there's two theories to arguin' with a woman. Neither one works. So…no sense arguing with Liv, son…she'll win every time."

Rawley threw Doc a dirty look.

Coming back into the dining room a few moments later, Liv gestured for the two men to follow her. Standing in the doorway, the three gazed at the two figures both sound asleep on the bed. Lacy was holding the little boy in her arms, her chin on top of his head and he was snuggled into her embrace.

Liv moved to wake Lacy. Rawley stopped her by touching her arm, "Better not, she gets a little testy, remember? I'll wake her." Moving to the bed, he squatted and prodded Lacy, "Sunshine, wake up, time to go home now," he said, shaking a shoulder and ducking as a tightfisted hand swung across at him.

A look passed between Doc and Liv as they tried to hold back their laughter.

"Cut it out Sunshine. It's me, Rawley. It's time to go home now."

Lacy cracked an eye open and groaned. She untangled herself from the sleeping boy, stumbling past the three.

Rolling his eyes at Doc and Liv, he followed Lacy heading towards the front door.

Grabbing her coat, she marched outside and then slid her arms into the sleeves. Lacy sat on the steps and leaned her head against the railing. She willed the cold air to wake her up.

Inside, his arms slid into the sleeves of his coat, Rawley turned to Doc and Liv, "Now you know why you don't wake her up," he said giving Liv a kiss on the cheek. "Thanks for the dinner, as always, it was excellent…'night."

Rawley opened the front door and shut it softly. Finding Lacy sitting on the steps, he asked, "You okay…Sunshine?"

Lacy looked up, blinking, "Yeah…I'm just trying to wake up."

Taking her arm, Rawley pulled the girl towards him, "Let's get you back to the office so you can finish your nap."

Chapter Thirty

WALKING BACK TOWARD the center of town, their ears picked up strains of a ruckus coming from Mike's place. The noise was loud enough to disturb the quiet nighttime of the little hamlet called White River.

Rawley picked up his pace, wool encased muscular legs pounded the frozen street. Lacy ran a few paces behind. He jumped the stairs landing on the walk with a surprisingly with a light thud, uncommon to someone with his height and stature. Lacy hurriedly followed, her legs lightly taking her up the three steps. Both stopped and peered over the swinging doors. They backed out of the way when one patron flew past them, landing in the snow. He got up and charged back in.

Lacy and Rawley looked at each other, and then peered again over the doors. A full brawl was in swing. Yells mingled with oomph's and ugh's as fists connected with work hardened bodies. Chairs clattered and tables flipped accompanied by the sounds of glass breaking, followed by more yelling. The sweet smell of spilled whiskey floated through the smoke drenched room. Lacy jerked around when someone exploded through Mike's front plate glass window, creating a dull thud when the body hit the walk and then rolled into the street.

Rawley muttered, "That does it!" Glancing down at Lacy, he said, "You stay put. You're not wearing a weapon." His large frame disappeared into the melee'.

Saturday night cigars and rolled paper cigarettes made the smoke thick enough to walk on, hanging half way to the rafters, drenching the patrons in its fog. Lacy's nose wrinkled at the strong odor, the pungent scent smelling like an old fire charred building.

Still standing on her tiptoes, Lacy continued to peer over the door. She watched as someone grabbed the marshal's shoulder, swung him around and gave him a right uppercut to the jaw that sent his hat flying. Recovering, Lovett returned the blow. Lacy just shook her head. Instead of breaking up the fight, Lovett continued slugging away. *He's as bad as the rest of these cowpokes and blue-coats from the fort, wanting to blow off some steam.* She sighed inwardly.

Apparently, she'd have to interrupt all this fun, gun or no gun, she decided, before someone really got hurt or worse yet, killed. Glancing to her right, she spied a cowboy with his back to her, slugging away. Crouching low, she slid through the swinging doors. Dancing between blows and dodging swinging punches and bodies flying, Lacy neatly lifted the man's gun. She sidled over and ducked behind the bar. Tucking the pistol in her britches, she crawled toward Mike who huddled against the floor, both covering their heads as shards of glass and whiskey showered them. Lacy shook the glass out of her hair and off her coat, catching a whiff of the whiskey that now covered her. She yelled above the roar that continued from the other side of the bar, "Sheesh! Mike, what happened?"

Mike gestured as he yelled back, "I don't know." He ducked again as a chair flew over the bar, hitting and exploding more bottles that sprinkled them again with whiskey and glass. The sour, sweet smell filled the small area behind the bar. Lacy looked around and spotted the sawed-off scattergun under the counter. Nodding at it, she asked, "That thing loaded?" Mike gave her a thumbs up.

She peeked over the edge of the bar, ducking as another chair came sailing toward them. It crashed against the front, shaking the sturdy wood. Lacy rose again, looking for Lovett, she spied him in the corner. He landed a solid hit to one man who fell against the hot pot-bellied stove. The blue-coat yelled, his arm flailing, knocking the stove pipe loose. It came crashing down. Soot and cinders flew, sending billowing smoke into the already thick haze from cigarettes, choking the air further. The sharp, unpleasant scent of burnt wood floated across the room.

Damn you, Lovett! Lacy thought. She quickly made a decision. *It's time for a little female influence.*

With one hand holding the scattergun, she stepped up on the shelf below the counter. She placed one boot on the bar top, followed by the other. Lacy stood and cocked both hammers with her thumb. Forefinger resting on both triggers, she aimed it at the ceiling and pulled. *Kaabooom!* The blast sent wood chips and chunks of ceiling showering down on the crowd. Lacy glanced at the big hole the scatter-gun had left. Dead silence permeated the room immediately.

Her eyes drifted back down, surveying the silent crowd, their mouths gaping, their eyes on her. Even the marshal had stopped. He too, gawked at the redhead.

Standing on the bar gave Lacy the height and attention she required.

She announced in that soft husky voice of hers, "Well…now that I have your attention, gentlemen, who wants to explain why you jackasses decided to tear up Mike's Saloon?" Handing the shotgun back to Mike, she whispered, "Load it up again, Mike." Nodding, he disappeared below the bar once more.

She took a wide stance, letting them know she meant business. She pulled the pistol out of her britches. Lacy held it muzzle down waiting for an answer.

A voice snarled from the middle of the room, "Who 'r you? I don't take orders from a girl…" the cowpoke said, wiping his bloody lip.

Lacy swung her eyes toward the voice, cataloging his face and stature into her memory before answering. A roughshod cowpoke stood staring back at her, his hand wiping a bloody lip as his other swept the long brown hair out of his eyes. From the

182

looks he kept giving her, he didn't like females that disrupted a good brawl.

Rawley pushed disheveled dark hair out of his eyes as he began moving toward the man. His hand wiped the blood running out of his own nose. He stopped in surprise when he heard Lacy answer the man's question.

"Your new deputy. Now who started this fracas?" She continued to let her eyes drift over the men before it settled on two faces that wouldn't look at her. They kept staring at the littered floor.

"You two there..." she pointed out, waving the pistol in their direction, "...Come here."

The two gestured to themselves, answering in unison, "Who? Us?"

Lacy nodded, waving them over with the gun. Squatting in front of them, she gave them one of her best blistering looks. They flinched.

"You...what's your name?" Lacy's eyes bored into his face, "Well?"

"Uh...Ma'am...it's Dickinson, Sully Dickinson."

Lacy smiled at the use of *Ma'am*, her gaze traveled to the next man, "And you?"

"Rip Warren..." the man replied.

Lacy continued to scrutinize the two men, "Well, Mister Dickinson and Mister Warren, care to fill me in on what happened here?"

Rawley's eyes swept the room taking in the dumbfounded expressions on the men's faces listening to this exchange. The room remained so quiet you could hear a pin drop. Rawley smiled to himself as his finger swiped at the blood still running from his nose, *So...she decided to take me up on my offer after all...*

"He started it..." Dickinson said and pointing, "...Cheatin' the three of us."

Lacy's gaze wandered over in the direction Dickinson pointed, "And you sir, your name?" Lacy asked quietly, now standing. The muzzle of the pistol still aimed downward.

The man's tiny eyes narrowed, and then he smiled, turning on the charm. "Why, my dear, it's Macgregor. Duff Macgregor, at your service," he replied giving a deep bow.

Lacy wasn't fooled for a minute, taking in the scuffed well-worn boots, stained striped trousers and matching coat with a threadbare grungy brocaded vest and shirt. Even from that distance, Lacy could see the dirt ring around a tired looking collar. His eyes were set too close together in his hawkish face, and long greasy, dark hair with a side part adorned his head. She wrinkled her nose at the thought of what the man smelled like up close. *Glad I'm not standing downwind of him.* His watch chain stuck in a buttonhole that ended in his frayed vest pocket twinkled in the lamp light. Her eyes tapered shrewdly, but she matched her charm to Macgregor's, giving him a coy smile and allowed two dimples to appear in freckled cheeks. She tilted her head, "Thank you, Mister Macgregor," she replied.

Turning back to Warren and Dickinson, she asked, "You said there's three of you boys he cheated? Who's the third one?"

Pointing behind him, Warren answered, "Him."

Leaning around, Lacy looked for the third man. Her eyes narrowed when she spied a small wiry fellow with tightly curled straw-colored hair, "Well…well, if it ain't Cody Brown, smack dab in the middle of trouble again. Seems every town I come to, there you are creatin' a roocuss," she said, exaggerating the word. "Thought by now, you would've growed up some," she finished, razzing him.

He went for his gun. Lacy fired, creasing his wrist. Bodies dropped to the scarred wood, boots and debris scraped the planked floor as Mike's patrons scrambled to clear the area around the man.

Flying lead had a way of doing that to folks.

Cody Brown yelped, dropping his weapon. The pistol

184

thumped against the floor, the noise loud in the now silent saloon. Brown stared at his wrist, then placing fingers over the wound he squeezed, trying to stop the flow of blood.

Rawley picked up Brown's weapon and tucked it in his britches while his eyes continued to sweep the crowd.

"Tsk, tsk, tsk, you know better than that, Cody. You know you don't pull a gun on the law. Shame on you, Cody Brown," Lacy finished, still using that soft husky tone. Addressing Brown again, "You and Macgregor in this together or did he cheat you too?"

Brown gritted, his wrist stung like fire, "He cheated me too..."

Sitting down on the bar top, Lacy began swinging her legs, "I see. Well...Mister Macgregor, what do you have to say for yourself?" Out of her peripheral vision, she saw Lovett moving, placing himself behind Macgregor. She acknowledged the move by tapering one eye.

Raising his hands, palms up, Macgregor smiled, "My dear young lady, I'm just a poor drummer hawking my wares. I just stopped due to the snow to play a few hands of poker. Surely you can't think of me as a card shark?"

Her legs still swinging, Lacy said, "Uh-huh, and those wares you're hawking, might they be marked cards?" tilting her head as she smiled coyly back at Macgregor, dimples deepening.

Rawley took that moment to pin Macgregor's arms behind him, taking him by surprise.

Lacy hopped off the bar and strode over to the scattered cards on the floor. Kneeling, she picked up some of them up. As her hand held them up to the light, she fingered the edges. Finding what she'd been looking for, she turned back to the three, "How much did he take you for?"

Warren answered first, "Twenty-five."

Dickinson offered up, "Fifteen."

"And you, Cody?" Lacy asked.

185

"Forty…"

Her eyes popped with surprise, "You had that much on you?"

Cody scuffed the floor with his boot, "Yeah, well…I jus' finished a job."

"Tsk! Tsk! What *ever* am I gonna do with you Cody Brown?" Lacy replied. Pointing to the scattered bills and coins on the floor, she said, "There's your money boys…pick it up." She watched them for a few seconds while they scrambled to retrieve the bills and coins.

Going over to the barkeep, she asked, "Mike…how much do you think the damages are?"

Mike, surveying the shambles his saloon had become, shook his head, "Don't know."

Looking around, Lacy said, "Well, give me a figure." Glancing back at Mike, she offered up, "How 'bout two hundred…think that might cover it?"

Mike gazed up at the hole in his ceiling, then at the pot-bellied stove still billowing smoke into the room. Broken tables and numerous busted chairs, the hole where a front window should have been, not counting all the liquor, he sighed, "Yeah…I guess that should 'bout cover it."

She picked two hats up off the floor and shoved them into Dickinson and Warren's bellies saying, "You two go around and get five bucks from everyone in here, including Marshal Lovett." She gave the Marshal a big grin, it growing wider by the look of surprise on his face. Walking past him, she whispered, "Should've been doing your job, 'stead of playing with the boys." Lacy continued on to Cody, taking him by a coat sleeve, she tugged him along with her, "C'mon, got a nice warm place for you to sleep tonight." On the way out, Lacy handed the pistol back to the dumbfounded cowpoke whom she'd borrowed the gun from when she'd first walked through the doors.

***

CODY CONTINUED TO give the new deputy a hard time for locking him up. Rawley followed in with Macgregor, shoving him in another cell. Metal doors clanked, tumblers rolled, clicking into place and locking the two doors. Rawley turned and walked back into the main office, heading toward his room. He needed to wash the blood off his face. While washing up, he couldn't help but overhear Cody's whining voice and Lacy's low calm one.

"Cody Brown! Whatever am I going to do with you? Why can't you keep a steady job? Settle down somewhere? Meet a nice girl, save your money, buy a small spread, and get married."

Cody just stared at this redhead preaching to him. He snapped, "You don't have room to talk...you gun toting little twit!"

Rawley came out of his room, towel in his hand wiping his wet face when he heard the voices rising. Standing in his doorway, he continued to listen.

"Cody...Cody, listen to me. You're good with horses and cows, small and wiry, light. There's got to be plenty of good places where you could work using your talents."

"I want a doctor now! You could've killed me...look...I'm bleeding..." Cody howled.

"Oh shut-up Cody," Lacy shouted back. "If I wanted to really hurt you, I would have. You got water in there, wash up and quit cher bellyaching!" Lacy said as she started toward the door. She suddenly turned and walked back to him. "Cody, I want you to think about going to work on some ranch or small homestead, why even here in town. It would be a good steady job for you. You think about it," she said, leaving the cellblock.

Lacy shut the door and leaned against it closing her eyes, heaving a deep sigh.

Still standing in his doorway fingering the towel, Rawley asked, "How long have you known this Cody Brown?"

Lacy groaned as she rolled her eyes and pushed away from the door, "Too long." Pouring herself a cup of coffee, she set it on the desk. Plopping in a chair, elbows on her knees, she buried her face in her hands, expelling a long noisy sigh. She repeated, glancing at Rawley, "Too long. He's a good kid really, but he either finds trouble, or it finds him. I hadn't figured out which yet." Sighing again, she slumped back in her chair. Absently, she began playing with the badge that had been left on the desk. Her finger spun it around, and then stopped it, only to send it spinning again.

Throwing the towel on his bed, Rawley walked over and poured his own coffee. Taking a sip, he continued to study Lacy and her fingers as they kept toying with the badge.

He spoke, "I think you and I have a little business to transact."

Lacy threw him a sharp look, "What?"

"You ought to smile more, show off those cute dimples."

Lacy rolled her eyes, again.

Grinning at her eye rolling, he said, "Well, since you announced to half the town tonight you were the new deputy, guess we'd better make it official."

"I…I was just saying that to…to keep their attention. I'm leaving soon's my money gets here."

"Uh-huh," he murmured, not believing a word the girl said. Opening a drawer, Rawley pulled out a Bible, laying it next to the badge.

"You keep a Bible here?" Lacy asked, stunned.

"Sure…even read it…especially during these long winter months."

"You read that thing," Lacy said, pointing at the book.

"Uh-huh, you ever read it?"

"No." Lacy said, firmly. *I don't believe in the damn thing,* she thought silently.

Picking it up, Rawley gazed fondly at the book. "Got a lot of good things in it."

"But, but, you…you're a half-breed," she exclaimed, waving

an arm at the ceiling. "You're supposed to…to believe in," her arm waving again, "Whatever the Cheyenne believe in!" She finished in a splutter.

"Not necessarily," Rawley continued, "Whatever someone decides to call a power greater then themselves, Wise One Above. God, Father, that's up to them. I believe in both what the Cheyenne believe and…" picking up the book "…What this says." Giving Lacy a long look, he took in the few emotions he saw flickering across the freckles as his eyes traveled over her face. "Let's swear you in," he said, holding the Bible.

Lacy hesitated, *This man is making me nervous again.* Before she could stop herself, she stood and her right hand automatically lifted. She caught herself, the left hand hanging over the Bible.

The marshal tilted his head. He could see the emotional war waging itself internally through her dark eyes.

Surprising herself, Lacy saw her left hand move to rest on the surface of the book.

Rawley spoke quietly, "Do you swear to uphold the laws of this office with the powers invested in you, so help you God?" He asked.

Lacy licked lips that had suddenly gone bone dry. She wanted to run, but couldn't seem to convey that message to her feet. Instead she exhaled softly, saying, "I do." It had been easier when she'd said those words to Sam.

Grinning at Lacy he said, "There now…that wasn't so bad, was it?" Rawley reached down and his long fingers picked up the piece of metal. He bounced it around in his hand before handing the badge to her, "Reckon you might be able to find a place to hang this?" He would love to hang it on her shirt himself, but knew she would probably swat him clear across Wyoming.

Taking the badge, Lacy just laid it back on the desk. Then she sat back down. Picking up her coffee, she took a sip, watching Rawley put the Bible away.

Turning to her, he said, "It's always in this drawer, if you want to read it."

Her answer was another quick swallow of hot coffee.

The marshal refilled his cup, settling back down at his desk. His chair squeaked again, *Gotta get some oil,* he reminded himself.

Rawley told Lacy, "We've got another little item to discuss, too."

Her head jerked up. "What now?"

His eyes took on a hint of amusement, "You owe me five bucks…"

"I do not!" She retorted, color ripening her face. "You were just as bad as the rest of those boys tearing up Mike's place!" Lacy sprang up and bent forward into his face. A finger began jabbing into his shoulder with hard strokes. Rawley leaned further backwards with each poke of that finger, his chair squeaking with each jab. "In fact, you ought to be over there helping him clean up!" She snapped, straightening and placing fists on her hips while she glared at him.

Rawley just laughed.

Her eyes narrowed into a venomous look. She spoke angrily, "You think it's funny tearing up Mike's business?"

Shaking his head as his smile went wider, making his eyes crinkle in mirth, "No…no…it's you. You're so easy to get a rise out of." he continued to chuckle.

"Lovett! I ought ta wrap two rattlesnakes 'round your neck and watch you hop," she threatened. Giving him one last black look, she flounced past him to her room, slamming the door.

Rawley heard a thud against the wall, then another coming from Lacy's room. Whimsy crossed his features, *Must be the hair brush and a boot,* he figured.

Chapter Thirty-One

OBSERVING A RAG tag boy warming himself by the stove, Lacy listened quietly.

The boy had long stringy brown hair, with a thin lanky frame. She noticed a lot of bare leg showing above worn string-less shoes; his britches being about three inches too short for his legs. Lacy tried to guess what size shoe the boy would wear. His coat sleeves ended about four inches from his wrists, exposing grimy skin. Her mind began to tally up items; *Shirt, pants, socks, underwear and a good warm coat. Maybe a bar of soap and a towel...too.*

"How was school today, Billy?" Rawley asked.

Raising thin shoulders, and then dropping them, he replied, "It was okay." Then he added, "Um...you got any work for me?"

"I would have if you hadn't done such a good job yesterday," the marshal stated.

Lacy's eyes softened at this exchange, and it had her volunteering, "I have work for you, if you want it?"

Rawley cut a quick glance at her, wondering what she had up her sleeve.

The boy's face lit up.

"I'll pay you a dollar a week to take care of Fancy, that is...if you want it."

"A dollar a week? Yes, Ma'am! When do I start?" Billy wiggled like a new puppy.

"Today, if you want, but there's one condition..."

Billy stopped wiggling, becoming wary.

Lacy continued, "...The money is yours. Not for your Pops to buy his liquor. If you need a place to hide it, you can take a

191

drawer in the desk. Is it a deal, Billy?"

Billy hesitated.

"I know you're doing the best you can to take care of your Pops, but…you earned the money…he didn't." Lacy added softly, "Is it a deal?"

A young face had bloomed bright red during the time Lacy spoke. Billy stood still, staring at his boots. "Yes, Ma'am," he breathed out quietly.

"Fancy likes you, she loves the attention you give her," she said, slumping back in the chair and stretching her legs out in front of her. "I know you will be good with her," Lacy assured him.

Billy just nodded.

Knowing she'd hit a raw nerve with the boy, Lacy decided to let the 'boys' have a little privacy, "Well, I've got errands to run," she said, rising to her feet. Lacy picked her coat off the back of the chair and slid her arms into its sleeves. Walking out the door, she closed it softly behind her, heading towards Ezra's store.

Looking out the window, Billy watched Lacy jump muddy ruts, then tiptoe through the mucky street, hurrying out of the way from a buckboard's wheels slinging mud. He said to Rawley, "Miss Lacy…she's nice."

"Yeah, she can be," Rawley replied. His forehead creased as he thought, *The girl seemed to have a real soft spot for kids; first Cotton Top and now Billy. And she'd found Cody Brown a job in town too, making sure he stayed out of trouble.* He thought he had figured her out, but she still surprised him at times.

192

Chapter Thirty-Two

WALKING INTO THE bank, Rawley handed over a bank draft.

"Must be payday," Bill Wilson, the teller, a mousey looking fella of small build, said. Light from the hanging coal oil lamp reflected off his bald head with just a fringe of hair circling the pink scalp. The wire ear pieces of his spectacles hung on big ears, shaped like giant teardrops. Lenses as thick as the bottom of two whiskey bottles magnified small beady eyes resembling the big round eyes of a horsefly. These glasses sat atop a long snout, portraying a very distinctive looking face.

"Yup," Rawley replied.

"Say, you know what that new deputy of yours did?"

"No telling," Rawley answered. Bill had always been a gossip. It seemed that and netting butterflies were his two passions in life.

"Well," Bill leaned in closer, looking around before speaking as if the bank had been full of customers. He whispered, "Took that bounty money and opened a trust fund for that little Howie Clancy. Yes, sirree," he said bobbing his head. "And takes part of her pay and puts it in an account for Billy Atkins. Yes sirree! That shore is mighty nice of her to do something like that...aint it?"

Someone could've knocked Rawley over with a feather at that news. Recovering, he answered, "She did...huh?"

"Yea-up..." Bill answered, his head bouncing up and down again as he handed the marshal back his change.

Rawley leaned into Bill and whispered back, "If I was you, Bill, I'd keep quiet 'bout that. Lacy can get pretty testy about her personal business. Otherwise, one day I might find you strung up and gutted like a hog at killing time." Rawley watched as the man's face paled, beady eyes popping out. He added for emphasis, "She would, too."

Bill spluttered, blinking like a barn owl, "Oh, I'll keep quiet...yes sirree...I'll keep it quiet."

Rawley nodded. "See that you do," he warned.

Fingering the bills, Rawley stood outside the bank. No wonder she always asked for an advance on her pay, buying Billy and Cotton clothes, making sure Billy ate. Even taking in that big scroungy looking stray dog and named it Baxter! What the hell kinda name is that for a dog?

Except for Bill's big mouth, he never would have known about her setting up those accounts in secret. Lacy existed like one of them desert lizards, changing color to fit a certain background so you couldn't see it. He knew in her case, she figured being secretive had about the same effect as hiding. But she didn't know Bill or the folks in White River. He did. In a small town, gossip flowed like a river, but in a circle, picking up new versions each time it was told. Nope, nothing could be kept a secret here in this town.

Chapter Thirty-Three

PULLING THE COLLAR of her coat up around her ears, Lacy walked through town doing final rounds. *Sheesh! It's cold tonight!* she thought, *Glad I'm not tracking in this, I'd freeze more'n my butt off.* Even the boards cracked with the cold as her boots drummed along the planks.

"Pssssttt! Psstt! Miss Lacy? Psstt!"

Lacy stopped at the edge of the steps and peered into the gloom between two buildings.

Billy stepped out of the shadows, coming to stand in front of her.

"Billy? What are you doing out here? It must be below zero."

"I need your help," he said, teeth chattering like a magpie. "Miss Lacy…it's Pops, something's wrong…bad wrong."

Placing a gentle hand on a bony shoulder, she asked quietly, "Alright, where is he?"

"The house," Billy said, taking off down the alley.

Lacy followed and entering the shack Billy called home, Lacy wrinkled her nose at the stench of an unwashed body, vomit and stale booze assaulting her nostrils. She paced slowly to where Clete Atkins lay.

Taking in a deep breath, Lacy gazed at the yellow waxy skin of his face. She knew he was dead but went through the motions anyway, for Billy's sake. Taking off her glove, she placed two fingers along his neck, feeling for a pulse she knew wasn't there. Holding her breath, Lacy knelt and rested one ear on his chest; no heartbeat, she knew there wouldn't be one. She stood, letting the air escape from her lungs. Her fingers took hold of the edge of the blanket. Lacy covered the face of Billy's father.

Turning, Lacy went to Billy, hands resting gently on the boy's shoulders, "Oh, Billy, I'm so sorry." She saw the sudden flicker of insecurity dart like a shadow across his eyes and quickly fill with tears.

Billy straightened and pulled away from her hands. Turning his back on Lacy, he asked, "What will happen to me?"

Taking a deep breath, she plunged into her next statement, "Nuthin'…Billy, you'll stay with the marshal and me. We'll take care of you." Opening the door she said, "Let's go back to the office and get warm." *Lovett will kill me but the fourteen year old kid needed to be reassured…and that's that!*

Rawley looked up as two figures entered the office. Concern darted across his face at what he saw reflecting from Billy and Lacy's faces.

"Billy? Lacy? What happened?"

Gazing at Rawley, she shook her head as Billy sank to his knees, taking Lacy down with him.

Squatting in front of the pair, Rawley rested a palm gently on his thin shoulder, "Billy? What is it? What happened?"

The boy choked back tears as he tried his best to act like a grownup, "It's Pops. He's dead," Billy said.

Rawley's eyes rose over the top of the boy's head to Lacy, "When?"

"Just now…you need to go get Doc, I'll take care of Billy." Seeing the marshal hesitate, she ordered, "Go on! Go on, get Doc!" When he didn't make any attempt to leave, her voice rose to a harsh whisper, "Move it!"

***

Soon after Doc arrived and was in Rawley's quarters talking with Billy, Lacy piped up, "We're gonna take care of Billy…he can sleep in your room."

"What?"

"I said…we're gonna take care of Billy, give him a good

196

home, better than where he did live," Lacy said, remembering that gawd awful shack Billy had called home. "He can't go back to living there…it's awful," she said.

Rawley turned around at what Lacy had just revealed, "Sunshine…we can't do that. This is no place to raise a boy. You're talking nonsense. He needs a real family."

"I am not talking nonsense! He's scared! He's afraid he'll be sent to some orphanage, away from everything he knows! He needs a home right now! And…and you and I can give that to him!" A light suddenly came on in her brain, "We'll be his family!"

"Us? You loco?" Out of the blue it dawned on him where Lacy seemed to be going with this fool idea of hers. "Sunshine…you can't keep taking in strays to fill a big gaping hole in your heart; first Cotton, then Baxter and now Billy? You're just trying to fill a void in your life. You can't gain back what you lost in the past." His voice resonated with softness as he added, "You can't do that…Sunshine. You've just got to move forward."

"What do you mean I can't do that?" she shouted, "Billy needs a man in his life!"

A slow smile began to form within his rugged features.

"…A good man! You're a man! You have to show him how to grow up to become a good man!" she cried. Stepping forward her fingers clawed into his shirt as she pointed out the obvious, "I can't show him how to be a man! I don't know about those man things! You do!"

Looking at her fingers gnarled into his shirt, then back at Lacy, he replied, "And you've chosen me for the job…is that it?"

Lacy reluctantly nodded, "Billy needs patience, understanding and kindness…" she faltered, "…Like…like…" she said, as her fingers slowly released his shirt and retreated. "Like…you've shown me," she whispered quietly.

One brow quirked up, "I see…" he said. "Didn't know you thought so highly of me Sunshine, what with all the fighting and arguing, bossing me around all the time." *That'll get a rise out of her,* he knew.

"I don't boss you around all the time! If you'd just do your damn job like Sam taught you, I wouldn't have to step in, digging you out of trouble half the time…" Stopping to heave in a breath, she opened her mouth to continue the verbal onslaught.

His eyes telescoped downwards. Lacy was getting wound up. Normally he'd ride out her lashing temper, but not this time. Leaning into the redhead, he interrupted, "…Do my damn job? I do my job, which is more'n I can say for you! All you do is collect strays and play with that fool horse of yours! Always begging me for advances on your pay, so's you can spend money on those two boys!" Rawley exclaimed hotly.

Lacy's eyes baked with anger, "Those two boys need me," she yelled. "They don't have anyone else! Miss Liv can't take on all those expenses by herself. I do what I can to help, which is more'n you do!"

Doc opened the door of Rawley's room and came out, closing it softly behind him. He'd heard the two going at it while he tended to Billy. He stood silently for a moment, listening to the continued heated exchange between the hot-tempered redhead and the black-haired giant. Finally stepping into the fray, Doc's voice growled, "Here now! You two cut out your jaw jacking with each other right now!"

Rawley spun on the Doc, pin-pricks of sparks shooting from blue flint, "You stay outta this Doc, this ain't none of your business!"

Doc's gravelly voice grew deep in response, "When it comes to the health and welfare of my patients, I make it my business! That young man in there needs rest. He can't get it with you two arguing all the time! Now knock it off," he crossly demanded, glaring at the marshal and his deputy.

Astounded by the old doctor's behavior, Lacy spluttered, "Why Doc, I've never seen you mad before."

His head swung around, hazel eyes boring into the redhead's face, making her rear back against their ferocity, "Yeah? Well...you hain't seen nothing yet! You two keep it up!" he said, threatening the two adults as if they were criminals. "Aww...hell...I've got a body to attend to..." Doc stopped midway to the door and turned back to face the pair. "Oh...for heavens sakes! Why don't you two just get married so's all this nonsense 'ill stop!"

"Married?" Two voices cried in unison.

"Yes married, so's I can get some peace and quiet!" Glaring at Rawley, "You coming?" Doc gruffly demanded, "We got a body to take care of...in case you forgot with all your damn caterwalling!"

***

RETURNING TO HIS office later, Rawley took off his coat, hardware and hat, hanging them on the pegs. He wandered over to his desk, where he stood for some time, thumbs tucked into his back pockets, studying Lacy. She kept playing with a pencil and wouldn't look at him. Finally easing himself down on the edge of the desk, he closed the space between them.

Lacy gave him a momentary look, then proceeded to ignore him some more by resting her forehead in her hand staring at the blank page of a pad of paper. His overpowering physical presence began to grate on her nerves, along with his wonderful masculine scent. Fresh cold air and pine seemed to engulf her. Lacy quit breathing through her nose so she wouldn't be tantalized further. She leaned back in the chair. It squeaked in response, pencil still twiddling between her fingers.

"How's Billy?"

"Sleeping."

"Lacy, we need to talk..." Rawley finally ventured.

Tossing the pencil across the desk, it bounced and clattered to the floor. "You've already said it all," she replied stiffly, continuing to avert her eyes.

"Lacy, I know how you feel…" he began softly.

"No…you don't!" Lacy rose, the chair giving its customary squeak. She moved further away. She needed to breathe, being that close to Rawley had cut into her air supply.

"You know nuthin' about me. Just because you're twice as big as me, you think you're twice as smart! Well…women have brains, too!" She retorted as an irate finger jabbed into the air emphasizing her next words, "And most of the time we're smarter than you men!" She hauled in air as she continued in her soft husky voice, "Your brand ain't on me…Lovett and don't think for a minute you can boss me around all the time either," she finished, defiantly crossing arms in front of her with her chin tilted in the air.

Tamping down the smile threatening to bust out all over again at the little copperhead's venom, Rawley said, "Don't think anyone will ever be able to tell you what to do, Sunshine. You're too independent and headstrong to allow that to happen."

Glancing down at his hands, he continued, "My folks died from the fever when I turned thirteen. I could have stayed with my grandfather, Little Elk, but decided to move on. For a long time, I had this big aching hole in my chest; I felt empty. No matter what I tried to do, I couldn't get rid of it." Taking a sip of air, he exhaled slowly, saying, "Then I ran into Sam and Sally and slowly that big hole began to fill up with the love those two showed me. After being with Sam for several years, an opening came up here in White River after Vern passed away. Sam recommended me for this job, so I took it. Both Sam and Sally taught me that with time, you will heal, if you allow it. That's why I don't carry around grudges and resentments. It keeps you from healing, from moving forward, living…" he paused then added, "…and loving…" Rawley looked across at Lacy, waiting for her response.

Once again, this big galoot had been able to put into words

what she couldn't; reading her mind again. Not wanting to let him know how much his words had affected her, Lacy hissed at him like a mad cat, "Don't you preach to me, Lovett!" Whirling, she ran down the hall to her quarters, opening and slamming the door shut behind her.

The marshal stood and poured himself a cup of stale coffee. Taking a sip, he grimaced at the bitterness, he set it down on the desk. Rawley continued to stare down the empty hall.

"Damn, she's stubborn," he muttered. Sitting, Rawley slouched in his chair as he propped his feet on the desk, crossing his ankles and tilting the chair as he did so. It squeaked when he leaned back. Closing tired eyes Rawley sighed inwardly, trying to relax. Abruptly he popped up as a thought flickered like a flame in his brain. All those years she had spent alone, it finally dawned on him. What Lacy really wanted was to feel needed and loved, to belong somewhere, to someone, or anything, even the four-legged varieties, like Baxter and Fancy.

Lacy is just one big aching heart looking for a home, Rawley finally realized.

Chapter Thirty-Four

EVEN THOUGH RAWLEY and Lacy had settled into a more comfortable rhythm with each other, he knew she still wasn't totally at ease around him. Digging through old case files seemed about the only time she actually did talk with him, picking his brain on this one or that, not willing and still afraid to step outside her comfort zone.

A little over three months ago, the fiery, short-tempered copperhead had landed in his lap. Not that Rawley Lovett had minded too much. Cute as a speckled pup she was, with burnt coffee eyes and a temper that reminded him of a disturbed den of rattlesnakes. Lacy Carrigan a/k/a Lacy Watson carried a secret deep within her soul. As of now, only he knew what that secret contained and it pained him that she didn't trust him enough to talk more about it.

Billy lived at Olivia's along with Cotton. Baxter had taken up residence there too, sticking to the boys like a tick on a hound dog.

Christmas morning dawned bright and clear, the light powder glistening like pearl dust.

Lacy didn't believe in God. If there had been one, her mother wouldn't be dead and she might have had a different life. Not the one she'd lived for the last nine-ten years. This just added to her belief that Christmas shouldn't be celebrated either.

Looking very handsome in his suit today, Rawley kept giving Lacy his reassuring smile. More than once during the morning he tried to convince her that maybe Liv might loan her a dress to wear for the day. *I'm not falling into his trap, and I'm not wearing a dress,* her mind bucked against Rawley's cajoling. Lacy hadn't worn one of those in a long time. *I don't care if it is Christmas!*

She wore her everyday clothes to Miss Liv's, but did leave her gun behind hanging on the peg. Both strolled toward Miss Liv's in the brisk, sunny morning. Rawley held a few small packages in his arms. Lacy being her quiet and non-communicative self, prompted him to ask, "When did you last celebrate Christmas?"

Lacy just shrugged and kept her thoughts to herself, *Too long ago to think about,* her mind gritted, trying not to think of the happier Christmases from her long ago past.

The girl's strung tight as a wire fence. Rawley cocked a brow at the silent answer, hidden vibrations bouncing off her as if someone had twanged the wire. In the three months he'd known her, social situations tended to make the girl clam up tighter than a locked trunk. *She's been by herself for way too long.*

The fact that Lacy was still afraid of trusting human beings continued to rip at his heart. But her fear was something she needed to work through herself. If he were to push her into trusting him, she'd just buck up against him even more.

The boys were so excited. This would be Billy's happiest Christmas in a long time and Cotton's first one since his family had been murdered.

Liv came out of the warm kitchen, hearing the commotion in her living room. Her cheeks rosy from the heat, she smelled of cloves, cinnamon and baked ham.

"Baxter!" she scolded the big wire-haired, scruffy dog. He turned and happily grinned at the woman, then began barking again. Liv rolled her eyes as she walked over to Rawley and Lacy. She gave the big man a hug and kiss on the cheek. He returned the gesture, then bellowed, "Merry Christmas, everyone!"

Lacy scowled, his enthusiasm grated on her like sandpaper

going the wrong way on a piece of wood. *Sometimes Lovett acted like he had peas for brains!*

Liv reached out toward Lacy, but she shied away and quickly sidestepped her childhood teacher, avoiding contact.

Liv's brow cocked, she glanced at Rawley.

He shrugged.

Draping himself over Baxter's back, Cotton's baby teeth smiled as big as the dog's. His little hands held Baxter's tail down, keeping it from sweeping everything in its path. The youngster slid off the dog's back and ran to his big friend, his arms stretched upward. Reaching down, Rawley swept the tow-head into his arms.

"Did Santa come?" he whispered into the boy's ear.

"Uh-huh…" the boy replied, nodding as he slid out of Rawley's embrace. Cotton took a big palm in his little one, tugging the dark-haired lawman over to the tree.

Big red bows and pine cone ornaments decked out the tree. Sprinkled with paper snowflakes and colorful paper chains made by Billy and Cotton along with some store-bought decorations, all this came together nestled amongst the thick branches producing a festive centerpiece in Liv's home.

Cotton proudly showed Rawley the little red wagon. "Gama Wivy said I can help her go shopping now," he declared happily.

Doc and Billy were concentrating on beating each other with Billy's new checkers set.

Lacy had sidled away, standing in front of the fire warming her backside. She kept watching the activity as if her body stood in another dimension, another time.

Other memories kept flashing through her mind's eye, clouding pretty dark eyes with the recollections of occasions such as this. Except instead of two boys, a small copper haired girl in a pretty green silk dress had been the one squealing with delight at what Santa had placed under the tree. Her mind's eye retrieved the memories of her Mama sitting on the sofa, her smile lighting up her beautiful features and wearing her favorite blue gown to accent her own copper tresses.

Shedding his coat, Rawley took a seat on the sofa, his arm draped across the back as one booted ankle rested on his knee. He looked around. During the holidays, Liv always decorated to the fullest extent of the law. He sniffed appreciatively, his nose tingling with the delicious smells coming from the kitchen. The fragrance of fresh cut evergreen boughs decorating the mantle with matching red bows and cream-colored tallow tapers lit added to the festive mood. *Except for one thing,* he thought, *Lacy.*

His eyes were drawn to the lonely figure standing in front of the warm fireplace. Her dark eyes were dim as though a fog shrouded them. Lacy had gone deep somewhere within her soul he knew, remembering other Christmases. He watched as she visibly shook herself.

Turning quickly, Lacy ducked behind the tree to hide her tears, swiping at them with a hand, while the other placed a small box underneath for Rawley. The item in the box was very precious to her and she knew the marshal would feel the same way, since it held unique memories for them both.

Cotton, playing around the tree, found the little box. He gave it to Liv.

Lacy's breath caught in her throat. She tried to swallow the little pebble that seemed to have lodged there. "That's for the marshal," she squeaked.

Surprise washed over Rawley's face. He took the box from Liv and opened it. "A watch?" he asked, glancing quickly in Lacy's direction.

The room seemed to close in around her, shutting off her air. Lacy rose from the chair, forcing her legs to move and create the much needed distance between the marshal and herself. Stopping in front of the fire, she turned around and stated quietly, "Open the watch." She saw the emotions flit across his eyes when he read the inscription: *To Sam Luebker for twenty-five years of ser-*

205

vice. Thank you.

"I thought you might like to have that," Lacy added softly.

His eyes questioning, Rawley asked quietly, "How? Where did you get this?"

Lacy heaved in more air as she tried to swallow the lump before speaking. Long moments later, her voice broke into the heavy silence that crowded the room. "His heart went out on him one day when we were rounding up strays. He died doing his second favorite thing in life, running his ranch. Being a peace officer had been his first love, besides Sally. He died in my arms," Lacy said, her voice cracking with emotion at revealing old bottled up memories.

Swallowing down the tears that clogged her throat became increasingly difficult. She stammered several times before finally saying, "Ss…Sally sold the ranch and moved back to be with family in St. Louis." Lacy looked down at her boots as she said, "She gave that to me, saying Sam would want me to have it. I…I thought you might like to have it now, too… to remember him by…" her voice trailing off to barely a whisper, she glanced up across at Rawley, tears glistening in her eyes.

One could have heard a pin drop in that room; the boys, even the dog were quiet. Liv's mouth hung open in a very unladylike expression.

Taking out his handkerchief, Doc blew his nose, the loud noise disrupting the extreme silence.

Liv cut him a strange look.

Rawley rose and deliberately walked slowly towards Lacy, hoping that she wouldn't run. When she didn't, he gently turned her toward him, taking a finger and tilting her face upward, making the tears spill from the corners of her eyes, sliding down freckled cheeks.

"Sunshine…that's the nicest gift anyone has ever given me," he whispered. "Thank you." His thumbs brushed the wetness from those cheeks. Then he kissed her lightly on her forehead. It took some doing, but Rawley held himself back, denying the embrace he wanted, the kiss he knew they'd both never forget.

Color slid up her face as Lacy's eyes darted down. She also pinched her bottom lip with her teeth and just nodded. Abruptly shying away, Lacy hurried to grab her overgrown coat. Opening the door, she ran outside slamming it in her wake.

At last, Liv closed her mouth. "Well!" she exclaimed, breaking the heavy silence. "That was something…wasn't it? C'mon boys, help me get the goodies out!"

Rawley still staring at the door, moved towards it.

Doc stopped him with his words, "Leave her be, son," he said as he wiped his nose again. "Don't crowd her. She'll be back when she's ready."

The marshal continued over to the window, gazing out on the street; still no Lacy. He returned his attention back to the activities in the house.

Lacy skedaddled around the side of the house, pulling on the coat. Her coat sleeve swiped at the wet tears, then brushed across her runny nose. She proceeded to wrap her arms around her middle, holding the coat closed instead of buttoning it. *I seem to be crying at the drop of a hat these days,* she thought, sniffling again.

Gulping in the deep breaths of brisk air trying to calm herself made her lungs hurt. Lacy leaned against the side of Liv's house. Then she slowly slid down, her butt stopped when it rested on her heels. With her arms, she gathered knees to her chest and allowed her chin to rest on them. Lacy willed herself to calm down. It took a while, but her heart finally quit knocking against her ribs. Dark eyes scanned the mountains in the distance, the clear air making them appear closer than they were. *Sprinkled with Angel dust,* she thought. Her mama always called the snow way up in the mountains, *Angel Dust.* Briskly Lacy shook her head, shaking the memories out, concentrating instead on the sun blasting the snow with a brightness that kept her eyes blinking, adjusting to the reflection.

The memories made Lacy realize, *I'm getting too entwined in this little community. No one except Rawley knows who I really am.* And so far, the town only knew her as Lacy Watson, not Lacy Carrigan. No one had suggested she could be someone else, at least so far they hadn't. But it was bound to come out one day, if and whenever her grandfather came to town.

Again, the thought of running flitted through her brain. Closing her eyes against the glare, she acknowledged this had been the longest she'd stayed in one place since Sam had died. As Lovett said, she'd begun to allow her boots to get a little dusty. Maybe the time had come to get rid of that dust.

Spring...spring... I'll move on, she decided. Pushing herself against the house, she rose and walked back into warm Christmas festivities, something she hadn't been a part of for a long time, a very long time.

***

ALL EYES WATCHED as she reentered the house, but remained silent. Shrugging out of her coat and laying it on the arm of a wingback chair, she noticed Billy, Cotton and Rawley were playing checkers. Doc was keeping his eye out for anyone cheating.

Cotton piped up from Rawley's lap, "Miff Wafy, I'm winning, thee!" Chubby hands held up the handful of checkers he'd collected.

Lacy acknowledged the towhead's words with a smile. Her gaze drifted to Rawley's face, causing her steps to hesitate, watching the questioning look slide across those piercing eyes. They seemed to be digging and probing into her mind while they tried to peel away her protective layers. Her eyes skittered away from his intense look, continuing on to stand in front of the fire, warming herself again.

Liv bustled in setting down a tray filled with goodies and hot cider. "Oh...Lacy, you're back. Good. Come help me in the kitchen."

Realizing Liv had just given her the chance to escape the over-powering physical presence of Rawley Lovett, Lacy followed.

Handing Lacy a knife, Liv said, "I need you to peel the potatoes." Sitting a bowl in front of the redhead, Liv slid a heavy cloth bag closer to Lacy.

Lacy stared at the knife, the bowl and Miss Liv's back as she stirred a pot on the stove. Color rose from her neck to the roots of her hair as she stammered, "I'm not sure I know how."

Surprised, Liv turned and saw the bright color in redhead's face. All at once, she seemed to understand, "Oh honey…it's not hard…" as she quickly showed Lacy how to accomplish the task.

Halfway through the bowl, Lacy mumbled like she had a mouthful of marbles, "Sure is a lot of potatoes for only six people."

Liv's delightful laugh filled the warm kitchen, "We've got two growing boys out there, and if you count Rawley, three boys. That man would eat you out of house and home if you let him. Billy's got two hollow legs, just like Rawley. I declare, I think Billy's grown two inches here recently."

Lacy hesitated, finally saying, "Thank you for taking care of the boys."

Liv turned, wiping her hands on a towel, "Oh, honey! I haven't had this much fun since I retired from teaching. Billy is doing fine in his studies now, and Cotton wants to learn whatever Billy is learning, a good sign."

A long-ago question popped into her brain, one that had bugged her from her school days, prompting her to finally asked, "Why didn't you ever get married, Miss Liv?"

"Oh…I don't know, never thought much about it, too busy teaching I guess."

"But…what about you and…and Doc, didn't…didn't you two ever want to get married?"

209

"Oh…we talked about it some, but we're both too set in our ways now so…we're just really good friends. He's someone to have supper with and do things together, that sorta thing…" Liv stopped and turned while she analyzed the girl concentrating on her task.

"Rawley's a good man…Lacy," Liv said softly, sliding into a chair across the table from her. "You couldn't ask for a better friend or husband." She observed the girl's hands go still. "He's got a heart that's as big as a washtub…" Liv smiled. "…It kind of contradicts what he does for a living…doesn't it?" she said lightly as she rose again.

Looking up, Lacy shook her head, "No. I'm not *ever* getting married. Besides, no one wants to marry someone who well…who does what I do…" she finished quietly, adding abruptly, "…Am I done here now?"

Liv nodded, watching the girl scurry just a little too quickly into the other room. Lacy had a lot of good qualities, Liv knew. But that damned past kept cropping up making Lacy feel she wasn't worthy of anyone. Sighing inwardly, she turned back to the task of preparing a big holiday dinner.

Chapter Thirty-Five

"PLAY YOU IN a game of checkers?" Rawley offered.

Lacy nodded, pulling her fingers out of her britches' back pockets and sat, sitting cross-legged on the floor. Rawley set up the board and told her to make the first move. Several games later, Rawley had won two games to her one. Lacy let a smile peek through, allowing the dimples to appear. "Guess I need some more practice," she said, readying the board for another game. This time concentrating, she smiled, the glow of winning shining in her eyes, "That's better!"

Rawley noticed Lacy warming up and relaxing some, "Well...I can't let a girl beat me now, can I," he teased, setting the board up for another game.

"I wouldn't want to ruin your reputation," she returned, her smile going broader, dimples deepening. Lacy suddenly realized. *I'm being drawn into this big man's gentle embrace even though we're several feet apart. I...I can't let that happen.* Prompting the veil to drop once more, hiding her emotions.

Rawley glimpsed something flickering through Lacy's eyes, and then it swam away before he could figure it out.

Cotton chose that moment to wiggle into Lacy's lap, breaking the tension between the pair, "Miff Wafy? Can I pway wif you?"

Planting a kiss on his soft cheek, she said, "Sure you can," not daring to look in Rawley's direction.

Chapter Thirty-Six

STROLLING BACK TO the office, Lacy marveled at how quiet and still the night seemed after the hustle and bustle at Miss Liv's house.

Even Mike had closed down for the night. Her boots squeaked and crunched walking through the frozen snow. Stopping in the middle of the street, Lacy tilted her face toward the stars, slowly turning as she took in the quiet beauty.

Rawley came to stand next to her doing the same, "Beautiful...isn't it?"

"Yes...oh look, a shooting star..." she said, pointing.

"Some folks believe it's souls reaching their final destination."

Lacy allowed herself to bask in Rawley's warmth. Although not touching, she felt somehow reassured with him standing alongside of her in the cold. A glimmer of another smile began to peek through, "When I was on the trail, I used to like to...to dream that was a big piece of black flannel up there, and...and the stars were just really peep holes in all that black..." Lacy hesitated.

"Go on..." Rawley urged her softly, stepping closer.

Inhaling deeply, she continued, "I...I used to...I wanted to believe Mama was looking through those peep holes and watching me..." realizing how much she'd shared, she stopped abruptly.

"Sunshine...if that's what you want to believe, then you should."

Without an answer Lacy just scuffed the frozen snow with the toe of her boot.

Rawley wanted to take her in his arms, hold her and help wash away all that pain and hurt she'd been concealing inside all these years. Stepping toward her, he offered, "Sweetie…let me help?"

Lacy froze, then her hand struck out quickly, slapping Rawley's cheek. Hard.

Recoiling at Lacy's unexpected reflexes, Rawley voiced angrily, "Damn it…Lacy what the hell did you go and do that for?" His hand rubbed his stinging cheek.

"You bastard! You don't call me that, ever…" she hissed, "…Ever again."

Anger and fear accompanied the bone chilling air, saturating the small space between the pair.

Rawley reached for her.

Lacy shied away. Quickly spinning, she ran inside to the safety of her room.

***

HE FILLED THE firebox full for the night. After that, his hand absentmindedly turned down the damper as his fingers lightly brushed his cheek where Lacy had slapped him.

She had slowly and surely been opening up until just a few moments ago, when he had said the word *sweetie*. Rawley knew the word had some connection with her grandfather, otherwise she wouldn't have slapped him as hard as she did.

His heart ached watching her run back to the office. That girl continued to carry one heavy wagon load of grief, shame and hurt around.

And damn it, he thought, *she won't let anyone help her carry that grief or ease her pain.*

The boys had helped some in loosening her up, causing her to not be so reserved and leery of most two-legged creatures, especially him. But then he would screw up, like he did a few moments ago, sending her scooting back behind that brick wall.

Maybe one of these days he might even get to hear her laugh. *Yeah…maybe in a million years, if I live that long,* he grudgingly thought.

Chapter Thirty-Seven

LACY KEPT TOSSING and turning, unable to still her tumbling mind. Lovett had a way of dragging things out of her, even when she should've kept her mouth shut. She would have to be more careful from now on.

She finally gave up and padded into the office. Lighting a lamp, she opened the files. Sometimes if she physically concentrated on something else besides the events of a day, it usually helped to ease her mind and relax her.

Papers crackled as she shuffled through them. She glanced up as Rawley's door opened. Lacy's eyes gazed at the virile masculinity of the man stepping out of his quarters. Dark eyes grazed across wide shoulders, then traveled down his shirtless torso. A dark thatch that matched his hair covered the broad chest. Her eyes slid down further, touching on his suit trousers and the band that accented his slim waist and flat stomach. His stocking feet poked out below the bottoms of his trousers. Her eyes traveled back to his face. Lacy felt silly, like she was a cow grazing in the direction of the choicest blades of grass. She could feel her face becoming warm. Her heart banging away against her ribs kept saying one thing, her mind another. She chose to ignore the heart part. Even so...*Dammit, he seemed to be doing that a lot here lately, messing with my heart. But, he said I didn't have a heart...but I do...oh shut-up!* Trying to cut off the cackling bouncing around in her brain, Lacy wouldn't allow her stupid heart to fall for this virile man's masculinity. *No...way,* her mind retorted. Her fingers dove into the files once again.

Laying a muscular arm on top of the cabinet, Rawley tucked a thumb into a back pocket. He'd seen the look she gave him, the rosy color that had begun to rise. But that hadn't been what distracted him. Lacy's hair had been taken out of that constant rope of a braid, now flowing loose across her shoulders and down her back. Copper tendrils curled across her forehead with one long strand tucked behind a delicate ear. She stood quietly in her pretty pink and white nightgown. The pink ribbon threaded through eyelet lace around the collar and midway down the front. The material swelled as she breathed, accenting the soft curves of her breasts and took his breath away. He wondered when she had bought the gown. For once, Lacy looked like the woman she really could be and not the man she opted for. Clearing his throat, he asked lamely, "Kinda late to be working, ain't it?"

"Couldn't sleep, decided to go through these files again," she finally replied.

"Uh-huh. That the only reason, Sunshine?"

Lacy gave him a quizzical look asking, "What's that supposed to mean?"

"Nuthin' just wondered is all." Tilting his head, Rawley added, "It's nice to see you finally showing your feminine side." Nodding at her gown he said, "You ever give any thought to, maybe…well…wearing a dress sometimes?"

There he goes again, wanting me to wear a dress. Her eyes tapered drawing the freckles closer. Color again stained her cheeks, making her ask abruptly, "You trying to pick a fight with me again, Lovett?"

"Naw…just wondering what you'd look like in a dress, hair all done up real pretty like, 'stead of you wearing men's clothes all the time."

Lacy knew he liked to get her riled. For some reason Lovett enjoyed teasing her. She'd never get to sleep tonight if she allowed him to goad her. Instead she answered, "I wear britches because it makes doing my job easier, you can't go chasing criminals in a dress, get your legs all tangled up. Besides…a dress and sitting a horse don't exactly go together," she announced firmly.

"I know a fair amount of women who can set a horse right smartly in a dress." Rawley continued, saying quietly, "You're not a man…Sunshine. I just wonder when you plan to quit trying to be one."

Lacy's color deepened at his words. Trying to control her temper, her hands crumpled the tops of the files instead, forcing her knuckles to turn white. Words hissed through clenched teeth, "I don't know what kinda game you're playing tonight, Lovett. Why you're trying to crowd me so hard, make me into something I'm not. There are reasons for the way I do things." Lacy's heart continued to race, making it hard to breathe. She'd taken to wearing britches when her grandfather…well…to her, it just felt safer wearing britches.

Waving an arm in his face, she said, "I just wanted to go through some files and… and you come out loaded up like a scatter gun, each little pellet striking, hitting me here, then there, like angry little bees, stinging…" she stopped only to heave in a breath.

Jumping in before Lacy could strike again, Rawley answered her, "Because the only time I seem to get you to open up or talk to me is when I get you angry. I know only what you allow me to know. When you realize you've given me too much information, you clam up, frustrating the hell out of me, and I'm flat out tired of it!" Walking over, he sat heavily on the edge of the desk, crossing arms across his bare chest. Eyes of cold flint stared at the girl.

Dark eyes watched him silently.

"I've tried everything I know; patience, trying to get you to crack a smile, to share a laugh or two. I've given you understanding, letting you have your space. I haven't placed you on trial because of what your grandfather did to you. But you should have warmed up to me by now." He added quietly, "I'm not the enemy, Sunshine." Rawley stood, and took a few steps closer to Lacy.

217

Warily her eyes followed his movement.

Not receiving an answer made him angry. He spoke harshly, "You've shut yourself down for so long, I doubt you'll ever be what most folks would call normal."

Lacy gasped.

Once again Rawley knew his choice of words had hit home, "You're right...you'll never give me or anyone else the chance to find the real Lacy Carrigan," he said, anger rising in him like the river after a hard rain. "No. You just go ahead and keep wallering in your self-pity, running...afraid to take the risk of opening your heart to let it heal. That's right. You just keep running...always being afraid. One of these days, you'll come to realize I'm right," he said, giving Lacy another hard stare.

She shut down again, her eyes dark and impenetrable, focusing at a spot on the wall over his shoulder. His anger suddenly disappeared when he noticed the veil had dropped covering Lacy's emotions.

Rawley gently laid a hand on her arm, his voice softening, "You can't keep running from the memories, Sunshine. They'll always be a part of you. But if you face up to them, the pain won't be so bad. You're allowing them to ruin your life, allowing them to eat you up inside. Facing them will let you be in control of them, instead of the memories controlling you."

His fingers entangled themselves in the thick silky mass brushing them off Lacy's shoulder, enjoying the feel of red-gold curls slipping through his fingers. Imagining how the silky wisps would feel caressing his naked body as they made love. Rawley caught himself before his thoughts continued along that trail. However, it didn't stop his hand from smoothing the fiery tresses down her back. His eyes smoky with emotion, probed the depths of the girl's standing in front of him. Tossing those tantalizing thoughts aside, he asked softly, "How 'bout it Sunshine...you willing to take control of those memories?"

The smooth caramel of his voice wrapped around her; she

stiffened against it as her hands clenched into fists. "No." Lacy whispered, retreating. "No. I'll never...those memories..." she said, continuing to shy away from him until the wall holding the clock stopped her, "Memories will...they killed my Mama!"

Images of making love to Lacy faded quickly as he watched pain filter through her eyes. The fleeting shadows laced with a constant fear of always reliving those memories tore at his gut while he gazed at the still grieving redhead.

"Lacy! That's exactly what you are allowing them to do to you! Can't you see that?" Stepping closer, Rawley argued, "You're letting them eat you up inside! What? You on a death march? Hoping one day to be killed, putting you out of your misery, like a horse with a broken leg? You're not making sense! I'm trying...."

Words came suddenly, expelled violently, "Shut-up! Just, shut-up!" Lacy's eyes came back into focus, her memory laced ones scrutinizing his angry blue ones. The words seemed to claw their way up her throat accompanied by stinging bile, prompting them to be expelled harshly, "No one can kill me anymore...Marshal." Swallowing back the awful bile, she announced, "Because...you see...I'm already dead. I died a long time ago, Mister Lovett. A long...time ago..." she said. Turning quickly, Lacy's bare feet carried her back to her room, her hand opening and closing the door softly.

Tucking thumbs in his back pockets, Rawley exhaled an exasperated sigh, gazing down the now empty hall. Half-turning, he slammed the drawer shut on the files. The papers crunched and pinched against the wood, making the drawer remained partially open at the resistance. Resting an elbow on the top, chin in his hand, he didn't know what he wanted to do with the girl, claiming to have died a long time ago. He knew that, it had been too evident in her face and actions. Rawley figured it would take a lot longer for him to break down that barrier now. He didn't know when or how long that might take, but it would be the biggest challenge he'd ever faced, *Well...one of the biggest challenges I've ever faced.* Hopefully Lacy would see that she could recover from her painful past and the shame that went with it. But until she realized that, he would just have to be satisfied with watching her run each time whenever he got too close. Not just physically, but mentally too.

Rawley groaned out loud, suddenly realizing he had become more then attracted to the little firebrand, allowing her to entwine him in her web. How this had happened, he didn't know. Most of the time, Lacy was more trouble than a pound of pennies.

He slammed his fist into the side of the cabinet, causing his knuckles to crack. Walking over to the wood stove, he threw open the small door; it banged against the side of the stove with a loud clank. Rawley shoved more wood into the fire box and shut the door. Turning, he walked into his quarters and slammed the door in his wake, causing the front window to rattle.

Chapter Thirty-Eight

SITTING ON THE bunk in her room, Lacy felt numb. She stared into the darkness, her mind descending into a black hole, the sides closing in on her as she plummeted into its depths. Her mind quickly flashed back to the discovery of her Mama's body. Lacy's world had plunged into a deep abyss that night, never to recover. The image of her mother's mutilated face floated across Lacy's eyes. The image continued with a young girl weeping and rocking the lifeless body, sobbing over the sacrifice.

Finally, gently laying her mama back down, she saw the envelope with her name on it. Ripping it open she began to read, her tears becoming so thick the words blurred. Remembering again how she had hastily wiped them away, leaving her face blood smeared. Then she read and re-read the letter as more tears cascaded onto the handwriting, the ink running with the moisture.

Her mama's final words to her:

My Dearest Lacy,
When you find this letter, I will have passed into a much better place. I am carrying your grandfather's child. I could not allow that poor child to be born into such a destructive home as this. I saw no other way out of this despicable situation. Please forgive me for my cowardly way out. You must leave immediately, run, run as far away as you can. There is money in your Grandfather's safe, take it and run - never to return. You, my darling daughter, are stronger than I am and you will survive; for that I am grateful. Never forget that I love you so very much and will continue to do so even after I am gone.
Your loving Mama

Even now, nine years later, the words were still burned into her mind as if it had happened only yesterday. Taking the pistol her mama used to commit suicide, it had become hers. She did as her mother had requested; never to return until now, becoming part of the little community she had left behind. Painful memories stuffed down so deep, she thought they would never resurface, but they had.

Lacy began to shake violently. It began with her toes pressed into the floor boards, then crawled up her legs and into her stomach. From there it veered, like a fork in the road, down both arms and finally reached her shoulders where it rested. Cold. So cold. This same reaction always happened after her grandfather had visited her. The sickening tightness grabbed hold of her stomach once again at the memory. She gagged.

Swallowing, she forced the threatening bile back down. She couldn't think, didn't want to think, but she had to. Glancing around in the dark with her mind rattled, she recognized the fact that Lovett had pieced her past together like a quilt, bringing all those horrible memories to the surface. Lacy still couldn't figure out how the big lawman had been able to do that, but he had.

Opening the trunk, her shaking hands pulled out her saddlebags. Lacy began cramming them full, and then hurriedly got dressed. Tip-toeing out the door she gathered the rest of her gear. Tip-toeing back down the hall, her glance rested on the snowshoes hanging on the wall. Without a second thought, her hand reached out and picked them off the wall. Going back into her room, Lacy took the deputy marshal's badge off her shirt, caressing it one final time before laying it next to the brush and comb set Rawley had given her.

Gazing around the dark room, she let her eyes come to rest on the rocker. She loved sitting there, rocking at the end of the day in this cozy room, brushing her hair. Giving herself a mental shake, she scolded herself, *Don't go there, your mind is made up.*

Her still shaking hands buckled on the Navy Colt her mother had used. Running again seemed the only answer Lacy could come up with. She would only hurt more people if she stayed; a risk she couldn't take. *Lovett is right…I'm just a blood thirsty bounty hunter*, her mind said. *My destiny has already been laid out for me.*

She pulled on two coats to ward off the bitter cold Lacy knew existed outdoors. Her shaking fingers stumbled, trying to push buttons into holes that seemed too small. She picked up her things and quietly walked out the back entrance, closing the door with a soft click. Her boots crunched in the frozen snow, rounding the corner of the marshal's office. Then her footsteps picked up their pace as she headed for the stable.

Saddling Fancy in the dark recesses of the barn, her only il-lumination were the pin-pricks of star light glancing off the hay strewn floor through the half-opened door.

Rawley's big bay nickered at the activity. Other boarders shuffled their feet in their hay strewn stalls, blowing.

Ignoring them, Lacy crooned to the mare in a soft voice, "Yes…we are going for a ride…a long ride. We're going up to the cabin and stay the winter. Come spring, we'll move on to new territory, maybe Canada, maybe the mountains of Montana, may-be Texas." She didn't know for sure. But she also knew Lovett wouldn't track her that far. Lacy swung into the saddle, and urg-ing Fancy into a trot, the darkness folded around the pair encasing them in its blackness as they disappeared from view.

Chapter Thirty-Nine

WALKING OUT OF his room the next morning, Rawley stretched. All seemed quiet, but the coffee hadn't been made, so he guessed Lacy chose to sleep in. He'd spent a restless night himself following another of their one sided arguments, dozing fitfully debating what had transpired between them. He decided to give her some space this morning.

Walking across to Maddie's, Luke fell into step beside him.

"Say, Rawley? You send that deputy of yure'n's out on a special mission?"

Rawley stopped, his stomach beginning to twist, "No...why?"

"Well...she took off outta here 'bout three this mornin'."

Rawley glanced back at his office. He spun, his boots pounded the frozen street leaving Luke standing there, his mouth hanging wide open.

Banging the door open, darting his eyes to where they both would leave their gear, he saw that Lacy's coats and hardware were gone. His heart continued to clatter around in his chest as he hotfooted it down the short hallway. Opening the door to her room, his eyes swept the interior and saw the trunk lid wide open. Her saddlebags were gone as was her rifle. His glance drifted to the dresser where he spotted the metal from the badge glinting in the filtered light from the one window. He strode over and picked it up. She was gone; Lacy was gone. He felt as if the air had been sucked out of his lungs with Luke's bellows.

I need to go after her, bring her back, but he was the one who had made her feel the need to run away again. He had pushed her, crowding her to face the past before she had been ready to. He just wanted to help, but instead had made the girl run.

Tossing the badge in his hand, he walked back into the hallway. Staring at the wall, he noticed something was different. *Fishing poles are still there,* he thought racking his brain, *What is missing... his snowshoes!* She'd taken his damn snowshoes! Now he knew where she would be, when he decided to chase her down. But right now, he needed to think, gather his thoughts together.

Chapter Forty

BILLY WAS PLOWING through the snow on his way to take care of Fancy when Rawley stopped him. "She's not there...Billy. Lacy and Fancy are gone," he said quietly.

"What? What'da ya mean...she's gone?"

"Just that...Billy. She's gone."

"But why? I was taking good care of Fancy...wasn't I?" Billy's words tumbled over themselves, "It was something I did...wasn't it? Miss Lacy left because of something I did...didn't she?"

Rawley shook his head, resting an arm on the boy's shoulders and steering him back towards Liv's, "No...you did nothing wrong...son."

"But I don't understand...I was taking good care of Fancy, wasn't I? If I didn't do anything wrong...then why did Miss Lacy leave?"

Rawley's hands took the boy by the shoulders and made him look up, "Son...you did nothing wrong. It...it was me. I said something I shouldn't have. I made Lacy leave."

"But...why? Why did you let her go? Didn't you love her enough to stop her?"

Rawley's voice echoed his surprise, "What?"

"I thought you loved her. Loved Miss Lacy enough to...to keep her from leaving? You gonna go find her...ain't cha?"

Out of the mouth of babes, Rawley thought. The boy was smarter and more observant then he had thought, seeing something he hadn't. "I couldn't stop her son...she left in the middle of the night."

Head down, Billy scuffed the snow with his boot. "You

could've you know, if you really loved her," he replied sourly, turning around and tramping back into the house.

The marshal jammed his hands deep into his coat pockets and stared after the boy. *Love! What did that boy know 'bout love?* Rawley thought, *Apparently, more than I do, 'cause it's a four-teen year old kid who pointed out that I, Rawley Lovett have fall-en in love with a little freckled copperheaded, venom packed vix-en.* He sighed.

When he entered the house, Olivia met him, flour crusted hands gracing her hips. "What did you go and do to that poor girl now...Rawley Lovett? You've got Billy all upset," she scolded.

Mouth dropping as she reprimanded him, Rawley finally closed it and answered, "Something I shouldn't have....I thought I was helping, but I made it worse, I made Lacy run..." he said, shrugging out of his coat.

Noticing the pain skittering across his face when he spoke, Liv said quietly, "Well, come in the kitchen and we'll talk about it." She led the way and Rawley followed, taking a seat at the kitchen table.

After washing her hands, Liv poured a cup of coffee and sat it down in front of him.

Rawley just stared into the brew.

Liv placed a hand lightly on his shoulder, making Rawley look up. "You want to tell me what happened?" she inquired soft-ly.

Rawley leaned back in the chair, his finger running around the rim of the cup. "I've been a damn fool. Last night...Lacy was prowling through the files like she does sometimes when she can't sleep. I came out to see what all the noise was about and there she was, looking like a real woman for a change. Her hair was loose, hanging down her back and she was wearing a pretty pink and white nightgown. She looked all soft and delicate. She kinda took my breath away, seeing her like that."

Liv smiled, hearing Rawley express himself.

Taking another draught of air and expelling it slowly, Rawley continued, "Well, I made a comment about, well…" he hesitated, gathering his thoughts together then saying, "…Had she ever thought about wearing a dress…that she wasn't a man and when was she gonna quit trying to be one." Closing his eyes, he rolled his head around on his shoulders, trying to work out the tension. "She accused me of trying to pick a fight with her."

"And were you?"

Glancing quickly in Liv's direction, "Yeah. Yeah…I guess I was."

"Why?"

"Because she's got to be the quietest damn female I've ever met! The only time she'll talk to me is when I get her mad…or she's picking my brain on those old cases…"

Taking a sip, he continued, "…But that's not why she left." He swirled the coffee around in his cup. "Lacy left…" he breathed, "…Because I spoke pretty harsh to her about not facing her past. All those memories she's been carrying around through the years wouldn't hurt so much if she'd just face them, instead of always running away from them."

"Ooh…Rawley, you didn't!"

"Yeah…yeah I did," he said quietly.

"It's too soon! You needed to give her more time to…to get used to us…to trust us. For heavens' sakes, Rawley! She's been riding the territories for years, with no one to lean on except her-self…afraid to trust anyone! And you expect her to learn to trust again in one easy lesson! I don't think so…Rawley Lovett!" Olivia scolded the lawman.

Rawley flinched saying, "I know that. I know that now. I didn't…when I was saying it. I just wanted Lacy to talk to me…you know…regular like…have a real conversation for once. Now when I see her again, she'll just clam up worse than before."

"I swear Rawley…between you and Galen," using Doc's given name. "…I'm gonna pull my hair out!" she cried exasperat-

228

ingly. Olivia plopped herself in a chair across the table from Raw-ley. Resting her head in her hands, she sighed deeply and shook her head. A few moments later, she began in a calmer voice, "Rawley, do you remember a conversation I had with you some months before, when I told you she was fragile?"

He gave a slow nod.

"This is exactly what I was trying to tell you. You can't push her, or crowd her as you men like to say. Lacy has to ease into this on her own terms and she surely won't do it with you pushing her! No wonder she ran away! You men can be so dense some-times," Liv said, giving the big lawman one of her best teacher looks.

Rawley winced.

The pitter-pat of little feet stopped at Rawley's side as Cot-ton's small hands gripped a thick arm. The marshal looked down into the little tyke's face, tears dribbling down his cheeks. "Miffer Rawwee? Miff Wafy....," Rawley watched the little face pucker trying to get the words out, "Miff Wafy? Thee go wif Mama? Go wif da angels?"

Rawley groaned inwardly, realizing that little Cotton had thought Lacy died. He felt as guilty as sin; first Billy, now this sweet little boy figured he'd lost someone special once again. Picking the toddler up and sitting him on his lap, Rawley held him tight and kissed the little towhead on his forehead, "No...son. Umm...she had to go away...to fix some things. She'll be back, I promise. I'll bring her back...I promise," he said, wiping the tears from Cotton's cheeks with his thumbs.

"You bing Miff Wafy back? You pomthis?"

Rawley smiled into the hopeful heart-shaped face. "Yes...I promise!"

"Inky thware," Cotton said, sticking his little finger in the air.

The marshal laughed, releasing the tension in his chest. He took the little finger in his bigger one and promised, "I pinky swear!"

Liv smiled at this exchange. She glanced up as Billy sullenly entered the kitchen. He stopped to lean against the doorjamb.

Cotton hopped off the marshal's lap, taking Billy's hand. Excitedly pulling, he exclaimed happily, "Miffer Rawwee, he bing Miff Wafy back…he inky thware!"

"That true?" Billy warily asked the marshal.

Rawley nodded.

"Bout time…since you love her," he said cockily, striding over to the plate of cookies and taking a handful.

Liv's mouth dropped open, very unladylike as she exclaimed, "Billy!"

Billy stared at her in disbelief, his mouth full of cookie, "You didn't notice? Shoot, it was written all over his face! About time he did something about it."

Rawley cocked an eyebrow and grinned awkwardly, "Guess everyone knew except me."

"You mean you hadn't figured out that you loved Lacy?" Olivia asked, placing the plate of cookies in front of the hollow-legged lawman.

Rawley shook his head, "No. Not till Billy brought it to my attention."

"I don't believe it…" Olivia teased Rawley. "…You're even thicker headed than I thought, Rawley Lovett," she laughed.

"Yeah…I guess, I am," he replied, stuffing cookies into his mouth. He smiled.

Chapter Forty-One

LACY HAD BEEN struggling with Fancy since they had hit the mountains, strapping on the snowshoes some time ago. Tying the reins around the saddle horn allowed Fancy the freedom to plow through the snow at her own pace. Lacy stopped often to knock the ice out of Fancy's nostrils, allowing the thick heavy steam to rise once again. She re-wrapped her scarf in a different position around her neck.

Both horse and rider were wearing down from the exertion of the climb and the belly deep snow. Lacy began jabbering at Fancy, not only to keep the big animal moving but to keep herself going as well. Lacy stopped and bent over gripping her knees, trying to catch her breath. Rising, she looked back at Fancy as the horse struggled in the deep snow. Nostrils wide, Fancy blew steam like a locomotive.

Swishing back to her only and best friend, Lacy patted her neck, "I know, girl…I'm tired too…just a little bit farther. We'll be at the cave soon, Fancy Girl…just hang in there. C'mon, you can do it! Then we'll both rest." Her gloved hand took a fistful of frozen mane, tugging and urging the horse forward. Lacy's snowshoes shushed next to her, keeping the big horse moving, not allowing her to give up.

At last Lacy stood outside the cave, heaving in cold air that burned through the scarf into her lungs. Taking a few steps inside the shelter, she saw that everything remained the same, just as she and Rawley had left it. Thinking about him made her heart tickle against her ribs. She swallowed and tossed him out of her head.

Fancy entered, blowing hard. Lacy took off her gear and rubbed the mare down good with the saddle blanket. She covered her with the spare blanket that she had in her bedroll.

Quickly Lacy laid the makings of a fire. Pulling an oil cloth bag from her gear, she opened it with difficulty as cold fingers scraped out two matches. Finally swiping the two across a rock, the phosphorous flared. Lacy lit the kindling and dried grasses, slowly adding more wood until she had a good fire burning.

Making coffee, she sat huddled close to the heat. Too tired to fix anything to eat, she just watched yellow and orange flames sizzle and spit into the air when gusts of wind blew into the small shelter.

She allowed her mind to wander back over the last forty-eight hours. Staring into the flames, they bounced and flickered against her face lost in memories.

Rawley Lovett had scared her again. Lacy didn't know how he did it but Lovett had been able to take pieces of her past, patching it all together, figuring her out. Hell, he knew her better than she knew herself, making her nervous and scared. *Nosy big moose,* she justified to herself. But he'd pushed her in the wrong direction two days ago, that becoming the last straw. *I could care less,* she lied again to herself. *I'm tossing him to the wind. I'm moving on, back to what I'm familiar with.*

Putting more wood on the fire, Lacy continued to sit and think. She hated that she couldn't say goodbye to Cotton and Billy, but...they'd just be hurt, they wouldn't understand what drove her away. Besides she never was good at goodbyes. She always disappeared in the middle of the night to avoid facing the attachments only she knew about.

She might try her hand at something else, what she didn't know. She'd helped Sam on his ranch, but not enough to become really good at it.

Nope. Handling a gun had become her trademark. Throwing or dodging flying lead were basically the only things she knew. Her fingers slid down, tracing the all too familiar rounded edges of the grip. Lacy had never given much thought as to what she did for a living. That is, until she had met that big gentle marshal.

Yeah…Rawley had been gentle with her and that made her even more scared and nervous. Her mind wandering again, Lacy remembered the two boys, Miss Liv's kindness, crusty ol' Doc, even the warmth of Maddie and Mike.

What a sorry mess she'd gotten herself into and not knowing how to handle it, she had run again. Lacy slid down onto the cold ground. Closing her eyes, she released the tears that had been threatening to overflow. They slid down her freckled cheeks. Exhaustion had her drifting off quickly.

Chapter Forty-Two

TIGHTENING THE CINCH on his saddle and attaching the gear bag to the saddle horn, Rawley tied his bedroll and saddlebags on back of the cantle, loading up to go after Lacy, *Bring her home.* His hands stilled, recalling what he had just said to himself.

Mike closed the saloon door behind him and strode to the edge of the walk. Hand shielding his eyes from the bright snow pack glare, he looked around for Rawley. He found him standing in front of his office, tying down his gear. He stepped off the walk, and hurried across the street. Coming alongside, Mike held up a small flask of whiskey, "You might need this. Gonna be mighty cold up there." Looking earnestly at Rawley he added, "You bring that girl home, ya hear? She kinda made a mark on this town. Has a nice way of busting up them barroom brawls." Mike flashed his toothy grin.

"Yeah...she does, doesn't she," the marshal smiled back. Taking the flask, he tucked it in his saddlebag, buckling it closed again.

Coming out of her establishment Maddie adjusted her shawl, pulling it closer over her ample bosom. She hustled towards the marshal. Arriving there, she held up a heavy bundle saying, "Ye be careful wit' me wee lass, 'eh, laddie?"

"Yes, Ma'am..." he replied. Taking the bulky sack, he said, "...Good, Lord...Maddie! This thing weighs a ton! You put that fifteen-ton fruitcake in here? I ain't gonna be gone that long," he teased.

Maddie gave him a scorching look. "Ye chust see ta hit that the lass eats..." the woman ordered. "...She's been ah needin' ah bit mor' meat on them bones, she has..."

Nodding, he attached the cord to the saddle horn, sliding it off to the other side balancing his load. "I will, Maddie..." he said, giving her a tight squeeze.

"What is this?" he asked seeing, Doc, Olivia and the boys coming his way. "You'd think I was leaving town for good..." Rawley said, smiling his greeting.

Doc harrumphed, tugging on his ear. Then his fingers scratched his ever-present stubble, "You bring her back! Just so's I get the pleasure of kicking her butt back to Canada!"

Rawley grinned some more, "Oh, no you don't! I get first crack at that...you crusty old coot."

Doc just harrumphed in reply.

Eyes twinkling as he squatted in front of Cotton, Rawley told him, "I'll bring her back, Cotton. I made you a promise." He ruffled the tyke's hair before he stood and faced Billy, "Take care of Miss Liv and thank you..." holding out his hand, he waited on Billy to shake it. *The boy is growing up.* He needed to be treated like a man.

Billy glanced down at the hand and asked, "For what?"

"For helping me to see something I was too blind to see."

"Oh. That tweren't nothin'..." Billy replied, taking the marshal's hand.

Rawley grabbed Olivia in a hug, stood back and kissed her on the cheek.

Olivia quietly stated, "Recollect what else I told you some months ago?"

Rawley frowned and waited for her to refresh his memory.

"I said...that if there is anyone who could give us back the old Lacy it would be you. Remember now?"

He nodded, "I remember...but that's a tall order, Liv, a lot will depend on Lacy." Turning back to the saddle, he tightened the cinch some more.

"And God..." Olivia intoned.

Glancing over his shoulder, he nodded. Vaulting easily into

the saddle, two fingers brushed the brim of his hat, "I'll be back as soon as I can…" Riding past Mike, Rawley threw out a warning, "Anyone tries to tear up your saloon while I'm gone, tell 'em they'll have my deputy to deal with when we get back!" Grinning, he gave Mike a mock salute.

Laughter rumbled up out of Mike's deep chest.

Chapter Forty-Three

SETTLING BACK INTO her own rhythm, Lacy had been at the cabin for three days now. But she still caught herself wondering what the boys were doing, remembering Rawley's warm soft caramel tone, Liv's affection and easy laughter and Doc's irascible but lovable, surly demeanor. Physically shaking herself like a wet dog, she tossed the thoughts aside and retrieved more wood.

Dark clouds continued scudding across the sky, indicating another winter storm as Lacy loaded her arms with wood. *Good,* she thought, *Rawley won't try to find me in this mess. If he's smart, he'll stay out of these mountains.* Her mind remembered the storms that had kept her snowbound so many years ago.

Scolding herself mentally, she walked back into the warm cabin and dumped the logs by the hearth. *Don't...don't... it's better this way, for all concerned, even the boys. Liv and Doc will take care of them and Rawley will help.* Later, after she had traveled far enough away, she'd wire the marshal about the boys' money so they could have it. Again, she reminded herself, *It's better this way.*

The wind had picked up, forecasting the blizzard about to descend, singing around the eves. The two windows rattled as the wind careened around the corner of the cabin. Whistling again, it blew over and under the porch beams. Shingles rattled like a den of agitated rattlesnakes, whipped by the strong blustery weather. The storm acted as a safety net around Lacy relaxing her. She looked around the small, cozy cabin. *No one will come out in this weather.* Looking back into her cup, her mind wandered again; she'd been thinking too much here lately. She didn't want to admit it, but she missed the boys, and even Rawley jabbering all the

237

time.

***

STRUGGLING IN THE deep snow wearing the snowshoes he'd borrowed from Ezra, he continued to cuss the redhead. Tugging on the big bay's reins, Rawley forced him to carry on, plowing through the deep snow. "Damn woman…" he muttered into his ice coated scarf. "I should 'a stayed down below, let her disappear like she wants to. Instead I'm traipsing after that damn copperhead because I love her."

***

THE DOOR EXPLODED inward. Lacy crashed backwards in her chair taken by surprise. Yellow and orange flames suddenly roared up the chimney as gusts of bitterly cold air and snow blew into the small confines of the cabin. A big snow-covered bear on snowshoes stormed through the wind and snow right into her sanctuary.

Scrambling up, Lacy eyed her weapons, *It's no use,* she realized, rifle and pistol were near the door. Backing up, her hand searched for the poker behind her.

The bear kicked the door shut with a snowshoe, only to have the wind bang it open once again. This time, the bear closed it a little more gently with a glove covered paw, closing out the ferocious wind. Kicking off the snowshoes, they thudded against the far wall. Taking off its hat that revealed dark hair, the bear flung that across the room. Lacy's eyes big as saucers watched a paw yank the scarf from his face.

Gulping, she squeaked, "You…"

A paw brushed the thick snow off his shoulders and sleeves, adding that to the pile melting on the floor. Taking off his gloves, he stuffed them into a pocket. Unbuttoning his coat, he slid his arms out of the sleeves. Rawley flung the coat and his scarf after the hat. He finally replied, "Yes! Me!"

"But...why?"

"What the hell did you think you were doing...leaving like that?" Rawley growled.

Just like a bear, her mind echoed.

Lacy turned around and began stirring the fire with the poker she still held in her hands just for something to do. His arrival had unnerved her. Leaning the poker back against the rock chimney, she placed another log on the flames. She kept trying to find her composure again to face Rawley Lovett and to calm her own damn heart from banging so hard against her ribs.

"It's for the best, I needed to move on," she said to the chimney stone. Turning back around towards the man she thought she'd never see again, she held her chin high with her arms folded, standing her ground against the towering presence of his physical frame and anger, trying to hide her turmoil from within.

With eyes just as cold and stormy as the weather outside, Rawley thundered, "Like hell!"

Lacy flinched as his voice boomed against the walls, his anger crackling like lightening in the small confines of the cabin.

"You'd better start giving me some straight answers...Sunshine!"

Lacy stood silently, watching the vein in his neck pulse against his skin with each heartbeat. She watched his eyes turn to a gunmetal flint with his fury.

Not receiving an answer, Rawley bellowed, "You fool! You know how many people you upset down there? Billy thinks it's his fault you left, that he wasn't taking good enough care of Fancy. And Cotton...why...Cotton thought you had died and gone to be with the angels like his Mama..."

Lacy groaned out loud, spinning to face the flames in the hearth, staring at them to avoid looking at Rawley.

"...Liv is upset 'cause you made Billy and Cotton think it was their fault you left. And Doc why...he's ready to kick your butt to Canada! You even upset Mike and Maddie! Baxter is

239

moping around because you upset the boys…" He paused to suck in air, "…Don't you ever think of anyone besides yourself?" Rawley demanded.

Stunned at what Rawley had just told her, Lacy whispered before she could stop herself, "And you? What about you?"

"Me?" Stepping closer, Rawley's physical presence leaned over her forcing her to retreat from his fury. "I'm mad as thunder, that's what!" he yelled. "Tramping all this way…you took my snowshoes! I want them back!"

Gawking at the man, Lacy finally closed her mouth then stiffly formed the words, speaking slowly, "That's not the real reason…"

Rawley interrupted her, "…No! It's not! I came because you hurt a lot of people in that town by leaving! People I care about…" he roared again, his deep baritone ricocheting off the walls.

Lacy shrank back further from the fury emitting from this man, "I'm sorry, I wasn't thinking, I just thought…well…it's just…better this way…"

"That's right you didn't think! If you'd think with your heart…instead of that fool brain…" he said, trailing off. "Damn it, Lacy…" he growled, jerking her into his arms and kissing her with a rough raw passion, telling her without words the depth of his feelings.

His icy cheeks cool to her hot ones.

Lacy didn't respond the way he'd hoped; the lack of her reaction to his kiss, the stiffness of her body caused Rawley to release her abruptly.

She retreated from his heated embrace as if she'd been touched with a red-hot branding iron. Lacy wasn't sure what to make of his sudden, powerful display of emotion. The back of her hand pressed against her lips.

The words she wanted to say, she couldn't. They remained jammed behind her teeth glued to the roof of her mouth. How could she tell this kind gentle bear of a man how much that kiss meant to her? She would never have the high standards Rawley Lovett had. *I'm not the woman he needs. I'm not wholesome, clean, worthy of him. I'm 'soiled'.* Her mind quickly choked on the word soiled. A hand pushed out as she backed further away, "Don't...please don't, you'll just get hurt. You want..." she began, heaving in more air. "I...I can't give you, what you want," she stammered, receding further away. "You, the others, want me to be someone I can't...never be. That's why I left so well...so I wouldn't hurt more people. It's better I...I move on now." Lacy finished quietly. She knew her words were lame, but it was all she could think of to say at the moment.

Tucking thumbs in back pockets, Rawley's eyes telescoped down at this stubborn female giving him all kinds of excuses. "You're not gonna tell me the real reason, are you?"

Whirling away from his stern gaze, Lacy's hands gripped the mantel, squeezing the wood until her hands hurt, "I don't think I know myself," she whispered. Turning back to face Rawley, she cried, "You're the one who's able to take my past and piece it together like a quilt, telling me things about myself I hadn't even figured out yet!" She felt as if her heart was ready to bounce right out of her chest, the feeling of those emotions scared her further.

Silence floated in like a thick fog, filling the small cabin. Lacy struggled to breathe. Flames licked logs, the popping and crackling loud in the ensuing silence. A log rolled back against the hearth, sending sparks shooting up the chimney. Lacy jumped.

His arms folded across the grey-pebbled wool shirt he wore, he continued to study his redhead. Rawley's thoughts turned inward. He knew that Lacy always struggled to express her feelings. The Good Lord knew she hadn't had much practice at it. Early on, Lacy had disappeared into the far reaches of the territories. So instead of being a carefree young girl who should have been spreading her wings, keeping a social calendar, dancing with the local young men and falling in love, life had given this cop-

241

perhead a bum steer, causing Lacy to turn to the only thing she felt worthy of, flushing fugitives out of the brush. Never trusting another human after her grandfather violated her, causing her a deep shame. Those actions from someone she had once trusted had made her feel like an outcast, a fugitive herself, and that had taught her to keep her mouth shut more often than not. She kept her past bottled up tightly inside along with her emotions.

Mentally shaking those thoughts out of his mind, he offered his lopsided smile, his teeth flashing white in a truce saying, "Sunshine…I do believe that's the most string of words you've put together since you told me about the Dillard boys."

Surprised at the sudden shift in conversation, Lacy puckered her face into a frown, "I've said more than that sometimes."

"Sure…when you're picking my brain about an old case."

Lacy's frown deepened, her teeth clamping down on her bottom lip as she glanced up, "That's not true…I talk to you…"

"Uh-huh, when I make you mad," he replied, his eyes twinkling.

Lacy started to retort, but realized he was teasing her again. Her eyes cast down towards her boots, then back up again. The corners of her mouth began an upward climb. She allowed a shallow dimple to peek through one freckled cheek, telling him, "Better put your horse in the barn, lock it up tight, I've had problems with wolves. I'll have your supper set out with fresh coffee when you get back," she said, getting busy all of a sudden.

Gazing at the slender back of this tough little woman, he retrieved his coat and hat. Giving Lacy one last long look, Rawley stepped out into the storm.

***

WHEN HE RETURNED, Rawley hung his gear on the pegs by the door, resting the rifle against the wall. He moved toward the center of the room. Maddie's bundle landed with a thump on top of the table.

"Wolves are pretty close by. Maddie sent that," he said, gesturing at the cloth filled sack, "It weighs a ton, I 'spect it might be that fifteen-ton fruitcake she prides herself on.

Lacy stopped the smile before it came into full bloom, "She did? Why?"

Placing open palms on the table alongside the bulging sack, Rawley sighed, leaning towards her saying, "Sunshine…you have a lot of people who care about you back there…"

Shaking her head, Lacy said, "No. No…they only know me as Lacy Watson. They don't know who I really am and one of these days they'll find out and, and…" her voice cracked. Swallowing, Lacy began again, "…It's just better that they never find out, letting them, letting them…" she wasn't able to finish, the words too painful to express.

Straightening, Rawley stepped around the table. Taking her arms, he turned her toward him.

Focusing on his shirt buttons kept Lacy from staring into his handsome face.

"Is that what this is all about? You're afraid of what the folks in that town will think of you if they find out your grandfather molested you?"

His words made her flinch.

Rawley's thoughts turned to other instances and other towns, where the community had basically blamed the woman for her own rape, whether the rape occurred by her husband, some stranger or their next-door neighbor. The law always seemed to support the men in cases like this. To Rawley's knowledge, it happened more often than not. The women and yes, the men of the town, vocally and physically shunned the victim, saying, *If she wasn't such a hussy, things like that wouldn't happen to her,* until she moved away or committed suicide. Lacy must have seen this exact same thing occur, further reaffirming her shame about what had happened to her adding to her already fragile emotional and mental state.

243

Lacy struggled to pull out of his grasp.

Tightening his grip, Rawley held her still, "Honey, I won't let that town put you on trial for something you had no control over. You couldn't fight off a full-grown man. You were just a little girl back then."

Lacy's head flew up.

Well...that got a response, he thought as suddenly more parts of the puzzle clicked into place. *Now I understand. She had no control back then, prompting her to try and control everything, now.* Ignoring his thoughts, he continued, "Sunshine...there's a lot of good people in White River, that's why I took the job there. Why Vern stayed all those years. Why I plan to stay, too...it's my home now. It could be yours too...if you let it."

Turning her head away from his steady gaze, she whispered, "You're asking more of me than I can give."

Rawley eased his grip, releasing her.

Lacy stepped back, "I can't..." she said, her eyes finally finding his. They pleaded with him to understand.

Rawley decided he'd pushed her enough for tonight. This had been the most she'd ever revealed about her feelings. "Okay...Sunshine...we'll leave it be," he said, watching relief slowly ebb across her body.

Changing tactics, he asked, "What's for supper? Traipsing after you the last few days has made me hungry. As Maddie says, I'm a growing boy!" Rubbing his stomach in an exaggerated gesture, he hoped to draw a smile out of a freckled face, but all he got was a cock-eyed look with lips locking up tighter then the Denver Mint, yet *again.*

Chapter Forty-Four

KEEPING UP A steady stream of one-sided conversation during supper, Rawley had filled her in on the entire goings on within the community since she'd left.

Lacy continued staring into her cup, not answering, her mind a million miles away.

Rolling his eyes to the beams above, he sighed inwardly. *Can't understand how I fell in love with her, she's always got that tongue glued to the roof of her mouth.* Rawley sighed again, *But I did.* Saying instead, "I see you've got two wolf pelts."

Keeping her eyes focused on her cup, Lacy just nodded. Her mind kept trying to wrap itself around the idea that Rawley Lovett had been able to peel away layer upon layers of frozen crust that had enslaved her heart so long ago. It was like scraping the scales off a fish one by one finally exposing the unprotected skin–illuminating her heart to sunlight once again.

"We could go get more, if you'd like? Make a nice little addition to Cotton and Billy's bank accounts," he said.

Realizing Rawley had been jabbering all this time, she asked, "What?"

Leaning back in his chair, one hand toying with his fork, Rawley said, "You haven't heard a word I said, have you?"

She could feel her neck becoming warm, then spreading upward into the roots of her hair. Ducking her head, Lacy kept quiet.

"You were a million miles away…Sunshine…" he said softly. "…Where did you go?"

Shrugging, Lacy still wasn't comfortable in revealing her thoughts with him.

Swiping a hand across his dark stubble, Rawley sat quietly for a few moments watching Lacy do her best to avoid looking at him. Finally, he said, "Alright, let's start this conversation over again. You with me...Sunshine?" Waiting for her customary silent nod, he got it. "Okay...I said...we could go get more pelts and add the money to Billy's and Cotton's bank accounts..." he repeated.

Jerking her head up, she asked, "How'd you know 'bout that?" Then it dawned on her. "That rat faced bank teller told you...didn't he?" Lacy groused.

Describing Bill Wilson in much the same way he thought of him, he grinned saying, "Uh-huh."

Rolling her eyes, she said, "Just what I need, to have more of my personal business spread all over town!"

"Oh...I wouldn't worry too much about that."

"Why?"

"Well...I kinda told him what you told Aubrey...that you'd gut him like a hog at killing time if he spilled the beans."

Her eyes popped. "You didn't?"

"I did..."

"Lovett...damn you..." she said. "...Now I've got to go around living that down!"

"Oh...so you're gonna come back with me then?"

"I didn't say that...you nitwit..." Lacy fumed.

Rawley laughed.

Lacy gawked at the man. "You rat! You big overgrown rat," she said, rising and aiming a punch at his shoulder.

Rawley grabbed her fist, his eyes filled with mischief. "Glad to see you've got your spit and vinegar back...Sunshine."

Raising her other fist, Rawley caught that one too. He stated calmly, "Temper...temper, Sunshine. You're quick, daring, gutsy, stubborn and bright, but you still need to get a handle on that temper of yours...okay?"

"Well then...quit taunting me..." Lacy said, jerking her

246

hands back, color deepening her freckles and eyes sparkling with anger.

"Oh...I can't do that, Sunshine," he said. Reaching into Maddie's overstuffed bag, he brought out two muffins. As he handed one to her he said, "You're too much fun to tease."

Snatching the muffin from him Lacy plopped back down in her chair falling silent as she popped small bites of Maddie's delicacy into her mouth.

The silence became so thick Lacy felt like she was suffocating. And it wasn't because of the heat coming from the blazing fire in the hearth either. She knew she needed to say something to break the tension, but what, she didn't know.

Finally, leaning back in her chair, creating the much-needed space between herself and Rawley, she softly stated, "I'm not who you think I am."

A brow cocked up as his head tilted. Rawley decided to wait her out see what she would say next.

When he didn't jump in with his usual jabbering quick comeback, Lacy cut him a sharp look. Swallowing she continued, "You can't stop what is my destiny. My...my circumstances surrounding my past forged what is now my destiny. You can't stop that, it is what it is...and...and I've accepted it. You need to accept it too..."

Lacy wouldn't look at him, just kept playing with what was left of her muffin, smoothing the crumbs into a neat little pile.

She continued quietly, "...Sam liked you a lot, talked about you as if you were the son he never had. He...he used to tell me how smart and quick you were about figuring things out. I knew all of this but I thought I could keep you off guard long enough to move on before...before you figured me out. I was wrong. You're every bit as quick and smart as Sam said you were..." she said, still focusing on her fingers pushing the pile of crumbs around. Her lips locked up tightly again.

"And Sam thought of you as the daughter he never had?"

247

Shrugging, she unlocked her lips only long enough to say, "I guess…"

"Did Sam know what happened to you?"

Lacy shook her head no.

"I'll bet he did. He and Vern were close."

Unlocking lips again, she replied, "If he did, he never let on…"

"No…Sam wouldn't. He'd let you come to terms with it on your own. Something I didn't let you do…" Inhaling deep, Rawley exhaled quietly as he spoke, "…Lacy…I'm sorry I forced the issue with you but you were driving me nuts…" he said.

Lacy nodded, "I know. But I'm not some flop-eared pup that needs to be prodded and poked till he knows all of his commands either," she said, a bit of a spark resonating in her voice.

That made Rawley grin. Then sobering, he spoke softly again, "Lacy…this destiny…this fate, that's got you thinking you're supposed to be drifting, roaming all the time, not having a home, you could change that if you want. Destiny is not what makes us, it's what we want to make of it," he said. Reaching across, he placed a warm gentle touch on her hand. "You're a strong-willed, independent young woman; you've got survival instincts that would put most men to shame. The way you handle Cotton and Billy shows me that under that tough exterior is someone who is kind and gentle. Why even you helping Cody Brown, when most folks wouldn't have given him the time of day!"

"Sunshine…" he said softly, "…You can't have a future until you've faced the past. But that doesn't mean you have to lose whatever dreams you might have."

Jerking her hand out from under Rawley's warm one, Lacy hissed, "Dreams? I don't have any dreams!" Her chair scraped harshly against the floor. Standing she moved toward the fire, staring into the flames. Whirling she faced the man sitting in his chair ever so still. "Dreams? What dreams?" Waving an irate arm

248

through the air, "Those disappeared years ago!" As her hands clenched into fists at her side with her body rigid, she spat out the words, "If you think I have any dreams left...you're a jack-ass...Lovett!" Her hot, angry eyes finally dragged themselves away from his perceptive blue ones. Lacy spun, facing the fire once again. She concentrated on the blue, yellow and orange flames instead of him.

Another chair scraped against the floor. Lacy felt the warmth of his body when he moved in behind her. Fresh air and pungent pine wrapped around her, enclosing her in Rawley's scent. The heat from his hands resting on her shoulders seared through the flannel into her skin like a branding iron. Squeezing her eyes shut, Lacy tried to block out the sensations of his touch, of her feelings reacting to his quiet, gentle act. A lump suddenly constricted her throat, tears pricking the backs of her eyes. She forced the words out, "I'm sorry..." she whispered in a small voice thick with emotion. "That was uncalled for...I'm sorry," she said.

His hands left a hot trail as they slid down her arms. Lacy groaned inwardly, her emotions were already in a tangled mess, worse than trying to unsnarl barbed wire. *And now this!* But she couldn't seem to push herself away. For some unknown reason, she wanted his reassurance that everything would be okay. And that made her heart bang against her ribs like a cattle stampede.

His warm palms enclosed her freckled fists and brought them up, crossing her arms across her upper body. Rawley wrapped his arms around her and pulled her against him, resting his chin on her fiery hair. Slowly, he felt the tension, the stiffness leaving her body eventually melting into his embrace. "I know...Lacy...I know..." he said.

His slow steady heartbeat pulsed through her shirt into her back, slowing her own to match his steady rhythm. Resting in his embrace, Lacy realized she felt safe, not afraid anymore, a feeling she had not felt in a very long time.

Abruptly, Lacy slipped out of his arms and moved away.

He frowned in puzzlement.

She didn't want to, but Rawley had been cutting into her air supply. Heaving in air for her starved lungs, she walked back to the table. Sweeping the muffin crumbs into her hand, she threw the remains in the fire. Sitting on the bunk, she took off her boots. Lying down, she turned her back to him pulling the blanket up to her chin. She closed her eyes and pretended to drift off to sleep.

Laying out his bedroll in front of the fire, Rawley realized he and Lacy finally had a real conversation for once. Not only that, he got to hold her and he treasured that fleeting memory. Tonight, he'd also seen and felt other emotions besides anger coming to the surface. He'd gotten more out of her in four hours then he had in four months. Lacy had begun making progress.

Rawley was tired from the trek up the mountain and began to settle down for the night. As his body began teetering on the edge of a deep sleep, a voice pulled him back from the edge of that quiet abyss.

"Lovett? You asleep? Psstt…you asleep?"

He stirred, coming off the edge to answer, "Umm…"

Lacy whispered, "Lovett? You telling me the truth about those folks in town missing me?"

He willed his brain to concentrate on her words. "Yup," he finally said. He paused before replying, "Lacy…I've never lied to you. I don't intend to start now."

She nodded into the air, "Night…Lovett," she said, rolling on her side. Pulling the cover back over her shoulder, she settled down.

Rawley smiled to himself, "Night…Sunshine…"

Chapter Forty-Five

SOMETHING STIRRED RAWLEY from way back under his, oh so wonderful deep sleep. Rolling on his side, he began to slide off into that wonderful abyss again, when he heard it once more. He lifted his head, concentrating. The shrill whinnying of horses, hooves banging against stall and barn walls reached his ears. He quickly sat up and pulled on his boots.

Lacy had heard it, too. She had bounced up and was already at the door. A soft click sounded as she cocked back the lever of that buffalo gun. Sliding a linen encased cartridge into the chamber, she closed the lever, emitting another sharp click, cutting the casing, exposing the black powder in the chamber. Cocking back the hammer, her fingers tapped a percussion cap over the nipple. Easing that back down, she grabbed a handful of linen cartridges and caps off the shelf next to the door, stuffing them into her britches' pocket. She pointed into the darkness as she opened the door, "You go that-a-way, I'll go around the other. That way we may be able to corner them," she said, running for the southeast side of the barn.

He checked the chamber on his Henry, *Load it on Sunday, and fire all week.* It held sixteen brass fire-rimmed cartridges. Rawley headed out in the opposite direction of Lacy. The horses were becoming more frenzied, their nostrils had picked up the scent of the pack outside the barn. Seeing a dark form out of the corner of his eye, he turned toward it. Aiming, he fired, his shot ricocheting in the still night. Satisfaction crossed his features as he heard a yelp and the shadow drop into the snow. Continuing, he spied another form running toward the shadows of the woods. Rawley fired again, hitting his mark.

251

Lacy heard the shots firing as she tried to climb the rock bluff alongside the southeast side of the barn. Her feet slipping on the frozen surface, hand clawing through the darkness, she finally reached her destination overlooking the back lot of the barn. Standing precariously at the top, she tried to maintain her balance on the slippery surface. Three wolves were still trying to gain entrance into the barn despite the rifle shots by scratching and chewing at the wood. Cocking back the hammer caused the intruders' heads to turn toward the sound. Lacy aimed while she whispered, "I've got you now, you flea bitten curs!" Her finger pulled the trigger.

Kaabooom! Kickback from the powerful rifle caused her foot to slip, losing her balance. Lacy yelped. The rifle went flying, as did her feet. Now she had nothing to defend herself with. Slipping and sliding on her backside, her head banged on an outcropping of bare rock rendering her senseless, a black wave overcoming her. Her body slid to settle at the bottom, covered in snow, out cold.

The wolves ran. The fire and noise exploding from the rifle scared them. Then they stopped when no other shots followed. Intelligent yellow eyes turned back, surveying the situation. Seeing the all clear, they trotted toward their new and easier prey.

He'd heard the lone *boom* coming from that thunder pipe of Lacy's before he'd stepped around the edge of the barn. The storm had moved on exposing a clear night sky. The only light in the darkness came from the pin-pricks of stars.

He squinted as everything seemed to blend into the velvety blackness. As his eyes adjusted to the even darker recesses in the landscape behind the barn, he saw the four-legged carnivores had zeroed in on a dark shape at the bottom of the wind break. He fired several more times, killing two and wounding another. He fired again after the wounded wolf, missing him as he took off into the dark undercover.

Rawley ran through the snow. He turned his attention to the

252

two downed wolves and the body beneath one. Grabbing one wolf by the scruff of his neck, he hauled him off Lacy. Blood greeted his eyes. Realizing the smeared blood came from the wolf, Rawley relaxed some.

Sliding his hand under her neck and lifting her head, he saw the blood splotched snow. Rawley raised Lacy's unconscious body into a sitting position. Fingers found a lump rising and the sticky ooze matting her hair. He looked at the blood staining his fingers, and wiped them on his coat. Retrieving the two rifles, Rawley swung Lacy into his arms carrying her back to the cabin.

Laying her on her the bunk, Rawley turned Lacy on her side. His hand reached for the coal oil lamp, moving it for a closer look. Rising, he hung his coat on the peg and retrieved the wash pan and a cloth. Filling the pan with warm water from the bucket, Rawley returned to Lacy's side. Wetting the rag, he began cleaning the wound, his fingers separating strands of hair as he continued to dab at the cut in her scalp.

"Oww...that hurts..." a small voice announced, trying to roll over.

"Not yet...Sunshine...I'm not done," Rawley replied pushing her back on her side.

"Cut it out...that hurts!" Lacy tried to sit up then fell back as a wave of nausea hit her. "Ooh...my head," she said, the pounding intensifying, throbbing with each heartbeat. "What happened?"

Rolling her back on her side, Rawley said, "You decided to take a sleigh ride...on your butt..." Fingers parting her hair again, he dabbed at the cut.

"I...what?" Lacy asked in disbelief as she tried to turn again.

"Lacy be still...will you..." he said testily, wrapping a clean bandana he'd dug out of his saddle bag around her head. "You don't remember?"

Shaking her head, "Ow..." she gritted, squeezing eyes shut against the pain. "I don't feel so good. I'm gonna be sick."

Rawley grabbed the bucket and held Lacy as she emptied her stomach. Laying her back down, his fingers smoothing the wisps of hair off her face, "You took a nasty crack to the head...Sunshine. You need to be still, or you'll get sick again. You understand me?" Seeing Lacy beginning to nod, two palms gently held a freckled face in his hands stilling her head, "A verbal yes or no will do."

Enjoying the soft gesture of his callused hands, she finally mustered out a "Yes..."

"Good." Covering her with the blanket, he noticed her wet socks, "Hell...Lacy! You went out there in your socks? No wonder you fell!"

Cracking one eye open against the pain, she squinted at the tall man, "Huh?"

"You went out there in your socks?"

"I don't know! Fancy was in danger! Ooh...you're making my head hurt worse. Can't you just quit jabbering for once? Be quiet?"

His mouth curved upwards. He had to hand it to her. Lacy had spunk. Removing the wet socks her feet felt like ice. His hands tucked the blanket tightly in around them.

Throwing a couple more logs on the fire, Rawley poured himself a fresh cup of coffee. Settling in the chair, he stretched his legs, his hand massaging and working the kinks out. He tried to rub the tiredness out of his eyes. It seemed Christmas Day had been ages ago, but in reality, it had been only six days. Gazing at Lacy, a warmth creased his features, softening them. She'd have a good headache for a couple of days, but she'd be fine.

Tomorrow he'd take the pelts from the four wolves; they should bring a good price. Settling back down on the floor, he pulled the blanket over his shoulder. Grinning, Rawley realized he wouldn't have anyone pssting at him now, Lacy had fallen asleep.

Chapter Forty-Six

AFTER TAKING CARE of the horses and retrieving the pelts, Rawley loaded his arms with wood. Entering the cabin, he closed the door softly. A quick glance told him Lacy was stirring.

Cracking her eyes open, Lacy watched the gentle lawman tending the fire. Once again, quick thoughts flitted through her brain, making her head hurt. She would never be able to live up to his standards.

Lacy needed to go outside. She tried to sit up, but then fell back as another wave of nausea swept over her. "Lovett, I need to go outside, I need to…well…you know."

Walking over, Rawley swung her legs over the side of the bunk. Sitting down next to her, he gently pulled her into a sitting position.

Lacy moved in closer, resting her head in the concave of his shoulder, breathing deeply of his scent: pine, cold air and wood smoke. One arm tentatively eased around his back, her hand gripping his shirt. The other rested lightly on Rawley's broad chest.

Lacy just wanted to be held, Rawley realized. Liv had been right. For all her toughness, Lacy remained vulnerable in a way, starving for affection and warmth. He pulled her in closer, allowing his cheek to rest against her forehead. And he thought, *This is only the second time that Lacy allowed someone close to her since she'd run away.* Remembering last night when she'd allowed him to hold her. *Progress…she's making progress.*

"Put your boots on, Sunshine. I'll get your coat," he said softly. Easing himself out of Lacy's embrace, he rose to get it.

She looked at her feet asking, "Where's my socks?"

Coming back with her coat, he asked, "You don't remember?"

Closing one eye against the pain in her head, she squinted with the other as she asked, "Remember what?"

He gave her a long squirrelly look, sighing "Never mind, just put your boots on."

Standing on the porch waiting for Lacy to finish her business, Rawley caught her movement out of the corner of his eye, prompting him to move toward it.

He bent down to help her as she crawled back on the porch. She stopped his hand and bent over the edge of the porch as she emptied her stomach again.

Rawley knelt by his redhead, gently rubbing her back and holding the thick red rope out of her way as she puked into the snow. When she finished, he swung her up into his arms, her head resting against his warm shoulder. Her aching head managed to grasp a fleeting thought; somehow, he made her feel safe, not nervous anymore.

Once inside resting on her bunk again, Lacy's teeth chattered like a disturbed flock of blue jays. She tried not to let it show, but it did anyway.

"Where's your fresh socks?" he asked, removing her boots.

"Sa...s...saddle ba...bag," Lacy chattered.

Wool socks went on small feet. Afterwards, Rawley covered the girl saying, "You feel up to some broth? That was a good stew you made. Where'd you learn that?"

"Sal...S...Sally."

"Yeah...Sally knew how to cook, 'bout like Miss Liv and Maddie."

"Water...I want some waterrrrr..."

Filling the dipper, he held Lacy's head while she drank. "Better now?" he asked after repeating the process.

Lacy gave a slight nod.

"I think you need to rest, sleep some...we'll try the broth later," he said tucking the blankets in around her. Rawley watched

256

as she drifted off. Wandering around the cabin, his eyes were drawn to the shelf with all the books piled there. Titles he'd heard of, but never read. Selecting one, *Oliver Twist,* he sat down and began to read.

Chapter Forty-Seven

FIVE DAYS LATER, the two-party team was ready to move out. Saddling the horses, Rawley mused, Lacy had clammed up on him again but she didn't seem as stiff this time. She didn't even argue with him about going back to White River, just giving her usual silent nod when he'd mentioned it. Rawley felt the girl just might be coming around to trusting him. *Well...maybe...I hope. But, I ain't gonna hold my breath. The way she takes two steps forward and three back all the time.* He sighed inwardly.

Strapping on their snowshoes, Rawley took the reins of his horse leading him away from the cabin. Lacy wrapped the reins around her saddle horn, letting Fancy trail her. She began to follow Rawley. Then suddenly, she stopped and turned back to face the tranquil scene they were leaving behind.

Noticing Lacy not following, Rawley shushed back over to her, standing quietly next to the bundled-up figure. Warm breath from two horses and their human partners mingled in the cold, still morning air.

Lacy felt his presence and without turning and began speaking softly, "This became my sanctuary when I first ran away. I went into town that night, after Mama...after Mama..." her voice stumbled, the words still too painful to say. "...Well anyway, I woke Vern up and told him everything. I showed him the letter my Mama wrote to me..." she faltered, then continued in a whisper thick with emotion, "...Her very last words to me..."

Inhaling deeply, she glanced at her snow encrusted boots. "At first Vern tried to talk me out of it..." she said, looking shyly at Rawley. Then her eyes darted back toward the cabin. "...I mean about running away, but when he saw he couldn't change my mind..." Lacy said trailing off. Taking in another deep breath, she continued, "...He was the one who suggested I change my name so my grandfather couldn't trace me..."

"Vern went over to the store and woke Ezra up and got me some supplies and boxes and boxes of cartridges for these two guns..." she said, tapping the butt of the rifle. "...This was Vern's old buffalo gun. He showed me how to load it and shoot it."

Her gloved hand caressed her coat, where underneath a Navy Colt laid nestled against her waist. "I...I didn't know anything about this Colt..." Inhaling a ragged breath, trying to gain strength, she continued, "...He...he was kind enough to show me how to load it, clean it, keep it in good working order so that it wouldn't misfire on me..." Eyes shifted away from the cabin to her snowy boots again. She said quietly, "...I guess in a way I owe him my life."

Lacy's head rose. Squaring her shoulders, she continued, "One of the last things he told me was to make sure that I practiced and practiced with these guns, that no matter what position I ended up in, I always hit my mark..." Still speaking in her soft husky tone, she added, "...So I did, hours and hours and hours, the same with that knife, until I became good, well...better than good. Taught myself that drop and roll, too. Dropping, rolling and firing till I never missed. I'm not proud of what I've become...but it's the only trade I know. I've never killed unless fired on first."

Taking in another shaky draught of air, she continued, "I took a thousand dollars out of my granddads safe that night, Mama told me to..." Lacy faltered. The memory still remained fresh even after nine years. She straightened, plunging on, "I...In her letter and I figured I had it coming after...after...well...with what all that had happened."

Lacy's eyes shifted again, taking in the forest surrounding the cabin. "Vern sent me up here...this is his place. I guess it was his hunting cabin. I call it my sanctuary, the place where I could get my thoughts together without being afraid. I knew if my grandfather ever found me he would probably kill me…he wouldn't want his dirty little secret to get out…" Lacy finished.

A heart nestled within a big chest felt itself tearing apart while Rawley listened to Lacy's quiet dialogue. He understood how hard it had been for her to explain those horrific events. "That means a lot to me…Sunshine, you opening up like that."

Giving the lawman a hasty look, she stated, "You deserved to know, helping me out like you've done. I'd be dead now…if you hadn't killed those wolves."

Lacy kept fiddling with Fancy's bridle, her hands nervously smoothing the big grey's forelock.

Rawley reached out with his own hand and stilled the ones fidgeting with the mare as he said, "That took a lot of guts and nerve to do what you did…Sunshine. Not many folks, especially a woman, would have been able to survive and do what you've done."

"I had no choice," Lacy replied.

After a few long moments, Rawley broke the heavy silence that hung deep in the cold air, "Well…I don't know 'bout you, but, I'm ready to get out of this deep snow, back where it's a little bit more normal…"

Lacy threw another quick glance at Rawley, saying softly, "It's Angel dust."

"What?"

"My Mama used to call the snows up here Angel dust…" she said. Glancing shyly at him, she explained, "…Because the mountains are closer to the Angels up here. She always told me they'd sprinkle the tops with snow like powdered sugar. So…Mama called it Angel dust," she said.

"Oh," was his only reply.

Two humans and their four-legged partners began the trek down the mountain, away from pristine *Angel dust* and back to the place Rawley called home. When she wasn't taking two steps forward and three back, he felt Lacy considered White River home too.

If Rawley Lovett had anything to do with the future between the two of them, he wanted Lacy by his side for the rest of their lives; to hear her laugh, to birth their babies and build a family and give her the home she never really had. However, one small problem remained in the way; Lacy and her ever-present fear. Somehow…someway, he needed to find a solution to that problem.

If he believed in hocus pocus, he'd mix up some witches' potion and force the swill down the girl's throat. Hopefully it would speed up the process of her figuring out that she loved him, too. He sighed inwardly.

He cut a glance at the quiet bundled up figure trudging beside him. Her hat shadowed any expression she might have been carrying on her freckled face. He thought back to when he first saw her ride into town astride the big grey who followed obediently behind her now. Lacy still remained the tough little bugger who'd slammed his back against the floor in Mike's saloon that day. Still ready to argue with him at the drop of his hat, but he'd seen a softer side too, one that made his heart melt.

One of these days he hoped to see her bloom into the woman he knew remained hidden behind her masculine façade and not the bounty hunter she'd become. Maybe one of these days Lacy Watson could be put to rest for good and Lacy Carrigan would finally come home. Rawley hoped this day would come sooner rather than later, but he knew a lot would depend on Lacy. He also knew in his heart that he would wait however long it took. Suddenly his snowshoes felt as light as his heart. With the promise of a bright future with a freckled venom packed vixen looming on the horizon, he took hold of Lacy's arm saying, "C'mon, Sunshine…let's go home."

THE END

Sneak Peek

Thanks for reading the **NEW REVISED EDITION** of *Freckled Venom Copperhead*, I hope you Enjoyed the Ride!

Thanking you in advance for leaving a review!

A LITTLE SOMETHING to whet your appetite with the second installment in the Freckled Venom Series, *Freckled Venom Copperhead Strikes!*

***

SLOW RECOGNITION DAWNED in Justin Carrigan's eyes, "Lacy? Lacy…is it really you? You've come home to me finally…sweetie?" He reached for her.

She dodged his hand and countered by thrusting him further into the street. Her tone grew softer and more deadly, "Yeah…old man, I finally came home. But not to let you continue where you left off."

"Lacy, I…I thought you were dead…" Carrigan said, reaching for her again.

Lacy's fist erupted, quick as a geyser bursting up from the ground. Her knuckles cracked when they made contact with his jaw. The force sent Carrigan sprawling in the dirt, his hat flying. The dust kicked up around him and settled back down across his clothes.

The momentum of her attack sent Lacy crashing against the steps. Rawley lifted her, setting the copperhead back on her feet. Lacy struggled against his grip, but he held on tightly. "Lacy…" he began.

She hissed like a mad cat, "Stay away from me, Lovett!" jerking away from his grasp.

Hastily covering the short distance to where her grandfather lay, she placed her hands on her knees. Leaning closely to the man she hated so much, Lacy spoke softly, but lethally, "Surprised, old man...that I'm still alive? Did I make your day, today?"

Carrigan blinked in surprise at his granddaughter.

Rawley remained where he stood next to the steps, but a crowd had begun to gather as the confrontation between Lacy and her grandfather progressed. His height enabled him to gaze across the gathering town folk.

The commotion caused quite a stir in the normally quiet town of White River. News spread quickly and at Mike's Saloon, Rooster pushed open the bat-wing doors crowing excitedly, "Hey, Mike...sumsing's going on between Ole Man Carrigan and that girl deputy down the street!" Chairs scraped and boots thundered through swinging doors, sliding to a stop at the edge of the well-worn planks. Mike shoved his way through curious patrons. Wiping his hands on the apron tied around his barrel middle, he also had eyes transfixed on the copperhead. His eyes searched the gathering crowd for Rawley. He found him not far behind Lacy, one big palm resting on the butt of his pistol. Mike breathed a sigh of relief.

Drug to the window by one of her girls, Maddie stared at the scene in the street. Jerking the door open, she muttered, "Chust, what 'cha think ye gain' ta do...lass?" Maddie stopped at the edge of the walk, placing hands on her generous hips. Town folk crowded onto the porch behind her, eyes wide as they gazed at the scene happening on the normally quiet on the street.

Luke moved away from his bellows in the livery as the noise outside increased. Standing in the door, he was surprised to see the large crowd gathering. Short in stature, Luke whirled, and headed toward the loft, picking up his scattergun on the way. He flipped it open, and saw it remained loaded. A flicking motion of his wrist snapped it shut with a click.

The marshal's sharp eyes caught Luke as he appeared in the opening of the hayloft. Luke waved his scattergun at Rawley, then rested it in his arms. Luke stood waiting and thinking, *Been a long time since this town's seen a shoot-out. Last one...Vern had still been alive...* He continued watching the drama unfold on the street below.

Acknowledgments

MANY THANKS TO my step-mom, Mary Ann Douglas who read the first raw version and actually liked it. My awesome daughter, Suzi, my handsome son, Ben and his beautiful wife Liz and her extended family, thank you all for your support.

Jack Phelps for suggesting the wonderful title.

Allen Edwards, antique firearms expert who so graciously explained the workings of the firearms to me that were used in the story. Any mistakes are mine.

My wonderful neighbors who surround Froggy Flats Farm. Jake and Jondra Shadowen and their little Cotton top, the protégé for my Cotton. Barb and Dick Page, who have been there for me through thick and thin. Sandra Lovett Cope, with her wonderful dry sense of humor and long ago forgotten sayings.

God has blessed me in so many ways. He showed me a talent I never knew I had six years ago. Without each and everyone of you continuing to encourage me with your love and support, this goofy boat washer's tale would never have made it to its final destination…into your hands.

I thank each and every one of you from the bottom of my heart. God Bless.

For being there with all my pesky questions and support, Jared McVay, fellow author and friend.

About the Author

Photo by Lois Cunningham, Benton, KY

Author Juliette Douglas is shown with white thoroughbred stallion Arctic Bright View who played **'Silver'** in the 2013 remake of **The Lone Ranger**.

Both hail from Marshall County, Kentucky.

Visit our websites:
http://juliettedouglas2016.wix.com/mysite
www.megsonfarms.com

Visit Juliette Douglas via Facebook:
www.facebook.com/author.juliette.douglas

SADDLE UP... LET'S RIDE!